Advance Praise for Johnny Diaz and
BOSTON BOYS CLUB

"Johnny Diaz brings to palpable life the ins, outs, ups, and downs of gay city life and its most dangerous pastime: dating. In chronicling the love lives—or lack thereof—of three good friends who meet weekly at a popular watering hole, Johnny Diaz gives us situations, hopes, fears, and, especially, characters that all readers will identify with, and may even recognize as themselves. At turns comic, touching, and tragic, *Boston Boys Club* is sure to serve as a testament of American gay life in the new millennium, and the timeless search for Mister Right—or Mister Right Now. An addictive read."
—J. G. Hayes, author of *This Thing Called Courage,*
Now Batting for Boston, and *A Map of the Harbor Islands*

"*Boston Boys Club* is racy, funny, and smart. With his unforgettable trio of narrators, Johnny Diaz ushers the reader through the sex-filled, weirdly skewed world of contemporary gay Boston. You're going to love this book."
—Scott Heim, author of *Mysterious Skin* and *We Disappear*

"Make way for the boys of summer! Johnny Diaz has written a sexy beach-read romp that you won't be able to put down."
—William J. Mann, author of *Men Who Love Men*

BOSTON
BOYS
CLUB

JOHNNY DIAZ

Christi,
Thank you for
your support and enthusiasm
for my writing. You're an honorary
member of the Boston Boys Club.
Cheers,
Johnny

KENSINGTON BOOKS
http://www.kensingtonbooks.com

KENSINGTON BOOKS are published by

Kensington Publishing Corp.
850 Third Avenue
New York, NY 10022

ISBN-13: 978-0-7582-1545-1
ISBN-10: 0-7582-1545-2

First Kensington Trade Paperback Printing: May 2007
10 9 8 7 6 5 4 3 2 1

Printed in the United States of America

BOSTON
BOYS
CLUB

Chapter 1

TOMMY

Another chilly night falls on Boston and the mercury is down to 30 degrees. Damn the thermometer! It's not too frigid to go to Club Café in the heart of the city's gay ghetto.

When I say ghetto, I mean that only in the most positive sense. The South End neighborhood is full of character and charm. Streets are lined with shoulder-to-shoulder three-story brick row houses, rounded with English-style bow fronts. First-floor windows sit a few feet from street level and the decorative cobblestone boulevards. Rose and orange flowers burst from the windowsills during warmer months. And there are Volkswagen Jettas, Beetles, and Mini Coopers parked on streets that have equally gay-sounding names such as Berkeley, Clarendon, and Upton. It's basically a gay utopia.

As twilight beckons on this city on a hill, I brave the cold in hot pursuit of the man-traffic on Columbus Avenue. Guys sport sleeveless shirts and chest-defining T-shirts underneath American Eagle wool coats and Gap corduroy jean jackets. The top layers come off as soon as they hit the lonely coat check dude and drop a buck or spare change in his tip box. Then they walk around the club showing off smooth, tanned skin as if it's summer, even though it's a bone-chilling November night outside.

Not me, the more conservative (and cheap) one. I take off my coat and leave on the Nautica red hoodie I bought on sale at Costco. (What isn't on sale there?) It's not that I'm ashamed of my body. I have it; I just don't necessarily think I need to flaunt it like Lil' Kim.

Thursday night is the busiest gay night here. An armada of men stand around creating a logjam of testosterone, in this bar/lounge that also serves a gay gym downstairs. You come here depending on what kind of workout you are looking for.

It's easy to think that this place has some kind of addictive magic. Each week guys come to drink, mingle, drink, cruise, drink some more, and perhaps, find manpanionship, a queer peer, a date, a potential partner/lover/spouse or whatever boyfriends are called these days, or just a play buddy for the night. No matter how often these guys see each other in the same spot, leaning at the edge of the bar, lingering around the coat check or S&Ming (standing and modeling, folks) under the TV monitors that blare Britney, Madonna, or the *Wonder Woman* theme song megamix, they never seem to tire of it. They never get sick of seeing the same perfectly shaved faces with mostly blue or green eyes and Salon Selectives hair, sipping their light Sam Adams or Corona beers or nursing glowing green Apple Martinis.

My reason for coming back is simple. After three Thursdays of coming here, chances are everyone will know your name as if you were in Cheers. But call this one Queers, where everyone knows with whom you last slept. So I try not to overdo it, at least the going-out part. Well, I try. Oh, and let's not forget our lady friends. They're here, too, in leather and denim jackets, jeans and winter boots. A small number wears skirts and high heels. But we men outnumber them by at least four to one. To the men, I say, You go girls!

Club Café is a perpetual rerun episode of *Same Sex in the City*. Each season or college semester brings a crop of new faces. So you never know whom you will meet. That unknown, an optimistic sense of possibility of meeting "someone," is what keeps guys revolving through these doors week after week, winter, spring, summer, fall, rain or snow. But even the ones who do meet that someone still can't seem to pull themselves away from Club Café.

"Howdy, Tommy Boy! What's up with you? I haven't seen you since what, last Thursday," says Rico as he walks in through the front glass, snow-stained doors that face Columbus Avenue. Rico fits the stereotype of the sexy, macho Italian to a well-groomed T. He's got thinning wisps of jet-black hair combed down Caesar cut style and eyes that easily match the green of the Italian flag.

Tommy is my nickname, short for Tomas, as in the Spanish pronunciation. It sounds like the Spanish word *toma* as in "drink," so I think I was appropriately named. Yeah, I'm the Cuban transplant to Boston from Cuba North, also known as Miami. Although if you think about it, Miami really is a piece of Cuba injected into the United States—but more on that later.

Just as I am proud of my Cuban heritage (my Jeep Wrangler's license plate reads QBAN) so is Rico of his family's lineage. The tattoo on his bulging right shoulder bears the design of a sailing Italian flag. It looks good with his blue T-shirt that reads ITALIAN STALLION. Rico is that kind of patriotic. This is Boston, after all, where everyone's proud of where they came from, especially the native Bostonians. But us newcomers have plenty of pride in our roots, too. Some people hate it, but I like that people here cling to their identities. Like the Puritans who first arrived here centuries ago, Boston today remains a city of immigrants. It's a revolving door of newcomers, including me. And I wouldn't have it any other way.

"Doing really well, Rico. Just hella good," I say as he stands by the coat check, peels off his coat, and unveils his guns—those killer biceps that frame his sleeveless blue T-shirt. Rico's body is hard, sanded, and sculpted like the sand dunes in Province-town. The great body is the result of his boxing hobby, which he says is stress-release from his accounting job in the financial district. Boxing is great for cardio, he always says, but I'll have to take his word for it. I'm a writer, not a fighter. Picture a more rugged and built Freddie Prinze Jr. before he went crazy-blond for the two *Scooby Doo* movies and that's Rico.

"Good to see you, dude," Rico says, handing his coat to the coat check dude and then giving me one of his rib-choking bear hugs that literally lift me off my feet.

"Want a drink, dudette? Let me guess, the usual, right?" Rico offers.

Vodka with Diet Coke, aka Skinny Black Bitch, is my tonic. I didn't name it; that's what the bartenders here tell me it's called. A black bitch is vodka with regular Coke and the former is all I order. Blame my predictability on my mild OCD—the one in the medical books. I always order the same thing at restaurants and bars and I get stuck in ruts like coming to Club Café on Thursdays after 10 P.M. (Just don't call me on Friday nights when *Dateline* and *20/20* are on the tube.) But some say I have another kind of OCD: Obsessive Cuban Disorder, since I manage to lace my everyday conversations with Cuban references or inject them into my feature stories. Plus, I love our Miami hometown girl Gloria Estefan.

But Beantown keeps growing on me. Although there aren't many Cuban-Americans here, I always wanted to experience the seasons besides summer, write for *The Boston Daily*, and get in touch with my inner New Englander. I traded *sopa de pollo* (chicken soup) for clam chowdah. And all the buildings here have stories to tell. Being in Boston is like living in an urban museum. With a walk or a jog, you pass buildings from differ-ent centuries, each with a unique history and sometimes con-nected to a famous or infamous figure. Miami, my hot endless summer for twenty-nine years, looks like it was just unpacked out of a box on CBS's *CSI: Miami.*

Rico and I are about the same height, five-feet-ten, and I have to say that the physical similarities end about there. I've got the tumble of dark brown curls and thick black eyebrows like two sculpted awnings that umbrella my Cuban coffee-bean eyes. People say I look a lot like a skinnier Ethan, the guy on *Survivor* who won the $1 million a few years ago and who plays soccer. I can see why people have told me that. Hey, I'm just glad that people don't get me confused with the other *Survivor* winner, you know, the fat gay naked guy who has been fighting the IRS for not paying taxes on his winnings.

"Any cute guys tonight?" Rico asks as I recover from his bear hug with a d-e-e-p breath.

We make our way deeper into Club Café, also fondly known as Café SoGay, which is a restaurant in the front, with a lounge and bar in back. We pass a row of guys, spectators in a parade, as they stand along the walls of each room.

Another crush of younger guys, sporting American Eagle T-shirts, Old Navy hoods, blue jeans, and baseball caps tilted to the side, plop themselves in the middle of the room, like an island of youth. Like piranhas, the older guys—awkward in youthful garb that doesn't quite disguise the fact that the salt in their hair pours out more than the pepper—circle around and watch their potential gay prey. Destiny's Child pops up on the monitor and Beyoncé, Kelly, and Michelle's voices ricochet off the mirrored walls behind each bartender's station.

"Can you keep up baby boy? Make me lose my breath . . ." the trio harmonizes.

"Yeah, there are some Twinks here and some new faces. Like Mary J. Blige says, let's go percolate around the club," I tell Rico. (For the uninitiated, Twinks are late-teen or early-twenty-something gay guys who are uniformly thin, wear tight A&F shirts, and who are new to the whole gay bar scene. They look

like any one of the boyish, teenage hunks you'd find on The
CW network, formerly The WB and UPN.)

Rico flashes his smile as he passes each guy, almost like a
Miss Little Italy would when greeting her public. His smile can
be compared to a gamma ray. When he smiles, which he does
often, you need sunglasses to protect your eyes. It's that bright.
He knows his smile is his trademark and he flashes it often, almost like a reflex, in a Tom Cruise sort of way. It's how he
meets guys. He smiles and they come, in more ways than one.
Problem is you never know what Rico's thinking when he
smiles. Whether he thinks you're an asshole, hates what you're
wearing, or doesn't exactly get what you're trying to say, the
smile appears. It's mischievous like a Cheshire cat. Even at fu-
nerals, the smile makes a cameo appearance. And he gets away
with it.

When Rico doesn't smile, he has mournful eyes that seem
to harbor something deep and dark. His smile seems to mask
some sort of pain, some longing. I can only guess because he'd
never talk to me about such things. He can be inaccessible
emotionally. We basically talk about guys and how to cut cor-
ners financially. Whatever he hides, he keeps it close to his vest
as he does his boxing gloves. He's never told me and I suspect
that lots of spontaneous sex is his panacea.

As Destiny's Child winds down from their booty-shaking
video, Laura Branigan suddenly appears on the monitor, belting her 1982 hit "Gloria."

"Gloria . . . I think they've got your number . . . GLORIA."

The music mixes with and seems to add new life to the
chatter from the scores of simultaneous conversations in the
jumping Club Café. By the entrance near the lonely $1.50-
service-charge ATM, a couple of guys seem to be whispering
to one another as they look up.

It's a bird. It's a plane. No, it's The Kyle, whose arrival is marked with his usual flair for dramatic entrances. By this, I mean he stands under one of the brighter lights in the bar and starts waving to people across the room like he is a victim drowning in a *Baywatch* rerun, just so people will know he's in the house.

This six-foot-three, lean, dirty-blond curly-haired former model from the Midwest walks into the place like a movie star of Brad Pitt caliber, waving to people and nodding his chin up to greet folks he doesn't necessarily recognize but who definitely recognize him. He stops to sign a few autographs. Really.

He's no movie star although he is a dapper dresser with khaki pants and long-sleeved Polo shirts. He's a reality show has-been whose once shining star has begun to fade and fall. Kyle still acts like a coterie of cameras shadow his every move, record his every word, and capture his every drama-dripping moment.

Kyle was the gay dude on the reality show *The Real Life*, which chronicles seven twentysomethings as they live together under one roof in Somewhere USA to see what happens when you put seven unstable opposites together with cameras all around them.

Kyle was on the Boston season, which airs in rerun hell on the weekends. Modeling scouts discovered him on the show, and he graced runways in New York, Miami, Los Angeles, as well as Milan and Paris. But as soon as the show wrapped up its fresh crop of new episodes two years ago, Kyle found himself without a televised runway to showcase himself.

Editorial modeling jobs and runway work dwindled, and his fizzling star dimmed and now barely flickers. His latest venture is to try to enlist in the *Battle of the Genders* challenge, which pits former *Real Life* contestants against one another in extreme sporting competitions. That season airs now and sometimes you can see it on the monitors here at Club Café. Kyle firmly believes the show will resurrect his career, whatever that may be.

Kyle (we call him KY for a sloppy KY Jelly incident inside a hot tub during a threesome on one of the most-talked-about *Real Life* episodes of all time) soaks up every stare and bit of attention he attracts wherever he goes. Tonight included.

Rico and I see him coming our way near the bar. Mr. KY spots us right away. Like a head-on collision, it's too late to avoid him. Kyle has always seemed like a good guy but his constant need for attention has made me wonder: What wouldn't he do to get it and what happens when no one cares anymore to ask him about the show? So I chitchat with him now and then to be socially diplomatic but I keep it simple and brief.

Rico, who doesn't care for Kyle and even rudely ignores him sometimes, manages to turn around. He focuses on flagging down the bartender and scans the rows of beer and liquor bottles that bedeck the wall mirror and shelves at the bartender's station.

I'm on my own here with The Kyle and there's nowhere for me to run.

"Tommy, heeeeeeeeeeeey, what have you been up to?" His words ooze out in a feminine lisp as he lords over me like a giraffe, looking around the room to make sure guys are looking at him. "When are you going to write an article about me in the *Daily*? I've got some upcoming projects in the works. You could put me on the front page or in the Features section. You write about everyone in this city but *moi!*"

I crane my head up to speak to this giant queen of a man and I "uh-huh" my way throughout the one-sided conversation. It's hard to get a simple word in when Kyle talks; he's a conversation hijacker. Finally, he takes a breath and lets me speak. "Yeah, keep me posted, Kyle. I'm really tied up with some other assignments but let me know if you get a big part in a movie or something," I say, noticing that Rico's V-shaped back is turned to us, intentionally oblivious to what is going on. "I can't guarantee a story. But I will let you know either way. Cool?"

Kyle, who is ever preening, can easily pass as a male version of supermodel Rebecca Romijn, you know, Mystique from the *X-Men* movies but without all that blue body makeup and morphing capabilities. He leans in for a double air kiss before he heads off to feed his ego answering all the inquiries and stares from *The Real Life* show's fans that are here tonight. "Great, Tommy. I'll have my agent send you an updated bio and press sheet. You're a doll!" he says, strutting off like Tyra Banks or a contender on *America's Next Top Model*, his favorite show.

I turn around and catch up with Rico at the bar as he waits among a throng of guys for the ponytailed bartender in the wife-beater shirt to come our way. "Hey, look at that guy, with the orange hoodie. He looks like your type. Pretty, skinny boy," Rico says. As I scan the rainbow of hoods and baseball caps, Rico smiles at the bartender, who doesn't even need to ask what he wants. "Sam Adams light, right?" Rico goes for the low-carb stuff. He nods back, smiling of course, as he fumbles for five dollars from his Urban Outfitters leather wallet and grabs his cool elixir for the night.

The guy Rico is talking about, the one I'm now scrutinizing like a Monet painting, resembles Ethan Hawke. He looks extremely boyish, sandy brown straight hair that really brings out his blue eyes, which sparkle like two small swimming pools. I watch him across the room bantering with his friends and taking a swig of Corona, and he laughs back. He's having a good time; he seems like a happy good spirit. His orange hoodie has a simple 10 on it. It agrees with him. I'm definitely interested. He looks my way, our eyes lock for one . . . two . . . three . . . seconds and we look away. As Rico turns around to talk to me again, I leer out of the corner of my eye and notice No. 10 looking back at me. We look away again. Reality bites in a good way.

"*Guao!*" as we say back in Miami. "He's sooo cute, Rico. He kinda looks like the prototypical American guy, the boy next door. Should I go up to him?" I look and look away from Mr. Ethan Hawke's clone.

"Yo, Tommy, why not just say hi to him when we walk by. Not everyone's gonna come up to you. For a reporter, you can really be shy sometimes. You just gotta put yourself out there. Let's go make the rounds. Let's walk, boyeee," Rico says.

So we trudge through the thick crowd of men and try not to spill our drinks. This place is packed! It's like a highway intersection of men, where Interstate 93 meets the Turnpike— during rush hour. In this traffic, you'll inhale a heady mix of aftershaves, body lotions, and colognes that the guys doused themselves with before leaving their brownstones or triple-deckers. I bump into Kyle again, who happens to be in the middle of the bar, babbling to some wide-eyed, impressionable younger guys about what it's like to be on *The Real Life*. I hear him saying "Yeah, we have microphones on *alllll* the time and there are cameras in the bedrooms. The only private place we have is . . . well, come to think about it, we don't have any areas off-limits to the cameras. So as I was saying, I . . ."

After Rico and I tap a few fellas on the shoulder to get by or squeeze in between some others, we approach Mr. Number 10, dead ahead at twelve o'clock. He sees me coming. We lock eyes once again, and we both break out in a grin at the same time.

"Hey, you're cute," he tells me, slightly tipping the top of his chin. "What's your name?" he asks in an undiluted Boston accent.

"Thanks, I'm Tommy," I respond, smiling and looking down. I can't help it. I get shy around cute guys. I get butterflies in my stomach, even if I interview police chiefs, mayors, the homeless, and strangers every day for work. "You're cute, too," I say, my inner butterflies flying away. "And you are . . ."

"I'm Michael but call me Mikey, everyone else does," he says, although it sounds more like "Mike-eee" with his accent, which hints at a Cape Cod/Plymouth upbringing.

I almost forget about Rico. These things happen when someone captures my eyes and, perhaps, my heart. I do believe in love/lust at first sight. I'm a dreamer. I'm a Pisces.

"Nice to meet you, Mikey. This is my buddy Rico or as I like to say *R-r-r-ico*."

Rico rolls his eyes at my cheesy joke (it's not the first time I've said it), smiles, and then turns to us and says, "Hey, I'm gonna make a round here. I'll catcha in a few." I wink at Rico, mentally thanking him for giving me some space with Mikey. That's the mark of a true friend, when he leaves you alone to chat up a cute guy. No sense in cock-blocking. Rico's not like that—and a good thing, too. It's hard to make good gay guy friends without breaking out into catfights over cute men. That's why I feel blessed to have at least one good hangout buddy here in this sometimes-unfriendly metropolis. My closest friends are back in Miami. My best friend Brian lives in New York and Miami, jetting back and forth on his helicopter with his partner. While we see each other only a few times a year when I visit *mi familia*, we e-mail and talk on the phone several times a week, kind of like the two women in the movie *Beaches*.

Rico disappears into the sea of guys as Beyoncé bounces her bootyliciousness on the video monitors mounted on each corner of the room crooning and hiccupping, *"So crrrazy in loooove. Uh oh, uh oh . . ."* And I'm here with Mikey, smiling and chatting up a storm in a corner of the bar, where cushy stools and small bar tables line up against a wall of windows, protecting the club goers from the freezing weather just on the other side of the glass.

Mikey is an elementary school guidance counselor on the South Shore, where he also grew up, just outside of Plymouth, as in the Rock. He is slight like the lead singer of Maroon 5 and a little hunched when he talks. I find it hard to believe he's thirty-three, only four years older than me. He looks twenty-five—probably because he has a head full of hair and exudes a boyish playfulness that seems endearingly innocent. Small freckles dust his nose and cheeks. When he says something he thinks is funny, he pops his tongue out and gently bites down. He's a cutie pie. *Que lindo.*

"Tommy, what do you do? Are you Italian? You look it, cutie," he tells me as I smile and glance away again. I need to stop doing that.

Folks here think I'm Italian or Greek, something that is bittersweet for me. In Miami, no question about it, everyone knew I was un *cubanito.* In Boston, my light olive skin allows me to blend in with the populace, allowing me to see how others are treated when they don't blend in and hear what others have to say about them. That's Boston for you. Almost thirty years after the divisive racial busing riots, the city still sometimes views itself through the old black-and-white prism. That surprises me because Boston itself is a minority-majority city. As for Latinos or Hispanics (depending on whom you ask), the townies don't know what to make of us, because we represent various shades of the ethnic spectrum.

Back in Miami, the city is a sea of Cubans. But in Boston, it's another story. Only a couple thousand Cubans, according to the Census (I know this because I am, after all, a reporter) and just a handful of gay ones. So when I tell someone I am Cuban, they look at me like I have a third eye. To others, Cuban sounds exotic.

Anyways, back to Mikey. I explain to him that I grew up in Miami Beach. I was born and bred there, by the sun, sand, and surf, and grew up watching Miami Beach undergo an extreme makeover. When I was a little kid, the city was more of a Jewish retirement community with the elderly lining the porches of Ocean Drive hotels with the best views of the beach. By the time I was eleven, the place had become gun-slinging, cocaine-cowboy country just like in *Scarface* and *Miami Vice*. In my teens, Miami Beach and tourists rediscovered and fell in love with the city's Art Deco decadence. The models came and so did the greedy developers. In my early twenties, the place became a gay subtropical capital and *the* club land on the East Coast. These days, SoBe is an international hip-hop playground with Missy Elliott and Usher considered as local royalty, and of course, JLo and Ricky "La Loca" Martin as part-time residents.

I am Cuban-American and speak Spanish (or more like butcher the *español*). I tell him I am a reporter for *The Boston Daily*, moved here a year ago to Cambridge, next to TWGU, The World's Greatest University (Harvard, folks), and I love the Boston way of life. It goes back to my college summer internship at the *Daily* in Living/Arts, my first time away from home and the happiest time of my life. I found my writing voice that summer, independence from my overprotective Cuban parents, and a whole new way to live. I also figure if I stay here long enough, I may absorb some smart rays.

"I love Boston, Mikey," I say as I break his stare by taking sips of my DCV (Diet Coke with Vodka.) "It's one of the prettiest cities I have ever seen. Big but not too big, or overwhelming like New York City. And the seasons make time fly and make me appreciate the moments in life. I love Miami, and it will always be a part of me, but sometimes, you need change to grow." I notice that Mikey's eyes are completely focused on me and every word I say, even as he chugs back his Corona.

He introduces me to his friends, one of whom is named Maria, who looks like she could have been a former Mario. She seems butch with her chiseled face but she's supersweet and gracious. Out of nowhere, though, she puts her hands in my curly hair, massaging it and feeling it and saying, "I love your curls. Ahhhh," as if she just placed her hands in a tub of Calgon. I love it when girls (guys, too) twirl my curls with their fingers but that's another story.

Mikey and I eventually walk over to the front lounge and sit at one of the two-seat bar tables and continue getting to know one another for the next two hours or so. He orders another Corona and I ask for another Diet Coke with Vodka. He laughs when the waiter informs us what my drink is really called. But I just can't get those words to pass my lips. It doesn't seem very PC and some of my biggest influences in Miami, from teachers and nurses, have been black women. Besides, many Cubans are black, too.

As we talk under the flow of a nice warm buzz, I notice, through the glass that separates the lounge from the bar, that Rico has found his hookup for the night. They are standing by the coat check, and Rico already has his hand on his new friend's bum. I laugh to myself because Rico is such a top, meaning, he likes to ride guys with his Italian Stallion.

Rico smiles the whole time they are in line and keeps his eye and his hand on his night's conquest, a toned guy, about twenty-three, with a crew cut of fuzzy brown hair and sea foam green eyes (at least from what I can gather across the room). He sort of looks like actor Josh Hartnett. I can tell he hangs off every one of Rico's words, that he's under his Italian spell. Before they disappear, Rico eyes me through the glass, waves, and winks. A few minutes later, they disappear off Columbus Avenue.

By 2 A.M., the crowd dims. The bar's staff begins to turn on the bright lights, which feel like minisuns, blinding everyone as they adjust their eyes like Gizmo in the 1984 movie *Gremlins*. (I have a bad habit of announcing the year movies and songs have been released. I think it's my OCD.)

Over the course of the last two hours, Mikey and I have talked about our families, careers, dating. I've been single for five years ever since I broke up with Tell-a-Lie Teddy in Miami, who was a serial liar. He swore he had a twin brother. (Lie number 1.) He swore his eyes were blue. (Lie number 2.) They were contacts. He swore he finished high school at fifteen. (Lie number 3.) He just stopped going at fifteen. And the list goes on and on almost infinitely like the math pie sign. "I'm just picky," I tell Mikey. "I know what I want. I want to settle down but I don't want to settle for less."

Mikey had been engaged to different women and then realized that he liked grooms more than brides. He became the runaway groom, calling off the weddings the day of the ceremonies. He says he's been casually dating men for the past three years but no long-term boyfriend yet.

We exit the warmth of Club Café and step into the chilly night. A crowd of guys stand outside, smoking Marlboros and Newports and trying to find a guy to hook up with at the last moment. We call this "the sidewalk sale." Mikey and I walk past them, under a light, sprinkling snow that is beginning to make Boston look like a holiday postcard. In the distance, a row of spires from the numerous city churches jut into the skyline.

"Where did you pahk, Tommy?" and I point to Berkeley Street, where my Jeep is around the corner. As we walk, we look up and smile at each other and then do it again a few times. He's so cute and he seems so kind. There's something good about him. I can sense it with every Cuban bone in my body. He's a guidance counselor, after all, so he must have a big heart and a lot of patience.

It's 30 degrees outside but I'm not feeling it one bit. I am too warmed by Mikey's presence. I wish we can walk the city for the rest of the night or perhaps go back to my place. But he has to get up early for school. I have an early interview with a local Santeria priest for an article about the growth of the

Afro-Cuban religion in Boston's Hispanic community. And besides, I don't want this to be just a hookup. After a while, those tend to be empty, hollow. Mikey seems to be worth more than that.

"Tommy, I want to get your numbah," he says as snowflakes quickly dot-dot-dot his cinnamon brown hair into white.

"Sure! Can I have yours as well?" I say as I lean my back against the door of my Jeep.

He grins. "You're the reporter. Where's the pen and paper?" he jokes, our faces two inches away from each other's.

I grab a *Daily* pen from my Jeep and he jots down his phone number on the back of a Trident gum wrapper. His writing is very elegant, like a schoolteacher's. I would give him an A+ for penmanship. I pull out one of my *Boston Daily* business cards and scribble my e-mail address, my home phone number, and my cell's digits. I draw a smiley face underneath the number.

"Well, I'll give ya a call, cutie," he says in his sweet accent. "It was really nice talking to you." He leans in to gently plop a kiss on my Strawberry Chapstick–covered lips. As he pulls back from the kiss, I tell him, "Same here, Mikey. Drive carefully, okay?" and I return another pop kiss.

We smile and lock eyes again. He then dashes to his car, a black Toyota Matrix sports wagon, across the street. We wave good-bye.

As I hop into my Jeep and drive back to Cambridge on the snow-caked Storrow Drive, my mind is on Mikey. I wonder whether he is wondering about me tonight as well.

And as I approach the desolate, snow-covered Harvard Square rotary, I'm thinking, I've got to e-mail Brian and tell him all the details.

Chapter 2

RICO

"Yeah, just like that. That feels hot. Whoa. Yeah." This kid on his knees giving me a hot blowjob is sucking Oscar like a lollipop. (Yeah, my penis has a name. Anything wrong with that?) This kid's tongue swirls all around it as we lie on my king-sized bed.

"Keep going, man," I tell him.

Shit, I forgot his name. But who cares? I'll just say "Hey" whenever I need to get his attention.

"Hey!" I tell him. "A little bit higher. Yeah, right there. *Yeah*," as wet slurping sounds fill my bedroom.

I'm just leaning back, enjoying the ride, the up-close and personal service. These younger guys are easy to take home. Tell them how cute they are, smile, stare deeply into their eyes, and slowly start to make your move. Put your arm around them or your hand on their ass. If they let you, you're in. You've hooked them. If they resist or move your hand, fuck them. They're a tease. Time to move on. There are plenty of other guys around here. This dude was mine within twenty minutes. I don't like to waste time.

I ditched Tommy Boy at Club Café. He didn't seem to care. He was shooting the shit with that skinny, pretty boy with the blue eyes after I took a lap around the bar. Shit, I forgot his name, too. So Tommy's cool. I'm probably gonna hear all the details, every quote, every detail, all of it, over and over again. Tommy can repeat the same sentence in five different ways and he'll say it each time with the same enthusiasm as the first. I guess that's what makes him a good writer or a bit of a cheezeball. You just have to learn to zone him out when he repeats himself.

I see the top of this guy's fuzzy head as it bobs up and down on me like a bungee cord. He loves Oscar, all eight inches of him. I'm not the Italian Stallion for nuthin'. I'm staring at the popcorn ceiling of my room with my arms cushioning the back of my head while this guy gives Oscar a wet workout.

Ahhh, man, this is heaven. He's a human vacuum cleaner. I could stay like this all night. There are so many dots on my ceiling.

Like boxing, Boston seems to fit me like a glove. I moved here at the beginning of fall from western Massachusetts, the Berkshires. Rich tourists go there during the summer and brag about it once they get back to Boston or New York. They bring traffic to the region, which some of us natives can't stand. But they also bring money, which helps the locals in the wallet.

Earlier this year, I graduated from college with a degree in accounting and landed a job I applied for through an online ad. It's a junior position, pricing stocks for the company's clients. I gotta start somewhere. You know, I'm twenty-seven and just getting my degree now, so I took whatever job I could to get my life in order again. I feel a bit behind everyone else sometimes. Most college students here in Boston graduate at twenty-two or twenty-three and get their master's. Most guys I know here have their own condos already. Some even have kids, though I wouldn't want one at this point in my life. I'm too young and there's plenty more playing to be done.

It was time to move on with my life. Also time to get away from Jeff, my lying, two-faced-shithead ex-boyfriend of two years. It was a toxic relationship. Unhealthy. You can't be with someone if he's cheating on you, and then you end up hooking up with other guys as a way of dealing with him having an affair with another guy. It was a total mental jerk-off. We weren't going anywhere except driving each other crazy. You gotta be true to yourself and no one else. If you're not, who will? Boston was a great place for new beginnings—and fresh faces to hook up with.

On megslist.com, where everyone posts rooms for rent, cars (even cats) for sale, or digital cameras to hawk, I found an ad for a room in a house here in Savin Hill, or what I call Stab N' Kill. It's a pretty neighborhood on a hill, full of Victorian and triple-decker houses with white picket fences and porches. From the top of the hill, you can see the whole friggin' city, even Fenway during a Sox game, and the Fourth of July fireworks exploding over the city from the Esplanade. I've taken some tricks up here in my Ford truck for another kind of home run and explosion. My Ford Explorer has become my Ford Exploder.

The neighborhood was called Stab N' Kill years ago when there was more crime and people wouldn't dare venture over the highway to the other side of the neighborhood, which is connected by a narrow overpass. They called that part "OTB," as in Over the Bridge, where thugs and gangbangers were robbing folks, stealing cars, and even burning down some houses. It was more ghetto back then.

At least this side of Savin Hill, the good part, has turned around, cleaned up as young professionals with families and some gay couples and their well-to-do friends bought up, refurbished, and renovated some of the depreciated housing stock and brought a sense of pride to these parts. Now these houses are worth more than double what they went for in the early and mid-1990s. It's a great moneymaking investment. Those fuckers! I wish I had done that years ago when I had some dough in the bank. But I chose to follow my adventurous Aquarius spirit, travel down to Virginia and back up the East Coast, taking odd jobs as a waiter and a hotel clerk to feel free and live life. You only live once so why not do it as much as you can in your early twenties? I could have been rich by now if I had invested my money; instead I'm renting a room, barely surviving check to check, and have a mountain of credit card debt from those years of running around the country.

"Ouch," I tell the Hey-kid. "You're using your teeth. Watch it!" The kid corrects himself and he's back to sucking me like an Italian ice.

I live in one of the bigger Victorian houses, right on the outer edge of the hill, where it overlooks *The Boston Daily*'s parking lot. Tommy comes over sometimes after work and we hit Boston Market for some carved turkey breast and macaroni. I love macaroni.

My roommate Bill seems okay although he can be weird at times, walking around the house talking to himself and bitching about his disability check not coming in the mail or about the heating bill getting too high. Bill is an older dude, in his fifties, with a nest of salt-and-pepper hair. He bought the first floor of the house as a condo conversion years ago when he was a more established events promoter and food critic. He doesn't do that anymore. He just does odd carpentry jobs in the neighborhood and spends the day painting some part of the house.

He charges me $500 for my room and tends to leave me the fuck alone, except when I bring too many guys over late at night. Then he makes catty comments in the morning like "What number was that this week? Forty-six?" in front of the guy as he leaves. What an asshole!

Besides, the subway stop is down the street at the bottom of the hill, parallel to Interstate 93, so putting up with Bill ain't too bad. I have another roommate, Peter, a straight college student, but I never see him. He works nights at the 24-hour pharmacy a few miles down. Sometimes, it doesn't even feel like he lives here. Our rent pays Bill's mortgage, I suspect, which explains why he doesn't work a lot and is always on the prowl for that state disability check.

This is not going to be my permanent home. No friggin' way. Once I pay down some of my credit card debt and school loans, I'd want a condo or a house around here as an investment and a home. Till then, I'm saving every penny I have. I collect my Sprite cans at the office and return them for cash. I take my spare change to the coin machine at the market. I don't buy too many drinks when I go out and I only take $5 with me, which covers a beer and a tip. Actually, Tommy's good about treating me when we go out. He's a cool dude like that. Besides, I'm sure he makes good money as a reporter at the *Daily* so if he offers to pay, then, hey, why not, right? It's not like I am asking him to. To save gas, I take the subway to work and I also encourage Tommy to drive. More gas in my tank.

For food, I load up on groceries at BJ's out in the western suburbs. Once a month, I spend $70 on food, chicken cutlets, meat for meatloaf, cookie dough, boxes of Sprite, and large cans of Gatorade powder mix to brew my own at home. I take my lunch to work (grilled chicken breasts I cook and cookies I bake Sunday night for the week) and my soda cans. I don't spend any money on food during the week. I save about $10 a day just by making lunch and eating dinner at home. For Boston Market with Tommy, I bring coupons. To pay him back sometimes for the times he treats, I cook him some stir-fry chicken with vegetables when we rent movies now and then.

I change my phone plan every few months when a better, cheaper deal comes along. I am so money-smart that if I squeezed a nickel hard enough, it would make the Indian on one side of the coin ride the buffalo on the other side, as the saying goes. If I have a date, I pretend to fight with the guy over who will pay and then I let him pick up the bill. This way, it looks like I made the effort to pick up the tab. I always say I'll pay the next time around but my first dates are usually my last. I lose interest in the guy once I have him for dessert. At least I get dinner and dessert without paying.

My cell phone starts singing.

"My milkshake brings all the boys to the yard . . ." I love that ring tone for my phone. Cool, huh? It's a text message from Tommy Boy. Go figure. That guy can talk all night if you let him.

"Hey! Me and the guy just kissed good-bye. He's sooo cute. I've got his number. He has mine. Hopefully, we'll have a date soon. What's new with you?" The text message ends with one of his trademark smiley faces.

While this kid's face is buried in my waist, still working on getting me off, and I am getting very close, I quickly punch in a message to Tommy, *"Yo! He's blowing me right now. TTYL!"*

I toss the phone on my desk chair, where a laundry pile of underwear and white T-shirts sits like snow on a mountaintop. I glance around my room and see all the photos of me from over the years, a black-and-white photo of me shirtless at twenty-one, with my thick Italian hair spiked up, and me sitting on a boulder on a hill back home.

There's a sketch of my body by an artist from Province-town who asked me to pose for him two summers ago. He paid me $50 and then sent me a copy of the drawing. There are photos of me pulverizing a boxing bag at a gym in high school, when I had a better body and looked younger. And then there's a photo of me during Halloween 2001, dressed as a shirtless GI Joe (I called myself GI Ho) with my camouflage pants. My abs were really tight in that photo, and my biceps were like two cantaloupes. I looked perfect, hot! I wish I looked like that again, so youthful, so beautiful. My hair has receded a bit. I have two runways opening my hairline by the sides of my forehead. So I cut my hair shorter on the sides and longer on the top. I wear a baseball cap sometimes to hide the obvious gaps.

The loss of hair makes me look older than twenty-seven. Shit. I'm getting old. I hate this crap. I started taking Rogaine here and there to get some growth back. I can't tell if it's working. But right now, I am feeling good.

"Oh, oh, OH GOD, *yeeaaaaaaaaaah. Molto bene,*" I shout out in Italian, releasing my load on this kid's face, making it look like a Krispy Kreme doughnut. I push my head back in my pillow and just take a few long deep breaths and savor the moment. That was hot. Nothing like a good blowjob after a night out and a week of brainless stock pricing. Any monkey can do that job.

The kid looks at me and grins. He crawls along my side and cushions his head into my bulging left bicep, as if to cuddle. No way! Once I get off, I want the guy to get out but I don't want to offend or hurt this guy. He seems like a nice kid but just not for me. I'm not looking for much more than a quickie these days.

I clean the white liquidity spill flowing on my abs, chest, and on my tattoo of the Italian flag with some Bounty paper towels. All cleaned up, I toss them into the trash near my computer's desk. I pop my back.

I'm shirtless with my boxers on, lying on the bed with this kid tracing invisible circles on my slightly hairy chest and all around my nipples with his index finger. I wish I could remember this kid's name. He seems like he wants to stay over or something.

He looks up at me. "Can I sleep over?"

I glance at my alarm clock and it reads 3:35 A.M. in large glowing red digital letters. And then I look at him again. "If it was a weekend night, that would be cool. But I work tomorrow. Gotta get up at 8 A.M. Sorry, man."

The kid hears me loud and clear, even though he seems a bit down now, like a puppy that has lost his way. In fact, his fuzzy crew-cut hair feels like the back of a puppy's head. He is such a cute guy, but not for me.

"Well, Rico, nice hanging out with you," he tells me as he puts his Abercrombie green T-shirt back on and starts to collect his clothes and J.Crew shoes from the floor.

"Want my number?" he asks.

"Yeah, um, sure," I say to be polite.

He walks on my wooden floors, loops around the bed, which takes up 90 percent of the room, and he writes his number down on a yellow Post-it. As I walk him out of my bedroom, I give him a kiss and a hug good-bye and wish him a safe drive. I escort him through the narrow hallway by the living room and out the front door. A quick arctic breeze sweeps inside the house before I close the door. My nipples harden from the chill. I hear the guy's footsteps crunching into the snow as he goes down the front steps of the porch and into his Honda Civic hatchback.

Walking back to my bedroom, I look at the Post-it with the number on it and I laugh. "Call me! Topher," the note reads.

So that's what his name was.

Chapter 3

KYLE

"I was represented by Model Citizens Inc. in New York last year and I've been featured in editorials for *Details* and *GQ* as well as print ads in Paris. See, right there in my portfolio. Those are the ads and catalogs," I explain to a trio of casting agents for a modeling job that could bolster my notoriety. There's a buzz about this hot, up-and-coming eighteen-year-old designer from Miami, and he's been getting good press all over the trade and entertainment magazines. If I score this modeling gig, I will be the face of his line of Spanish couture called *Papito Clothes Inc.* It could be huge! Stores are being planned in all the major metropolises: New York, Chicago, San Francisco, L.A., and even Boston. Billboards and a national television ad campaign are part of the deal. I deserve this job. It's what I've been dreaming of forever!

Thing is, I'm as Latino as Nicole Kidman. Truth be told, I'm as Anglo as the lineup in a typical *Friends* rerun. I don't even speak the *español*. But I have to try. The potential payoff is too great. Exposure. Acting jobs. More fame. Stardom. You know it!

I have to work it, flip it, and reverse it. Get myself out there. *The Battle of the Genders* has been airing new episodes featuring *moi*. Perfect timing for maximum exposure. That's why I keep bugging Tommy to write a story about me in *The Boston Daily*. That article would run all over New England and get picked up on the news wires and probably get published around the country. I could even include that in my portfolio, if they send their own photographer to shoot me. I really need to get Tommy to write that story. This ad campaign would be a perfect timely peg for an article. Just perfect.

"Mr. Kyle Andrews, your photographs are quite striking," the stern, gray-haired woman tells me from the middle seat of this long white-clothed table. "The camera just loves you. You have a classic look. You photograph differently in every shot." Two other men are perusing my modeling portfolio inside the lobby of the Hilton in Cambridge. It's quite warm in here, so warm that it's easy to forget that just outside is Memorial Drive and the icy Charles River.

The woman looks like a former ballerina with her slender build. She speaks with a slight Spanish accent. I'm guessing she's probably Puerto Rican, like many Hispanic women in Beantown. The two other men seem like corporate types, with their dress shirts, ties and reading glasses, and their curly dark hair slicked back with lots of gel. They are obviously representing some of the investors as they assist in the search for the new face of this clothing line. But no worries. I can hold my own with anyone. This trio does not scare Kyle!

"Gracias," I tell the woman, trying to win her over with some basic *español* I learned from my ex-boyfriend, José.

I right my posture, arching my back as I patiently watch them marvel at my pictures. I'm not the only one here, of course. There are rows of guys, also models, sitting behind me in fold-up chairs, waiting for their chance to show off their portfolios as well. They're all coiffed, clean-shaven, with dabs of makeup to cover up their unexpected blemishes. They share similar jutting mandibles and too-good-looking faces to be part of this planet. They could easily star in a Benetton ad. Like me, they are all sitting upright, perfect posture, and with elegant statuesque demeanors that silently scream, "I'm beautiful. Watch out. I'm getting this job. Booh-ya."

I'm relieved as I scan the rows of heads behind me. I'm not the only white boy in the room. There are some red-haired guys, brunettes with dark tans, black sculpted models (They always have the best bodies, right?), and hunky Asian guys with their spiked-up black hair. So I'm not the only one trying to push the envelope to be the face of a Latino ad.

As the woman and the two men "Hmm" and "Ahhh" their way through my portfolio, they close my book of pictures, hand it back to me, and smile. Then the woman, whose thin, penciled eyebrows furrow a little, shoots me a quizzical squint, asks, "Mr. Andrews, um, were you on that show *The Real Life?* Jou look bery familiar."

Yay! She recognizes me. I'm more famous that any super male model around these days. Not many people can name one right off the top of their heads, besides *moi*.

"Why yes!" I answer proudly, as my right eyebrow lifts a little. That's my trademark "interested" look. "That's how I was discovered as a model. It happened totally by accident. Destiny, you know." I flash her a smile. This is so easy!

She glances down, nods, and shoots me another curious look like she just found the missing word to complete a crossword puzzle. "*Sí*, I know the show bery well," she says, with an almost constipated face. "My teen daughters watch it. There was some crazy stuff in those episodes, especially one that was *muy*, how do I say, vulgar."

Oh God! Just great! She must have seen my threesome episode, the one with the KY Jelly and the two other guys including José. This is going to torpedo my chances for representing Papito Clothes Inc. Who'd want a guy who got it on with his Puerto Rican boyfriend and a cute Brazilian barback from Club Café. Shit!

She takes off her black-framed glasses, holds them in her wrinkled hands, and says, "I remember it well. It's something we will all have to consider. This is a new line and we don't want to send the wrong message to young teen buyers, our targeted demographic. Mr. Andrews, thank jou for coming in and we will be in touch with jour agent shortly, either way."

She graciously reaches out to shake my hand and the other two silent brooding corporate men do the same but they seem reluctant now to return my handshake since it was part of a former threesome episode. I grin, maintain eye contact with all six eyes, grab my portfolio, and push the chair back under the table.

"Thank you so much for taking the time to review my work. I look forward to hearing from you all very soon and, hopefully, to be working with your client. *Adios!*" I smile and walk away, showing them my runway walk. I pass by the aisles of male models; most are dabbing their faces with powder from their compacts as they wait for their names to be called. Good luck, suckers!

Once I'm out of the conference room, I take a seat in one of the so-cushy-your-ass-sinks-into-the-seats chairs in the lobby of the hotel, which overlooks the ash gray Charles River. Another soft snowfall sprinkles the water as people walk and cycle on the ribbon of concrete that hugs the river on both sides, Boston and Cambridge. The redbrick and brown Boston University buildings on the Boston side of the river are cloaked in white. It's a gorgeous scene. This place is a winter wonderland. But I'm not really feeling it the way I want to. It's just another winter afternoon with my chances of getting this job now falling with each snowflake.

That threesome episode is going to haunt me for the rest of my career, my life. What was I thinking when I brought José and Paulo back to *The Real Life* house and into the hot tub? We'd just met up at Club Café during Pride Week, and we all had too many Apple Martinis. What can I say? They're always to blame. On that June night, the guys standing in line on Columbus Avenue wore pride beads (in rainbow colors, of course), tank tops, shorts, and sandals. It was hot! Because of *The Real Life* cameras, the crowd parted for us like the Red Sea did for Moses as we cut to the front of the line. José and I made a dash to the bar and ordered drinks. I was so in love with José then. We'd been dating for two months, and things were going well, but sometimes, we got a bit wasted at the bar and created a bit of drama, on and off camera. This night was no exception.

Alcohol brought out the weird aspects of our personalities. Sober José was a shy, mellow, easygoing guy who produced a nightly radio program for the nationwide public radio station. He was a perfectionist and proud of his Puerto Rican roots. He organizes the float for the annual Puerto Rican parade and he speaks English and Spanish fluently. I picked up some *español* from my Puerto Rican lover. *Ay, Papi!*

Everywhere we went, from the grocery store, to the mall and the movies, we held hands and kissed openly. We wanted people to see that it's okay for a gay couple to be out and open. And with the cameras around, no one would dare pull a stunt or strike a punch because it would be recorded and possibly used in a court of law. The cameras were like our guardian angels, watching us.

After a few drinks, though, José transformed into a frisky, aggressive guy who was always looking to push his sexual boundaries. By this I mean the guy wanted to have acrobatic sex, hanging upside down while I stood upright or using objects like coat hangers and lots and lots of feathers. I'm all for experimenting. It's hot, but even I thought his ideas were, how shall we say, out there like Anne Heche.

For a few weeks, he had mentioned how great it would be to have a threesome. He thought it would bring us closer. Hmmm. I didn't see how bringing a stranger into our bed would bring us closer, but José and I tended to see things differently sometimes.

I can be a bit loud and melodramatic and somewhat obnoxious but, hey, that's me sober. When I drink, it's Kyle squared, me to the second power. Don't hold it against me. I've been known to flirt with other guys' boyfriends, in front of them, just to cause trouble because I know I can. No one wants the most popular gay guy at the moment to be talking to his boyfriend. You know what they say, meet them in a bar, lose them in a bar, which I learned the hard way with José after the show ended.

So that Thursday, José and I were at Club Café, guzzling down the liquor as cameras surrounded us in this chaotic carnival of men celebrating our right to be gay and free. Around midnight, by the front bar, José noticed a young stud, a Brazilian guy (They're everywhere in Boston. Who would have thunk it?) with his toned copper arms, black wavy hair, and eyes so dark that they reach deep. You couldn't tell where the circles of his pupil began or ended. José in his drunken stupor grabbed the guy on the ass and pulled him over to us. He then whispered to Paulo if he wanted to go back to *The Real Life* house with us on Beacon Hill and hop in the hot tub. The guy, apparently intrigued by the cameras and the powers of my model looks, said he was about to get off work in a half hour and would meet us outside.

Jealousy consumed me as fast as I had consumed those three Apple Martinis. I told José, "Why? Am I not enough for you? Why have another guy with us? You always want more and more, sugarplum!"

José grabbed my face, caressed my cheeks with his olive-hued hands, and said in his slurred tropical voice, "Honey, I love you. This has nothing to do with me liking that guy. It's about us, enjoying another man together, to make our union more alive. This does not change how I feel about you. Please, let me do this for us. You will love it, I promise, *papito!*"

I was just drunk enough to buy it. So stupid of me—and I totally forgot the cameras were taping all of it. Geez! Just my luck.

As soon as we stumbled into *The Real Life* house, the three of us stripped down to our birthday suits, tossing our clothes and jackets all over the wood floors. We then jumped into the steaming hot tub on the second floor. No one else seemed to be home; the other roommates were out. We had the house to ourselves: José, Mr. Brazil sex toy, and me. The camera crew, aka Big Brother, was watching us doing the dirty deed.

We wrestled in the hot tub, splashed water all around, and then out of nowhere, José pulled out a big jar of KY Jelly from a bag. He smeared it all over his ass as well as Paulo's as if he were about to wax a car.

"José, what are you doing with that?" I asked, paranoid about what was to come.

"Watch, you'll see, baby. You are going to looove this, *papito!* We will remember this for a long time," he told me, with his intense smoldering stare. José could turn me on with just one look from his beautiful Caribbean-sun-kissed face that re-sembled a butcher Ricky Martin. But like Ricky Martin, we were about to live *la vida loca.* (That's another new Spanish phrase I learned.)

Next thing I know, José, who is standing up like a sentinel, positions himself behind me and places Paulo in front of me.

We're like a manwich and I'm the meat. They both start grinding me from both ends, up and down. It was really hot. I was so turned on. I was slipping and sliding between both of them like a well-oiled car piston.

It was getting hot and heavy, with lots of heaving, breathing, and moaning, our bodies in sync, kind of like Madonna's threesome photos from her *Erotica* video with Naomi Campbell. Lost in the ecstasy of it all, the rhythm of the body grinds, we completely forgot about the cameras mounted in the corner of the wall amid our drunken haze.

And then a voice interrupted.

"You disgusting faggot! GROSS! *Que sucios!*"

It was Giselle, my conservative, bitchy, hot-tempered Latina roommate from Los Angeles who aspires to be a politician. "What the hell are you guys doing in the hot tub? We all have to use this. Disgusting!" she yelled at the top of her lungs.

I was so embarrassed and shocked, I froze, unable to utter a word for the first time in my life. José managed to dash to the bedroom and then ran out into the cold. Paulo grabbed his clothes, slid down the former fireman's pole to the first floor (the KY Jelly made it easier for him to go down), and ran out the door, too.

Amid the chaos, it turns out there was someone home, no, make that two other roommates, Rick and Flo, who awoke to see me in the buff full of KY front and back.

That episode, till this day, even with the blurred fuzzy cover-ups, has garnered the highest ratings of all time for *The Real Life*. Even now, people still call me KY behind my back.

Despite that embarrassing televised moment in my life, I need this job. When you are on a reality show, especially on a cable channel, you're only paid a stipend because the rent is free, as well as the electric bill. By the end of the six months I lived in the Boston firehouse, the network paid me about $6,000. Since the show has a six-month delay, my modeling jobs poured in just as the show began airing two Januarys ago. I've been able to live off that money, by renting a room in a three-bedroom apartment in the South End where most of the gay guys (about 97.9 percent) in the city live.

I don't have a car. I take the T everywhere with my monthly pass. I guard my savings and try not to use them too much. Because of the show and my fame, I've been asked by colleges and universities around the country to speak to their incoming freshman classes about my experience as a gay man in such a reality bubble. Those engagements pay about $1,500 a pop with travel expenses included.

So I've managed to live off my relatively short time in the spotlight. But I need to make it last. I don't want to go back to Oklahoma and be a nobody. Just as I was looking to do something with my life, after graduating from Princeton with a degree in sociology (What can someone really do with that degree anyways?), there was an open casting call for the show on campus. I made an audition tape and stood in a line of hundreds of students for a shot to meet the casting directors. I was different, articulate and fun, and most of all, openly gay. The show hasn't had many openly gay guys; and I know I am cute to boot, too. What else could they ask for?

Three weeks after that audition in September 2004, the producers called me back and flew me out to Los Angeles to interview me some more, but this time, they taped what I had to say. They asked me about my childhood and why I really wanted to be on the show.

I explained how constraining it was growing up in Oklahoma with the Catholic, Midwestern sensibilities instilled in you from conception. It didn't help that my older brother was straight and butch with athletic prowess while I was a skinny, tall, gay kid who loved to act in school plays and pose for cameras wherever they popped up.

I told the casting directors that ever since I saw the first

Real Life season based in New York with Ron, an openly gay guy, I felt like I wasn't alone in the world. Here was a guy, gay and proud of it, which was, like, normal. And he had a boyfriend on the show! If he was a role model for me, perhaps I could be a role model to some other teenager struggling with his or her homosexuality and society's views of us.

"I also want to be famous," I bluntly told the producers. "I'm not going to lie. I don't hold back. I make no apologies."

I believe my sincerity scored points with the casting directors. In January 2005, I got word from the network. I'd made the final cut. I packed my bags and headed to Boston, to live with six other dysfunctional roommates in a former Boston firehouse in the city's tony, historic Beacon Hill neighborhood.

Two years later, I find myself jobless. Money in my bank, while there, won't last forever. More is going out than coming in. The account dwindles.

Now, I look out on the forlorn Charles River from the Hilton lobby as the snow continues to fall. That whole threesome episode and how it will cost me future jobs is weighing heavily on my mind. I almost wish I could somehow toss it into the Charles, where it could be swallowed up and forgotten forever. Then I feel a vibration in the pocket of my Levi's. I pick up the phone with the gusto of a twelve-year-old girl.

"Hi, this is Kyle Andrews, may I help you?"

When I hear the other voice, I do mental cartwheels of joy. It's my best friend Eric calling from San Francisco.

"Hey, Kyle. What's going on?" he says. Hearing his voice reminds me of OK. (That's Oklahoma, people!). We grew up together in OK City and his mother, Bella Sols, was always like MOM (my other mom) or that's what I liked to call her. I came out to Bella first, even before my own parents, because she is so understanding and accepting. She happens to be the most fabulous radio psychologist in the Midwest. Eric is like my gay brother so I am always happy to hear from him. He also looks a lot like a butcher Ryan Seacrest from *American Idol* but with a better body and much taller, about six-feet-one.

"It's so good to hear your voice, Eric. I'm here sitting in the lobby of a hotel feeling crappy about this potential modeling job," I tell him as the snow dots the glass of the hotel's aquarium-like windows. "I don't think I'm gonna get it. I need the extra money. I need me some Benjamins."

"Listen, Kyle, I have a publicist friend who is looking for a well-known gay celebrity to emcee a pool party at the White Fiesta early next year in Miami. Of course, I thought of you," Eric says, always looking out for me. "They will fly you out and pay for your hotel room in South Beach. The job pays about $3,000. Not much, but hey, it's a nonprofit and for a good cause. Interested?"

"Of course!" I blurt out, jumping up and down inside the hotel as all the other models eyeball me and wonder what's going on with me. I can just see myself, the white boy surrounded by all those Latin lovers in Miami for the hottest circuit party on the East Coast. This is just what I need.

"Sign me up, pronto!" I holler into the phone.

"Cool, Kyle. I'll have the woman call you with the details," Eric says. "I know you'll be a hit as always."

Miami, here I come.

Chapter 4

TOMMY

It's amazing how snow can just get out of hand. At first, it's cute, sprinkling down like the powder a baker generously dusts on a fresh-baked pastry. But then, the white stuff just keeps coming and falling and then coming and falling down some more. Two days later, I'm still wondering, how can it still be snowing? Mother Nature, what's up with that?

It fills sidewalks, streets, even the insides of my shoes. I have to punch holes with my feet in deep mounds of Mother Nature's dandruff as I walk from brick-paved block to block. The parking lots at the *Daily* and for my building in Cambridge look like icing on a vanilla cake, with the cars and us humans as decorative figurines.

Mikey laughs when he hears my winter observations because this is my first winter in New England and, well, I've still got my native Florida skin. You can leave Miami but Miami never leaves you. It stays in your blood. I wish I could say the same thing about the tropical weather. Why can't I bottle up those tropical south Florida breezes and unleash them in my apartment whenever I feel homesick or supercold?

"Tommy, you need a thickah coat. That thin windbreakah won't do," he says, standing in the middle of my Cambridge studio as I ready to go out on our first date. I like how that sounds, our first date. Hopefully, it won't be the last one.

"It's thirty-five outside, not fifty-five. Heah, take my coat. I've got another one in the cahr," he says, helping me put on his Navy-like black wool coat. "You Floridians know nothing about wintah," he teases.

Yeah, it's 35 degrees outside—again!—and the wind is whipping, again! All I have on is my Nike red sweatshirt and a black Gap windbreaker. I hate layering myself like a ball of yarn, just to go outside for a few minutes before hopping into a car.

"Okay, you're the native heah," I say, imitating his Boston accent.

As I put on his coat, he grabs a black scarf of mine and twirls it around my neck like a strand of pasta on a fork.

"Now see . . . that's much bettah, cutie. Are you ready to go?"

"*Sí*, lead the way." I smile back and open the door for him.

I only met Mikey last night but things seem to be going pretty smoothly. We seem to click, like matching ends of a pair of dominoes. So it's only been one night but he just seems like such a good guy. He called today after work, just as I was about to watch an NBC *Dateline* episode about how everyone has gone carb crazy. We talked for a bit and he asked me if I wanted to meet up for dinner tonight.

I said, "Sure, that sounds like a plan," tickled by the thought of seeing him again so soon.

After we hop into his Toyota Matrix, we dash off to Bertucci's, my favorite Italian restaurant. Okay, it's a chain-restaurant found almost everywhere in New England but Mikey doesn't seem to mind. He is so easygoing. No fuss about where to go and what to do.

Fifteen minutes later, we walk into the red-bricked one-story restaurant in Harvard Square; the aroma of freshly baked dough fills every inch of this place, which is mostly frequented by families or students from nearby Harvard. It's not the most romantic place, but hey, the food is good and so far so is tonight's company.

The hostess escorts us to our table by a window that overlooks the subway stop and the trickle of cars on Massachusetts Avenue. Mikey pulls my seat out for me and I catch a trace of his cologne, a Tommy Hilfiger brand that smells of a clean powdery scent, like a newborn baby.

"You're such a gentleman!" I compliment him. A brief smile flickers across his face as we both sit down at the wooden table for two.

He orders the pasta with chicken and sun-dried tomatoes and a nice cool Corona. I order the margherita pizza with chicken and Diet Coke, of course.

I ask him about his day and Mikey begins to describe helping a student at his school.

"There's this one kid, super smaht but he can't seem to focus. He's been slipping in his grades. His teachah, Mrs. Berg, sent him to my office to find out what's going on," Mikey says in between sips of his cool tall Corona. The indoor lighting illuminates Mikey's blue eyes more than usual, making them look turquoise, like two slices of a bright blue sky. "You wouldn't believe what the problem was, Tommy."

I put down my Coke and ask, "What's his problem?"

"The kid hasn't been getting much attention at home because his father has been working a double-shift at the Gillette plant. I figured it out because I had him draw a picture of his family and his dad was standing the farthest from everybody in the group," Mike says, animated as he talks. His eyes seem to convey what he was thinking and feeling. Right now they show a genuine concern about this boy.

"When I asked him what he wanted most these days, the boy looked at me and said, 'I miss my daddy.' It broke my haht, Tommy. It broke my haht."

"So what did you do?" I ask, just listening to him talk as I rest my chin under my fist like I was hearing an old short story during a reading group in elementary school. I like the richness of Mikey's voice, the sincerity that comes through when he talks about work. I could listen to him all night. He seems like he truly cares about these students and I find that more compelling than his sweet blue eyes and cute face.

Mikey puts down his beer and continues.

"Well, I told him that if his daddy is working so much, it's because he loves him and his family so much. He wants to give them everything he can. So I told him not to worry, that I'm sure his father will make it up to him, but in the meantime, he could focus on his schoolwork and bring up his grades and that would make Daddy proud. The kid said he would try harder. I told him I'd speak with his father and mother about what we had discussed in my office."

"So you deal with that on a daily basis?" I ask Mikey, who orders another beer from our waitress, Candy, a Goth-looking college girl with nails the color of coal.

"Yeah, some days are busier than others with office visits, but other than that, I end up filling out a lot of paperwork and coordinating with the teachers about student files and their progress. Like I said, we sometimes provide the most stability for these kids. We're their other home," he says. "Anyways, enough about me, how was your day, cutie?"

I tell him about my interview today with a local Santeria priest who is trying to promote the religion in Boston and bring it out into the mainstream by performing more public ceremonies like on a beach, even during winter.

"This afternoon, the priest had a ceremony in his house to celebrate his twenty-second birthday as a priest. He offered apples, bananas, and other sweets to the orishas, or patron saints. You had all these followers kneeling and praying to the shrines and offering fruits and sweets as gifts inside his living room. It was quite a show but that's what I love about my job, writing about old things in new ways or discovering new things about old Boston," I tell Mikey, who again is completely focused on every word coming out of my mouth. I can see why students at his school open up to him. He's a great listener.

"I knew a little about Santeria while living in Miami and how it has parallels with Catholicism but nothing on this level because it's always been such a secretive religion. I want people in Boston to feel enlightened about what I write. I want people to feel like they've learned something new or feel enriched by reading this story."

"Well, Tommy, I'd definitely read that story," he says, mixing up his pasta and chicken and sun-dried tomatoes in his dish.

"Thanks. It runs next Sunday in the *City* section of the *Daily*. Um, I can save you a copy if you want? But you don't have to read it just because I wrote it. I write articles every week. It's no big deal."

"Well, I want to see what you do. It's obviously important to you that you moved up heah to keep writing. That's wonderful. You're the first reportah I have evah met and the cutest by fahr. You should be on TV. I'll definitely buy your article," he says, gently reaching out to my hand and tapping it. "You seem to like what you do, which is great, Tommy. I like that."

After we finish up our dinner, we head outside and walk around the outdoor-mall-like Harvard Square and marvel at all the two- and three-story buildings that ribbon the crimson university.

The wind has died down and there's fresh snow on the ground, making Cambridge look like a winter wonderland.

"You know, I've been thinking about you the whole day,

cutie," he says, his icy breath curling from the cold weather. We walk side-by-side on the brick-paved sidewalk by the huge Victorian estates on Brattle Street, just on the outskirts of the square.

"Yeah, me too, Mikey." I glance at him and then look down at my snow-covered brown J.Crew shoes. Whenever I look up, I see Mikey eyeing me, studying my face. He's probably never met a Cuban before or someone from Miami. I wonder what progress report he will write on me tonight!

"Cutie, seeing you tonight made my day," he says as we approach his car.

"Ditto," I answer back. Butterflies begin bouncing around inside my stomach when I realize he was thinking what I was thinking.

We arrive at his car and stand outside for a moment. I look around before my eyes finally rest at his blue ones, the kind that soothe yet stimulate at the same time. And then we both move in closer to kiss, kiss, and kiss some more.

We fall into a strong embrace, my nose tickled by his straight hair tucked behind his neck. He gently grips the back of my hips with his hands. And we kiss some more like two lips that don't seem to want to let go. I want to invite him back to my place but I decide to hold off. When guys hook up right away, they lose something, a sense of mystery, a connection with the other person. I don't want that to happen with Mikey so I'm trying to be patient. So it's just kissing, well, at least for tonight.

He drives me back to my studio and we hold each other's hands the whole way. My fingers rub the insides of his palm as it rests on the car's gear shifter. He plays his Sheryl Crow's *Greatest Hits* CD.

I hear her crow, "*The first cut is the deepest . . .*" as he tickles the insides of my hand in return and smiles my way.

Mikey parks in an empty space in front of my building and

I can't get enough of his sweet lips. I feel the slight stubble of his chin rub against mine whenever our lips touch, almost like Velcro, but I don't mind at all. He asks if I have plans for the following night.

"I don't have any plans," I answer. "I was going to stay home and rent a movie Saturday night. Nothing big or fancy."

"Well, do you want to go out tomorrow night?" he says, lifting his eyebrows, which makes his forehead crunch up a little.

"Shoah," I say, trying to mimic his accent again.

"Tommy, you have a horrible Boston accent. Let . . . it . . . *go!*" he jokes. "It would be like me trying to imitate a Spanish accent, not that you have one or anything."

We both start laughing.

After one more five-minute kiss good night, I step outside the car and into the entrance of my building. I walk in and I look back and see Mikey looking back as well, as if he's waiting to make sure I get in okay. Then he pulls away and his car grows smaller as if it were a Hot Wheels model in the distance. As soon as I head upstairs to my studio, I plunge into my head and hug my pillow as I was hugging Mikey.

Then a text message pops up on my phone, causing it to twitter electronically.

"Good night, Tommy. Sweet dreams, cutie!"

I can't stop thinking about Mikey for the rest of the night, and I fall asleep reliving and relishing his kisses in my mind.

The next day about 8 P.M. Mikey comes over again and my stomach is fluttering with anxious anticipation. When he walks in, we tightly hug and kiss like it had been weeks since we had seen each other. It's only been twenty-four hours but who's counting? He looks so handsome in his royal blue, long-sleeved button-down shirt and blue jeans. Both make his eyes more intense, like the blue of the waters off Cape Cod. We did not make any big plans besides him coming over. So after he walks in, we find ourselves lying on my big blue sofa, giggling and enjoying each other's company. He twirls one of my longer curls with his index finger as we talk about what to do.

"I love your hair, Tommy," he says, stretching out one of the longer curls in the front. "You look so cute with it," he says, his lips softly kissing my forehead, then slowly down to my nose and then finally reaching my lips. He caresses my cheek with his right hand.

It seems like we are going to stay here, just like this, which is perfectly fine by me until Mikey says, "Let's go out and get some drinks."

I look at him, wondering, "Hmmm. Again?" We drank Thursday when we met, and a little bit last night at the restaurant, and now Saturday, he wants to go out and get some more drinks. I know he is a counselor and that's one of the most difficult jobs around, but so is newspaper reporting!

But then he looks at me with those beautiful, sigh-inducing blue eyes, sticks his tongue out, and bites down on it, which makes me lose my mind a little and surrender to him.

I say, "Sure, Mikey! Where do you want to go?"

Half an hour later, we stroll into Club Café. He says that some of his friends are going to be there and he wants me to get to know them and have them get to know me so I oblige. I can't deny it, I'm curious about his friends.

There's an old saying my mom would tell me in Spanish, "You are who your friends are," or "Show me your friends and I will tell you who you are," or something like that. She always has some sort of old school Cuban adage to share about any situation.

So on my third night out with Mikey, I meet his friends, a lovey-dovey couple in their early thirties named Patrick and Will; they seem really nice. Patrick is a physical therapist who reminds me of comedian Jon Lovitz because of the way he talks. Will is an accountant (so many accountants in Boston) with bright red hair and the freckles to match every strand.

They immediately recognize my name from the paper when Mikey introduces me. We chitchat in the video bar, where Ciara dances and gyrates on the screen to her *Goodies.*

Things are going well until I notice the Jon Lovitz clone and the redhead growing drunker by the minute. They each make three visits to the bartender to buy drinks for themselves (mostly Cosmos) and Coronas for Mikey. Like watching a slow train wreck, I see what's happening and I stop drinking after my second DCV. I have a feeling I am going to be the only sober one here, not what I had in mind for a second date. Patrick and Will are a riot but they're bumping into other guys accidentally, slurring their words, and they almost break out into a fight with The Kyle, whose crisp chambray Izod shirt now sports a reddish splash from Will's spilled Cosmo.

Kyle glares at him the same way a coiled-up cobra does before attacking its prey, which would have ruined everyone's night. I step in and defuse a potential fight. No one wants Queen Cobra flexing her fangs right now. I try to keep him from wielding his verbal swords.

"Kyle, hey, it was an accident. If you go to the bathroom now, dilute it in water, and hold it up to the fan, you won't be able to tell," I explain to him as I try to play down the whole thing. "Haven't you accidentally spilled something on someone? There are so many guys here tonight that it's bound to happen." The last thing I need is a giant diva arguing with two drunken guys and Mikey stepping into the fray.

Kyle turns to me. "Tommy, your friends are as drunk as Joan Crawford in *Mommie Dearest.* They're making a scene and a mess here. If he bumps into me ONE MORE TIME, he will pay for a new shirt," Kyle says just before he struts toward the bathroom in full diva mode while Will and Patrick laugh away and venture to get yet another round at the bar.

I notice Mikey seems to be getting tipsy as well, cracking jokes that really make no sense.

"Tommy, is Fidel Castro a long-lost relative of yours?" he asks in his slurred speech and laughs back.

"Um, no, Mikey. That's not funny. If he was a relative, he would have been disowned a long time ago," I snap back.

"Are you like Puerto Ricans and Mexicans?" he follows up with a laugh.

"Um, *no!* We just share a common language, but no, Cubans are not like Mexicans and Puerto Ricans. We're all Hispanic but from different cultures and nations."

He hangs off my arm whenever he laughs. He now wears the Corona like cologne. I smell him from a few feet away.

I look around the bar, and to my surprise, I spot Rico in the corner about to order his own drink.

"Dudette, what's up with you? I just got here. Any hot guys tonight?" he says, peeling off his coat and showing off the tight green shirt that hugs and defines his body as if he were an anatomy textbook. The shirt brings out his green eyes even more than usual.

"I'm here with Mikey. It's our second date or well, our third time hanging out if you count Thursday. He's so sweet, Rico. We're here hanging out with his friends over there by the veejay booth," I say, pointing in their direction.

Rico looks around and sees Mikey with his drinking chums. A few seconds later, he tells me, "Your guy Mikey looks a little wasted. So do his friends. They're all slumped up against the wall over there, getting rowdy and singing. Is the dude drunk?"

I feel embarrassed for Mikey and a little for myself.

"Yeah, they all had a bit to drink and Mikey seems pretty buzzed," I tell Rico, looking down at my virgin Diet Coke on the rocks.

"That's not cool. He should be having fun with you on this date, not with his pals. Be careful is all I'm saying. I don't want you to get hurt or something. He should be sober and enjoying your company, bro. You deserve that, not him trashed like this," Rico says before grabbing his beer from the bartender.

"I hear ya, Rico, but that happens to everyone. Let me get back to these guys before they bump into someone else and create a bar fight the likes of *The Dukes of Hazzard*. They already splashed *Real Life* Kyle with their drinks."

"Oh no, God forbid that queen gets wet. It might ruin his *Cover Girl* close-up!" Rico fires back, unleashing his trademark devilish grin.

"See ya later, man," and I head back to the other side of the bar.

Rico pats me on the back in his rough but affectionate way. "Have fun and be careful! I know I will!" Like a shark, he must have picked up a cute guy with his sonar, or gaydar.

It's 2 A.M. and the three amigos are now definitely the three drunks. Patrick and Will stumble outside. I get them in a taxi back to Patrick's apartment in Charlestown, once he finally fessed up his address. Now I have Mikey to deal with, telling really unfunny jokes and talking gibberish. He wants to drive home, which is 28 miles south of Boston in the town of Duxbury or what people here call Deluxebury because of its grand estates, homes on hills, and somewhat snobby attitude. But I know what a trek that is after I got lost there once on my way to Plymouth, which borders it. The snow-covered roads and the fact that Duxbury's back roads have no streetlights make the idea of Mikey driving even more unappealing. The only lights you see there on the snaking, curvy roads are from other oncoming cars.

And besides, Mikey lives with his parents, both educators, and his younger sister, a realtor. I can't let him go home like this. I have to rescue him.

"Mikey . . . Mikey . . . focus for a second. We're going to 7-Eleven to buy you some water. I'm going to get some water, too, okay?" I say to him outside the club, trying to be patient, logical, and reassuring. I hold his hands and I make sure he looks straight at me.

"Yeah, that's fine, TOMmy b-b-b-boy! Damn, you're such a cutie." He beams his incandescent smile at me. Although he is talking to me, I sense Mikey isn't really here with me. It's as if another person possesses his body. He's not the sweet and sober Mikey I met two nights ago or even the guy from last night. He has a glazed look in his eyes like one of the drunken characters I've seen on one of those ABC after-school specials when I was younger.

Outside the 7-Eleven, I make him drink the bottled water. Minutes later, he is still lit as the streetlight above us. Then he becomes all apologetic. Where is all this coming from?

"Tommy, I'm sooo sorry. I drank too, too much. This will never happen again. I'm so, so sorry. You are so nice to me. I don't know how this happened. The guys kept buying me drinks," he says, wrapping his arm around my neck, leaning in for a kiss as his words slur some more. He looks at me with his deep blue I-need-you eyes.

I look at him and take a serious tone. "You had six Coronas. It will take six hours to get that out of your system. And you drank them in two hours. You can't drive home. I won't let you drive home. I know you don't know me that well but you can trust me. I'm a good guy. We'll go back to my place, I will make you a turkey sandwich, give you more water and some Tylenol, and you can sleep this off. I promise you, nothing will happen. I just don't want you driving home like this. You'll feel better in the morning. Now give me your keys."

We walk slowly to his Matrix (he drove tonight from my place) parked on Berkeley Street, around the corner from Club Café. In the passenger seat, Mikey looks at me, lifts his eyebrows like a pensive little boy, and says, "Tommy, thank you.

You're such a sweet, sweet, sweet guy. I had a good feeling about you when I first saw you. I'm so, so sorry about this."

"Shhh. Don't worry about it," I say as I start the car, which has a really cool futuristic-looking dashboard with all the circular knobs and buttons. It's so different from my bare-bones Wrangler.

"You overdrank. It happens to people sometimes. Don't worry about it. What matters now is getting you sober and feeling better. We'll be at my place in about fifteen minutes. Just relax. You'll feel better tomorrow morning, I promise. Okay?"

I turn the radio on, and just by luck, I hear Olivia Newton John singing "A Little More Love," her 1979 song on her *Greatest Hits* CD. I love that song and play it almost every day in the Jeep. It tends to put me in a good mood, even though the song is about a woman who can't seem to say no to a toxic man in her life.

"And it gets me nowhere to tell you no, and it gets me nowhere to make you go . . ."

It's Sunday morning and the sun slants through my red window shades, warming my face. I wake up to the aroma of bacon. I turn to my side and Mikey's gone. I prop up in my bed and rub my eyes in circular motion to wake them up. I look around and I see Mikey walking toward me with a plate and a big grin.

He hands me the plate, which has two eggs positioned like two yellow eyes and a curved bacon strip underneath them as if it was a smile. It's a breakfast happy face. How adorable! I smile back at the smiling plate.

In his other hand, he carries a nice tall glass of lemon-lime Gatorade.

"Cutie, I made you breakfast. I thought this smile would put a smile on your face. All you had was wheat bread, Diet Coke, and Gatorade in the refrigerator so I went to the store down the street and bought some bacon and eggs while you were sleeping," he says, sitting beside me on the edge of my queen-sized bed and running his hands through my curly hair, which probably looks like a giant Chia Pet right about now.

"You didn't have to do this. That is so sweet of you. No one has ever made me breakfast in bed before," I say, breaking off a piece of the bacon with my fingers and shoving it in my mouth. I don't like eggs or bacon but I can't tell him that. So I fake it and just eat them up.

"Well, you were so good to me last night when I got trashed. I acted so stupid. I'm sorry if I said anything obnoxious. I wanted to thank you for taking care of me. Thank you, Tommy, or as they say in Spanish, *gracias*," he says, plopping a kiss on my bacon-smeared lips.

"How are you feeling?" I ask, washing down the bacon with the Gatorade.

"Thanks to you, I feel great. The turkey sandwich and the Tylenol helped me a lot. I feel fine, cutie. So do you want to go to Providence today? It's only a fifty-minute ride. I'll drive!"

I couldn't resist. I have always wanted to take a drive down to Providence, ever since I began watching the NBC show of the same name on Friday nights at 8 P.M. When I lived in Miami, it reminded me of Boston and inspired me to try my best to get hired at the *Daily*. Now I meet this incredibly sweet and supercute guy who wants to show me around the city I've always been so charmed by, at least on TV.

"Yeah, that sounds like fun but let's go in the Jeep. Let's give your Matrix a break for the day."

"You got it, cutie!"

As I finish up breakfast and get out of bed, Mikey, wearing

a Miami Hurricanes white T-shirt of mine and my orange boxer shorts, looks my way and holds my hand.

"You know, Tommy Perez, I like you," he says with a gentle squeeze.

I turn to him on my bed. "I like you, too, Mr. Breakfast-in-Bed!"

Chapter 5

RICO

The blue glow of the computer lights up my bedroom. The radiator hisses like a snake in the corner. Too bad it's not a long big hot snake. This radiator sucks. It's just warm enough but it doesn't get any hotter in here. I have to wear a sweatshirt and sweatpants to stay warm. And I have to sleep with two comforters on my bed. The hair dryer comes in handy to heat up the pillows and comforters before I hit the sack. A chilly draft somehow manages to leak into my side of this old crappy house. You get what you pay for.

Just another night to manhunt on Bawstonboyz.com. It's 25 degrees outside and I'm not going out tonight. No way! Even if it's Thursday night, the good night at Club Café. Shit, I don't want to spend any money or gas tonight. Screw that. So this Italian Stallion is staying in the stable tonight.

I text-messaged Tommy Boy but he's probably with his boy Mikey tonight, because I would have heard from him by now if he wanted to go out. They've been dating a week now and the guy got shit-faced with Tommy on their second date the other night at CC. Not cool! Tommy deserves a better second date than that. Shit, anyone does. So now, I don't like that Mikey guy. But it's none of my business. Tommy is too nice sometimes. If it were me, I would have dumped the dude after that second date. No one wants a sloppy drinker on his hands or sheets.

My cell is ringing. A text message from Tommy. Speak of the devil and he instant-messages you.

"Hola, Rico! I'm with Mikey tonight. We're having dinner and renting a movie. A quiet night at my place. No CC tonight. He's sooooo sweet. I'll talk to you tomorrow. I hope you have a good night. Don't be good. Be bad!"

I instant-message him back, "Howdy! Staying in tonight too. Going on the computer. Have fun. Later!"

I log on to the website and start scrolling through the ads like a cyber photo album of porn. That word sounds hot. Porn. Porn. Porn. It just rolls off my tongue. The photos get me hard and horny. So do the names, well, some of them.

There's CUMNGETME. Another is UPMYBUTT. One ad is called PISSONME. Some of these dudes don't have any shame showing shots of their asses and dicks.

But who am I to talk? My screen name is EXFELON. Guys like that. They like the danger, the suspense, the bad boy image of it all. I look pretty rough in my profile photo. It's a shirtless picture of me, from the backside, hitting a boxing bag. If someone wants to see something else, they gotta e-mail me and start up a video camera link. I'd never put my picture out there for someone to copy. It's my face. No one else's. You never know where your face shot may end up without knowing it. Better to be safe than sorry.

My "You've Got Male" cursor blinks and I hear the computer beep. It's a message from a guy named CUMOVER. I open the e-mail. This should be good.

"Hey, what's going on tonight? Just out of jail? LOL! Hot photo. Looking to top? Lemme know."

I open up the guy's profile. He's forty-two, overweight,

balding. A troll. NOT! Why would he think I'd be interested in him?

I respond, "Thanks. Not interested. Later!"

My computer beeps again. Another message from the same guy. I sense this response won't be as nice as the first.

"Well fuck you, too. You're probably ugly since you won't show your face. Asshole!"

This is what you get for going online, but hey, it beats going out in this wicked weather. I keep scrolling through the ads in Dorchester. Most guys here are older, as in late thirties, forties, and fifties. You have to be older to afford one of these historic Victorian or Cape Ann houses. Most of the young guys here are in college and room together in triple-deckers, to save money on the rent.

Once in a while, you strike gold and find a cute hot guy who comes over to your place to play around. But to find that cute guy, you have to look at tons of fugly dudes on the site. It's like weeding out the bad to find the good.

I get hit with another "You've Got Male!"

The name on this one is LOOKIN4LATINOS.

"Hi Papi! You're one hot guy. Want to strap me up and hit me with a whip."

I don't even want to look at his profile. He already sounds like a weirdo.

I type back, "Me no espeaki English."

And another e-mail follows his.

The name on it says REALGUY.

"Hey Italian Stallion. I've seen you out. You're Tommy's wingman, right? I recognized the back of your head. Sexy guy. What are you doing tonight? Want to play reality TV? We can play Queer Factor or I could be your Bachelorette! Wink Wink."

Euuuww. It's Kyle, the *Real Life* dudette. I'm surprised he's not parading around Club Café tonight. He's cute to look at until he opens his big mouth. Then the image falls apart. He's such a queen and so superficial, always dropping names, including his own. I've never liked him so why is the dude e-mailing me here? Doesn't he get the hint that I'm not interested in his pretty *Real Life* ass. It's so obvious it's him, too. The first giveaway is his screen name: REALGUY.

Then there are his four photos. One's from his modeling ad for The Gap. Another is an image from *The Real Life*, of him and his ex-boyfriend. The other Kodak moment is him shirtless on a Provincetown beach, where he is sporting a bright blue Speedo and loud Elton John–type glasses. Kyle is holding out his hands to say, "Look at me! I'm fabu!" And then there's the X shot, of him and his bubbly toned Oklahoma white ass.

I tap the keys of my computer to respond and press "Send."

"No thanks KY!" I laugh to myself. Who'd want to be called KY! Ha! And who would want to mess around with that guy, after that threesome episode. Everyone saw it. Gross. Besides, everyone in town has been with him. I don't want to give him bragging rights that he's been with me and Oscar. No way. Ain't going there.

Kyle responds back.

"Don't be a stranger Rico Man. See you out soon," he responds. More like, avoid you sometime soon, Kyle.

I get hit with another "You've Got Male!" I guess I'm not the only one staying in tonight. I suspect Club Café is dead tonight since the chat rooms are crowded tonight at 9:30 P.M. The snow's falling pretty hard and there could be black ice on the roads. I'm gonna have to shovel the snow off my truck in the morning. What a drag but that's winter for you in Boston.

The name on this e-mail is "YOUNGHOTBOSBOY." This one looks promising. A quick hookup. He seems like a combination of a mineral and an animal from first glance.

I rate guys based on three categories: Mineral, if they have substance/brains. Vegetable, if they don't have smarts. And animal, if they are just hot but lack the substance and the smarts. Most of the guys in Boston are minerals but don't have the looks to match. It's hard to find two out of three. They may be hot and stupid or smart but with Frankenstein faces.

I continue reading his profile. I'm getting harder.

It says he's twenty-three, five feet eleven inches tall, white guy, dirty blond hair, brown eyes, a business student at Northeastern University. He's negative and looking to have fun or meet cool guys to be friends. His face is cute in that Matt Damon *Good-Will-Hunting* way. He has two body shots. One shows his tight abs and nice smooth arms and surfer-guy-type blond chest hair. He has a tattoo of a shark on his right shoulder. He looks pretty yummy. His location is South Boston, two subway stops on the red line or about a mile from me by car. But heck, I'm not driving tonight. He has to cum here, so to speak.

His e-mail reads, "Hi. Nice profile. My name is Joey. How's it going tonight? Cold?"

Wow, no "how hung" questions. No "top or bottom" question. No "my milkshake brings the boys to yard" comments. He seems cool so far. Cute name, too.

"Just staying in tonight, staying warm. Rico here. Nice to meet you dude. What are you up to?"

He responds, "Likewise. Thanks. Kind of bored tonight. Taking a study break. No one wants to go out tonight. Some news of a blizzard on the way according to Channel 7. I'm from Worcester but I live in the city for school during the school year. Are you from here? Are you a student? What do you do for fun? And why are you called ExFelon or is that just your gimmick? Did you serve in Alcatraz or something? Inquiring young minds wanna know!" He ends that sentence with a smiley face.

This guy actually wants to chat and he seems kinda funny.

I was looking for a quick hookup but Joey could be a possible date or a good fuck buddy. Did I just say that? A date. Shit! Tommy must be rubbing off on me.

"I'm from the Berkshires and moved here a few months ago. I work in accounting in downtown. I like snowboarding, watching movies, getting into snow fights and getting arrested. Just kidding on that last one. Never been in jail but wouldn't mind going either. I thought the screen name would get people's attention. It obviously got yours," I write him back with a facial expression marked by a winking right eye.

We talk until midnight, first on the computer and then later on the phone. He said he'd like to come over a bit but first he has to dig out his Toyota pickup truck buried in the snow.

"What do you wanna do, Joey?" I ask him, staring at his hot shirtless photo. I tuck my hand down between the layer of my underwear and sweatpants. My eyes, though, keep scrolling up to look at his smile. It's so bright and electric.

"We can play cops and robbers or we can just talk for a bit. Want to keep me warm tonight with conversation?" he says, in a butch yet tender voice.

"I'll e-mail you my address. Should take you about ten minutes," I tell him.

I hang up my cell, and at twelve past midnight, Joey's at my door. I let him in, excited that I am about to get off but more curious about what this guy is like in person.

At my door is this handsome guy, taller than me by an inch or so, and sandy hair covered in snowflakes that really bring out the brown in his eyes. I like brown eyes, especially on a cute face. I shake his cold hands, invite him in, and escort him to my room in the back of the house.

I take his corduroy jacket and scarf and toss them on my desk chair.

We hardly talk. We immediately start making out and let our bodies do the talking. They have a lot to say.

Something about this guy makes me feel relaxed and good. Good thing it's only for a little while. I don't want the dude to get attached or anything, even if he is adorable.

We roll around in bed, wrestling one another. I strip off his shirt and see his lean muscular skin. I pull off his jeans and yank off his blue Hanes underwear and gaze at his erect seven-inch cock saluting me back. Cut, just the way I like them. We're naked now, our bodies grinding, making our own type of indoor heat. I mount him and press my hands on top of his, tease him with my cock in between his legs. Damn, that feels so hot. I poke Oscar all around underneath his balls. I press my lips to meet his.

I then flip his long, soft, hairy legs behind his head. His eyes are completely locked on me, looking almost surprised yet thrilled, exhilarated. I lean in and softly whisper in his ear, "Nice to meet you, YoungHotBosBoy."

And the Italian Stallion rides again.

Chapter 6

KYLE

"Of course I will. It's my pleasure," I tell the events coordinator for the annual White Fiesta in Miami. I was in the middle of plucking my eyebrows in my bathroom mirror and attempting to pop some zits when I got the call on my cell. (Yes, even models have zits. They just airbrush them out for the editorials. You should see Tyra sans makeup. Whew!)

White Fiesta coordinators are planning a hot pool party at a South Beach hotel and they want me to be the emcee, thanks to Eric. "So all I have to do is open the party, tell everyone who will be there, and introduce each person or music act, all under the Florida sun?" I repeat back to her.

It's a no-brainer. This is, after all, for a good cause—me!

The coordinator, Sheryl, seems euphoric on the other end of the line in Miami, where it's probably, like 80 degrees and not like 20 in this December frozen tundra called Boston. Why did I stay here again? Oh yeah, because it's where I am most known from my reality TV fame and it beats being back in OK City.

"Kyle, you have such a following among many of our guests and you seem to be a natural for these kinds of events. So I will forward a contract to your agent to look over and you can fax it back to me after you've read it and signed it," Sheryl says in a very robotic corporate but friendly tone. "We will pay for your travel and room expenses. Again, thank you for doing this."

"No, thank *you*, Sheryl. Talk to you soon. Buh-byeee!" I tell her as I hang up the phone and start vogue-ing from sheer glee in my South End apartment.

Whew! This is exactly what I needed, a few days in Miami to soak up the sun in January and, more importantly, a paying job. Okay, so it's a temporary gig, one day of work, but it pays enough to cover some bills and gives me some exposure besides the kind from the freezing cold.

I haven't heard back from the modeling scouts for Papito Clothes since my casting call last month so I can't do anything about that there. So this hosting event is just want I need to lift my spirits and my profile.

Who knows, maybe Cher will be there or Elton John will make a cameo appearance. They've been spotted at these events before. And lots of gay men are producers and directors so my visibility as the emcee will get my face out there. I'm gonna have to visit Eric in San Francisco sometime soon and take him out to dinner, as a big thank-you.

Kyle, you have to work it, work it, work it, gurrrrl, I tell myself in front of the mirror. I stare up and down my lanky mirror and start to think of some funny lines I should say as host of the event.

"Let's all partake, partake," or "Seamen, come up and join me in welcoming RuPaul," or "Come one, come all!" or "Welcome to my party. Treat yourself to some gifts," I rehearse with an invisible microphone in my hand like a reporter for *Entertainment Tonight*. Now that would be a great job. Are you listening, *ET*?

I could just imagine all the hot Latino men and out-of-town white boys with their chiseled chests and thongs lounging around the pool areas, sipping their low-carb beers and Sex on the Beaches and staring at *moi*, as I disseminate information, among other things. (Wink.)

The White Fiesta is the hottest gay circuit party in the country. It's the biggest fund-raiser for the AIDE AIDS organization. Monies raised from the smaller parties such as the pool party I will be hosting help rake in $1 million in much-needed funds for the agency. As a host, I will also be granted an all-access pass to the crown jewel event, a formal evening party at Vizcaya Gardens, where everyone must dress in white.

As emcee of the pool party at the fabulous Raleigh Hotel, where all the stars are known to frolic, I feel it should be my queer duty to project a good image for my fellow gay sisters out there, I tell myself as I flex in the mirror.

I now strip down to my thong and hold my hands at my waist like a gay superhero.

I definitely need to work out before the Fiesta. I need to spend endless hours at the gym to prepare for said party and then spend a few hours at the tanning salon and at a Back Bay spa for a facial and some needed pampering.

I am heading to Miami, where everyone wears itsy-bitsy, teeny-weeny, tiny swimsuits, including the women. Wearing anything more would be a slap to the subtropical, bare-it-all culture. Here, less is more, as the motto goes. Perfect bodies are as common in these parts as the plastic surgeons who are on call to nip and tuck their every body part.

I plan to wear a little royal blue Speedo (to bring out the blue in my eyes and, well, the bulge in between my thighs). I just have to tone my abs (stop consuming those Frappuccinos and $1 pizza slices from the Italian shops on Boston street corners), and I have to cut back on my Cosmos at Club Café.

Now keep in mind, I am (a) thin like a telephone pole and (b) just as tall. I do not have the physique of your average *Playgirl* boy toy or *International Male Model*. Nor do I want one but being able to successfully sport a bathing suit is like one of those challenges on *Fear Factor* (or *Queer Factor*, in my book). And my body needs serious toning, like Pam Anderson or Brooke Burke.

After dressing myself in a loose blue Hollister T-shirt and sweatpants, I hop on my futon and dial my agent to tell him the good news and that we should milk my appearance at the White Fiesta for all it's worth.

"I'm going to type up a new press release and start sending it out," Bill, my wonderful agent, tells me.

"Send one to Tommy Perez at *The Boston Daily*. He said that if I do something big, he might be able to get a story about me in the paper!" I suggest to Bill, who has regularly landed me speaking gigs since I appeared on *The Real Life*. "And I think this is BIG, me being the emcee of one of the biggest gay circuit parties. And send a release to *OUT* magazine and *The Advocate* while you're at it. Maybe they'll give me a plug or something. They've already written small stories about me being the gay guy on *The Real Life*."

"Right on it, Kyle! I'll e-mail you a copy of it with the media blitz."

"You're fabulous, Bill. Keep up the good work," I tell him, my feet kicking up like an excited little girl. "I'm gonna get going to the gym to drag out the Brad Pitt body that is hiding inside this one. Have I told you how fabulous of an agent you are, Bill?"

"Yes, Kyle, you have, over and over. I'll talk to you soon. Have a good day!" Bill says before hanging up.

"Buh-bye," I tell him and toss my cell on my Ikea wicker chair.

I throw on some sneakers, grab my parka and gym bag, and start to walk the two blocks to The Metro Gym, below Club Café, for my extreme body gym makeover.

Forty-five minutes later and I am surrounded by pure testosterone. I can smell the musty, sweaty scent in the air. I love every minute of it! Sweaty, muscled men flex their cantaloupe-sized biceps while doing curls. Beefy hairy-chested men squat and squeeze every ounce of muscle power from their calves to the sounds of Usher and Gwen Stefani. The gym's pumping music blends in with the pumping iron as people step up and down on their step machines with each beat.

"*I ain't no hollaback girrl,*" Gwen hollas from the speakers.

"I aint no hollaback girrl, either," I sing back to the invisible Gwen in the gym.

I love coming here. It's like Club Café except you have bike machines and barbells instead of beer and bar stools. After thirty minutes on the elliptical machine, which makes me feel like I am skiing in place or moonwalking, I throw myself on the carpeted ab area and complete 1,000 crunches. Okay, not really, it was 100, but one more zero won't hurt. Boo-ya! All the while, the TV monitors play a marathon of my *Real Life* episodes. They just showed the episode where I met José, my Puerto Rican ex, and our first date to a Thai restaurant in Brookline called Bangkok Bangkok. What a name! I ordered the Kiss-Me-Chicken and José definitely followed up on that order with many kisses that night. (Sigh!)

I look up at the monitor, catch my breath, and recover from the painful burn aching in my belly. I am reliving the magic of that first date for a second when I hear a voice.

"Hey, isn't that you up there?" a rich, masculine voice asks from behind me. I turn around and come face to face with a ruggedly handsome hunk.

"Um, yeah. That's me. Hi, um, I'm Kyle and that up there was my life," I tell the hunk, who is six-feet-one and beautifully sculpted as if a Greek god had molded his body out of clay to perfection. He has dark brown hair in a crew cut style with some salt on the sides. Thick eyebrows and eyes as dark as night. He has olive skin, probably Italian or Greek, and I see some dark hairs poking out from under his tank top. I get a

boner just looking at him so I cover my frontal groin area with
the latest copy of *The Boston Daily*, which I grab from a nearby
machine.

"Um, and you are . . . ?" I ask, trying to regain my composure. This guy is so handsome that I find myself speaking as if I
had speed bumps on my tongue. I keep um-um-ing.

He holds out his hand, his *big* hand, to greet me.

"I'm Tony. I've never seen you here before but I've seen
you up there, on TV, during my workouts. You're a star here!"

"Why, thank you! But that was two years ago. It's gone into
rerun hell," I say as I eyeball him from head to toe and then
back up again. Okay, one more time. I scan him up and down
again. I couldn't resist. This guy is so my type, butch and
brawny with a Latin or Moorish look. I feel an electric crack-
ling tingle course through my body just from looking at him. I
want to put him in a cup and suck him hard through a straw
like my own personal milkshake. Hmmm. Delicious!

We're standing near the rows of elliptical machines as other
gym bunnies glide back and forth, sweating and grooving to
their iPods.

"You did great on the show," Tony continues, folding his
arms and grinning at me with a deep intensity. "Was it uncomfortable walking around with all those cameras around?"

"You get used to them after a while. They become like a
bug in your blind spot. You want to shoo them away sometimes but they always seem to be there so you just accept it.
Besides, I never felt alone. I always had a camera guy, a boom
guy, and a producer nearby me at all times. It was part of the
job, you know."

He nods as I explain my reality TV job description.

"What do you like to do for fun?" asks the hunk, whose
veins look like ropes bulging along his forearms from his recent workout. His black eyes twinkle from the fluorescent
lighting in here.

"I like to go to the movies, work out. I go upstairs to Club Café on Thursday nights to hang. I like to work but that's more sporadic. I just finished my cardio and abs. I'm going to be a host at the White Fiesta in a few weeks in Miami so I'm getting ready for that. What do you do for fun or for work?" I ask, finding myself unable to peel my eyes off this man. He's probably in his late thirties but he doesn't look a day over thirty. I can picture myself ripping his Nike black sweatpants right off, right here, right now, and going down on him.

"I'm an investment banker. I had a slow day today so I came to the gym earlier. When I'm not in the office in the financial district, I like to work out, and run along the Charles River when it's warmer. But for now, it's indoor running. I also like tall, lean, cute guys to throw around my bed," he says, leaning in as we stand under the row of monitors. "And you're definitely my type, *Real* man!"

I can totally picture dating this guy and I imagine him taking care of me. I'd wake up early in the mornings and brew him some coffee and bring it to him in our king-sized bed covered in a duvet and the newest Martha Stewart sheets. I would rub his back with a deep massage and oil as soon as he got home from the gym or work. We would spend weekends eating at the finest restaurants in Boston or taking drives down to New York or up to Provincetown for quick getaways. I can be a perfect wife to him.

We're standing so close, that I feel his breath on my face, which smells minty, like Winterfresh gum. I could lick those red juicy lips right now if he'd let me.

"Well, on that note, do you want to get out of here?" I ask, still hiding my boner with the *Daily*. At least Tommy Perez can't say I didn't pick up the paper today.

"Sure." He smiles back with a mischievous grin. "Do you live nearby?"

"Yeah, two blocks away. We can hang out. We can walk if

the cold doesn't bother you. It's about thirty-five outside but at least it's not windy."

So we both walk over to the brightly lit locker room with the rows of red lockers, small step benches to change on, and the tiled black floor. I stop a few lockers away from him, where I see him putting his hands beneath his head and curling his tight biceps up in a stretch before grabbing his gym bag and coat. I can't wait to see him shirtless, hugging me, holding me. That body!

A few minutes later, we're outside, walking toward my third-flood walk-up studio on Dartmouth Street. My place could easily have been a small one-bedroom if there had been an extra wall to divide the living room from the bedroom area but that's what you get for $750 a month. It's a bargain for this neighborhood.

"Do you want anything to drink? I've got some wine," I tell him as I take his wool coat and my red parka and hang them on the coat hanger. My back is turned.

When I turn around, I see Mr. Hunk whipping out his cock, which looks Italian from what I can tell because of its thick texture. He wags it around and smiles at me.

"Wanna suck it, Kyle?" he asks but it sounds more like an order. "I'd love to feel that pretty mouth of yours all over it. You're so cute."

Of course I do, but I don't tell him that. I move closer and start kissing his lips. I feel his tongue slip into my mouth and our lips lock. I love kissing, feeling his stubble against my smooth chin. But then he puts his hand behind my head and gently guides me downward to his cock. I guess he wants me to go south.

"Yeah, kiss that, Kyle," he says. Oh, what the heck! He's turning me on so much.

I kneel down on my weathered hardwood floors, look up and grin back, and marvel at him from this cat's-eye point-of-view.

I respond to his request by shoving his whole dick in my mouth like a long popsicle, in one take, all eight inches of it. I'm glad *The Real Life* cameras aren't around to tape this because then I would have one of those *One Night in Paris* videos floating around the Web, as if my threesome episode wasn't scandalous enough.

I stroke Tony's tiger up and down with my mouth, tasting every bit of him, swirling my tongue all around the top of his warm head in a clockwise motion. I hear him moan above me, guiding my head back and forth with his big hands while I create a wet vacuum between my mouth and his cock. I hear him grunting, his body jerking back and forth and twitching as I hold on to his waist for balance. I then feel his muscular, curvy rump with my hands. They are like two volleyballs, hard and round.

After ten minutes of sucking his dick, he starts to moan loud and grunts faster and faster, with heavy breathing.

"I'm gonna blow, man!" he shouts.

"Go for it!" I order, temporarily leaving my penis post, and then returning right back to it.

I then pull my mouth away and stroke his cock with my hand, so fast that it looks like a blur. I am eye-to-eye with his big round mushroom head, which seems to be staring at me. I mentally say "Hi" to it.

"*Yeah,* Kyle, yeah, Kyle, just like that, man, I'm gonna *co* . . ." And the white rapid shoots out from his cock and onto my face, warming every bit of it.

"Yeah, Kyle, that's just how I like it. I knew you'd be a hot lay," he says, breathing in deeply as his cock goes limp like a deflating balloon. He tucks his dick back into his sweatpants. He leans his head back and closes his eyes to savor the last moments of pleasure.

"*Yeah* . . ." he says. "*Ahhhh.*"

"Wanna jerk me off or suck me a little?" I ask him as I get

up from the floor and stand before him. I am still feeling all horned up. I want to come as bad as he did.

"Um, no offense, Kyle, but I already came. I lost the mood. Sorry," he says curtly. I try to look at him in the eyes, but whenever I do, his eyes suddenly dart away from me now, escaping mine. "Do you have toilet paper or something?" he asks, looking down.

"Sure," I say, crestfallen with my face dripping with his cum. I was hoping we could play some more.

"I'll be right back." I head to the bathroom to clean my face up. He really shot a big load because it takes me two face washes with soap to get it all off. I dry my face with my blue Martha Stewart towel. My face is still wet, though. I hand him some tissues and he grabs them abruptly.

"Do you want some water or something to eat?" I ask Tony, who is now fixing his hair in my mirror and shoving his T-shirt into his sweatpants. The dude has a crew cut. There is nothing to fix but he seems to think so.

"Thanks, but I'm gonna get going," he says. I see him pull out a ring from his gym bag. He puts it on his finger. Hmmm.

"Would you want to hang out some other time? Maybe see a movie or dinner? I know this great restaurant down the street that serves great Italian food," I ask him, all hopeful, as I sit on the corner of my futon, looking up at this fine creature of man who just minutes ago appreciated and craved me and looked at me like I was the only boy in the gym, or in Boston for that matter.

I'd love to wake up next to him sometime or brew him some coffee. Okay, so I would really buy the coffee from Starbucks down the street, but hey, it's the thought that counts.

"Kyle, you're super cute but I'm not looking for anything else. Sorry. I'm not interested," he says, grabbing his coat from the coat hanger by the front door. "I just thought you were cute on the show and you got me curious. Besides, I'm married. I have a husband."

I suddenly feel I just got sucker-punched but why am I surprised? I guess I knew deep down inside this would be just a hookup. We met at a gay gym after all. But maybe, I was hoping for something more. It's so rare I meet a guy that fits my type the way this guy does.

"Oh . . . I didn't know. I was just thinking we could have gotten to know each other better but not if you have a boyfriend," I tell him in a tone that tries to cover the disappointment in my voice. I should have asked whether he was single. Guys this hot usually have a boyfriend. They just don't always tell you right away.

"I love my husband. We got gay-married this year here. Besides, I'd never date someone on reality TV. No offense but everyone knows your business and I don't want to be a part of that," he says, grabbing his gym bag from the floor and throwing it over his shoulder. Again, his bicep bulges with the quick action. "I'm a discreet kinda guy."

He walks toward the door.

"There's more to me than what was on that show. But I guess you're not interested in finding out," I snap back. I open the door, and he walks into the hallway.

"Take it easy, Kyle. That was hot. See ya at the gym," he says, patting the top of my right shoulder awkwardly like I was a pet or something. He waves goodbye and then starts walking down the three flights of stairs that squeak with each step to the ground level of Dartmouth Street.

"Yeah, take it easy, too," I say but he's already gone. I close the door and look around my empty apartment.

Yeah, it would be nice to have a boyfriend again someday, someone who likes me for me and not the celebrity of me. Just because I'm a star doesn't mean I'm not a guy who wants his heart to be touched and be loved for all the right reasons. Well, one day it'll happen again. (Are you listening, George Clooney?) I loved José, but once the show aired our episodes together, he changed. The fame, even though he was on the show as my boyfriend and because of me, went to his head. He was recognized everywhere he went in Boston and he began meeting other cute guys. No more use for Kyle! He dumped me and moved on to his legion of twink fans, even though he was a peripheral character on the show. *Adios*, José, and now, *ciao*, Tony!

Anyhoo, it's just me and The CW's *America's Next Top Model* tonight. Tyra announces the final three still in the running to become *America's Next Top Model*. But everyone knows the winner in the show is really La Tyra. Maybe one day, I'll have my own reality modeling show. I'd call it *Kyle's Angels*. The theme song would say, *"Once upon a time, there was a cute little model boy from Oklahoma. His name was Kyle."*

As I sing the imaginary theme song to my fantasy show, I walk over to the fridge. I swing the freezer door open covered with my *Real Life* magnets and photos of me and Eric on horseback in OK City, and stare at what I absolutely know will make me feel better: a pint of Ben and Jerry's milk chocolate ice cream with swirls of peanut butter. Yum yum *yum!* I grab it along with a big spoon, plop myself on my red futon, and turn on the TV. Tyra and her crew are on. I could easily be a guest judge on that show and teach Miss Jay, Twiggy, and Jay Manuel a thing or two about posing and makeup. As I watch the new castmates cat-fight about who had the better *Cover Girl* commercial (It was Danielle, people!), I can't help but wonder if there is someone out there for me besides these hollow tricks. I'm feeling better with each spoonful of the chunky chocolate ice cream, the sugar tingling on my tongue. One day, I'll find a man who will take me away and adore me and forget that I was on that stupid reality show. He'll like me for me, even if I get fat from eating all this delicious chocolate ice cream or, God forbid, if I ever end up looking like Miss Jay. (I call the he-she Miss Gay.) Here comes the good part—Tyra's about to pick tonight's winner—but we all know who that really is, every season.

Chapter 7

TOMMY

"Which way, Mikey?" The sun bears down on us as we bop on Interstate 93 in my Jeep on the way to Providence. I'm so excited! This is my first time visiting the city that my favorite show of all time, *Providence*, is based on. The sun's so bright that it reflects off the highway and creates a blinding sheen. So I put on my sunglasses to reduce the glare. Mikey is riding shotgun, browsing through my collection of CDs.

"Just follow the sign to Providence when it comes up just ahead," he says. "Then we'll hit 95 south and we'll be in Providence in no time, about half an hour."

"Ah, okay. That doesn't sound too far at all. I can't wait, Mikey!" Although my eyes are focused on the road, I occasionally sneak a peek at Mikey and just marvel at his profile. *Que* cute! As he leafs through my CDs, he looks confused, lost in thought for a second.

"Um, Tommy, all you have heah are Gloria Estefan CDs. Her *Greatest Hits*. Then her *Greatest Hits*, part two. Then Gloria-sings-her-favorite-Christmas-songs CD," he says, his eyebrows rising, which form small wrinkles in his forehead. He thumbs through the individual discs while looking for something he might actually like. I doubt he will.

"Oh wait, you do have something else. I just found the soundtrack to the show *Providence*. What a coincidence! You weren't kidding when you said how much you liked that show. And what's with the Mandy Moore's greatest hits CD? She only had one good song!" he says, his eyebrows lifting again as to emphasize his point.

"You're too much, cutie! Don't you have Justin Timberlake or anything that is *not* Gloria Estefan?"

I smirk back at him.

"Well . . . I tend to listen to the radio a lot, too. Do you like country? I love Shania Twain, Faith Hill, and Dolly Parton. Their songs put me in a good mood." I fidget with my radio dial, which still has a tape player. It's an old Jeep, okay!

"I'll pass on the bumpkin music," he says, tuning into Boston's local top-40 station, which is now playing, of all coincidences, Justin Timberlake.

"Leave it there, yeah. I like me some Mr. JT," Mikey says, grooving to Timberlake's "Walk Away." The boy, meaning Mikey, seems to have no rhythm as he grooves awkwardly in my passenger seat with his hands but it's cute.

Now this is the Mikey I like. He's sober, calm, cool, and collected (white-boy rhythm dancing and all). He's just adorably sweet, not the loud lush from last night. This is our first day trip and I can't wait to see how the rest of the day unfolds.

"So what do you like to do for fun besides making fun of my taste in music?" I look over at Mikey, who is lying back in his seat after giving up on finding anything he might actually like in my CD collection. The sun pours through my plastic windows and highlights the soft golden brown hairs on Mikey's arms and a patch of light brown stubble on his dimpled chin. The Jeep rattles the whole trip because I have a soft top, which shakes and billows with the highway wind as if a giant invisible hand were rattling it back and forth.

"I love to ski, Tommy, in Killington, Vermont. That's why I bought the Matrix, because it has all-wheel-drive for the snow. We should go skiing sometime. Killington has like two hundred trails over seven mountains. I can't imagine you know how to ski, being from Florida," he says, trying to hide his yawn. It's one of many since we left Cambridge. I guess last night's revelry is finally catching up to him. If I had drunk as much as he did last night, I'd still be in bed, hiding under the covers and clobbered by a vicious hangover. But then again, I'm a liquor lightweight. Two Vodkas with Diet Coke and I'm pretty much set for the night.

"You're right. I don't know how to ski but I can ice-skate, if you can believe that."

"You ice-skated in Miami Beach?" Mikey asks incredulously. "No way! It's too hot down there."

"We had an ice-skating rink at the Miami Beach Youth Center, where I would skate during summer camp when I was little. I'm pretty fast. It's like in-line skating but you have to wear a jacket and you can see the puffs of your breath." As I talk, I steer the Jeep onto Interstate 95 and follow the sign that says PROVIDENCE, 33 MILES.

"So, you like to ski, what else? Tell me more," I ask Mikey, gently squeezing the top of his left knee.

"I love surfing on the Cape during the summah when the waves are high and the water is warmah. It's such a great feeling being out there, riding a wave and being free and no one to bothah you. You don't have to talk, or explain or listen to anyone except the sounds of the ocean," he says, his eyes seemingly drifting away as if momentarily reliving those aquatic moments on his surfboard. "That's another reason I bought the Matrix, I can stuff my surfboards in there. It's a great cahr and not as bouncy as this one, though. I feel like a Bobble Head in heah."

As he says this, he taps the top of my dashboard, which has a small Beanie Baby of a shark that Brian gave me back in Miami. "Do you surf, cutie?"

"Nah, not a surfer boy but I love to swim. Maybe it's the Pisces in me. I grew up swimming in Miami Beach with my parents and Mary and in the Olympic swimming pool at the youth center. I was pretty good free-style and with the back-strokes. I'm like a fish. Put me in water and I'm right at home." I look over at Mikey and he's resting his head against the plastic side window, relaxing yet listening to everything I have to say.

"Well, maybe this summah we can go swimming and I can see how good you really are, Flippah," he says, playfully poking my cheek with his index finger. He gives me a bemused smile at our playful banter.

"Seriously, I'm a seaman." I return the grin.

"I'm sure you are and I'm sure you like seamen!" he teases back.

"Ha, you know it! Pisceans are very intuitive besides being water-friendly."

"Oh yeah? So tell me, what does your intuition say I'm thinking right now, Tommy?"

"That you wished we had taken your car for this trip?" I chuckle.

"You're right," he says, making his head bounce up and down like a jackhammer or a cute blue-eyed Bobble Head named Mikey.

Half an hour later, I take Exit 22C off I-95 into downtown Providence. It looks like a mini-Boston, with the small forest of red-bricked skyscrapers and buildings that flank this gargantuan mall called Providence Place. We drive along the riverfront as it snakes along the spine of the city. Mikey explains how the city hosts "fire nights," on Fridays during the summer and fall. That's when a series of fires are lit in the middle of this narrow river, illuminating the water as people walk the river-front from Providence Place. He directs me to drive up toward this hilly area of buildings and homes that overlooks the river and the mall.

Just before we reach Brown University, we sit at a red light, where the uphill street is so steep, I feel like we're inside the Space Shuttle *Columbia* about to launch. I have to give my old Jeep a lot of gas just to climb this incline. We pull up to a parking meter next to Brown University and walk around.

"This looks a little like Harvard Yard," I tell Mikey, who points out the different charming academic crimson buildings on campus. Students sit on the benches and trek back and forth between the buildings. It's just warm enough to do that, at 40-something degrees with a cool breeze that occasionally lifts Mikey's soft brown strands of straight hair up above his forehead. The sun licks our cheeks like soft flames warming us in this chilly weather.

"There's Thayer Street ovah there where a lot of the students hang out. Lots of places to eat ovah there," he says, and so we cross the street and stroll that way. The whole time, I am just tickled that we're here in Providence, just like in the TV show. Maybe I'll see the Hanson family featured in it. But I feel so touched that Mikey brought me here. It was such a nice thing to do and I'm glad I am experiencing it for the first time with him. My own personal tour guide.

After trekking around Brown University, we hop back into the Jeep and drive a few blocks to Wickenden Street, another hilly street (so many of them here) but full of shoulder-to-shoulder eateries, cafés, bars, pubs, and art stores. We stroll in and out of the artsy shops.

"How do you know so much about Providence, Mikey?" I ask as we walk by a colorful pet store on the corner with a front façade painted like an ocean with vibrant goldfish, something right out of *Finding Nemo*.

"My ex-girlfriend went to school here so I spent a lot of time here," Mikey says. "That was a long time ago, but if you live in Massachusetts, you naturally learn about the surrounding states and where to go." We both cup our eyes with our hands to peek into the front window of the pet store and watch the fishies swimming back and forth.

"Was that ex-girlfriend your ex-fiancée?" I ask him, feeling a little bit like I am playing reporter even though I am off the clock right now.

"Yeah, that was the first one. We don't talk. She was supah angry after I changed my mind about getting married. I told her I didn't feel ready to commit yet and I just had a change of haht. She doesn't know I'm gay."

We peel ourselves away from the pet store's front windows and walk downhill on Wickenden Street.

"Mikey, does your family know you're gay?" I ask as we carefully maneuver ourselves around the small piles of snow that line the edge of the sidewalk.

"No, they don't. I'm not ready yet. My family is die-hard Catholic Italian and Irish, and although I'm sure they suspect, I just don't want to open up to them about that. It's hard, Tommy. I'm the only son and I'm the apple of my parents' eyes. They're so proud of me. I don't want to disappoint them. It's just hard sometimes, almost suffocating."

I put my hand on Mikey's back and gently rub it as if to say, I understand.

"Well, when it feels right, you'll know. I'm the only boy in my family and my dad is one of these old-school Cuban macho types so I know the feeling." We walk by a coffee shop teeming with college students with their books opened up.

"So they're cool with you being gay, Tommy?" he asks as if searching for a long-lost answer to a crossword puzzle.

"It took some time. I told them when I was sixteen, in the eleventh grade. I've always been close with my parents and felt

I could tell them anything. They noticed I wasn't smiling as much and asked me what was wrong. I simply said, 'I don't know if I like boys or girls.' "

"No way! You just told them like that, point blank?" Mikey asks, his eyes expressing absolute surprise as if what I did was foreign and unimaginable in his world. "That was very brave of you, Tommy. That took a lot of balls."

"Thanks, but yeah, they were shocked. They always thought I liked girls; so did my older sister Mary. So after that, they sent me to a psychologist, and after a few weeks, my parents noticed I was smiling and being my chipper self and I began writing for *The Miami Chronicle* as a high school reporting intern around that time. Right before my last therapy session, the psychologist told my parents to leave me alone and to not pressure me, that I know what I am and what I like, and that if they pushed, I had the grades and gumption to move away and be my own person. He told them, 'If you want your son to be happy, let him be. He will find his own path.' And so they did. We just don't talk about my being gay. It's almost like a Latin code of silence. We know you are but we don't have to know every detail about it. It comes up when my mom gives me the occasional HIV talk whenever she suspects I have a boyfriend or what she calls '*un amigo*.' They trust me, Mikey, and that's all I can ask for. I don't rub it in their face and I don't fag out in front of them, not that I fag out all the time or anything. I respect them and they respect me," I explain as we find ourselves standing in front of a majestic old church with golden wooden doors used by local Portuguese residents.

"Well, maybe one day, my parents will be the same with me. I just don't want it to get all weird with them, you know," Mikey says as we sit on the stoop of the church, our shoulders touching.

"Your parents love you, Mikey, and they will love you no matter what. Always remember that. It may be awkward at first but they will come around. If you're not comfortable with being gay, then they won't be. But remember, you can't be a hundred percent happy in the closet. No one ever is. When you're ready to tell them, you will and you'll feel this weight lifted off your skinny shoulders." As I say this, Mikey plops a nice sweet kiss on my cheek and nudges the back of my neck with his nose. The moisture of his lips tickles my skin.

"Well, I guess I won't be sleeping over at your house anytime soon," I tell Mikey with a grin and a wink.

"Yeah yeah yeah, very funny, cutie. Very funny!" he says playfully, messing up my curly hair.

We walk back to the Jeep, which was parked at the top of Wickenden Street, or less than a mile away, and we head to Providence Place, flanked by Macy's at one end and Nordstrom's at the other. The state's capital building sits down the street and overlooks the train station and the rest of the city as if it were a giant white church.

We hit the main stores, The Gap and Old Navy, and try on new hoods and jeans. When no one's looking, I sneak into Mikey's dressing room to steal a kiss and a hug. We then head upstairs to the bustling food court and hit Ben and Jerry's ice cream. We both share a large chocolate chunk brownie shake as we roam from one floor of the mall to the next. In the middle of the mall, we stop and gaze at the postcard view of the city. It's like seeing Providence through giant aquarium glass windows. You can see Brown University, where we just walked by, as well as the charming Victorian houses that surround the neighborhood there. They look like tiny colorful dollhouses that you can cup in the palm of your hand.

At 7 P.M., we try to leave this colossal mall, which looks like a stacked cement wedding cake from I-95 with its various parking levels. But we can't find my Jeep in the mazelike parking garage.

"Tommy, you sure it was level three?"

"Yeah, I'm sure. It's like someone stole it. It was right there," I say, pointing to the space where a Jeep Liberty now sits. We walk up and down each level but no luck.

"I can't believe we can't find your Jeep. I'm a counselor and you're a reportah. We're educated and we can't find a simple Jeep," he says, catching his breath from going up and down the stairs and from laughing.

"I know!" I bellow from the top of the stairwell. "We're like that 1995 movie *Dumb and Dumber,* or is that *Dumberer and Dumbest?*" I say between my bellyaching giggles that echo in the stairwell.

"Oh my gosh, maybe someone stole your cahr?" Mikey says.

"I doubt it. It's so beat up. Let's keep looking. It has to be around here somewhere."

After an hour of fruitless searching, punctuated by much laughter, we surrender. We flag down one of the uniformed security officers bopping in a white golf cart. I explain to him where I swore I parked the car. He tells us to jump into his golf cart. Within two minutes, he drops us off in front of my Wrangler.

"That always happens here," the security guard says. "You were in the wrong place at Providence Place. You were parked on the city side of the mall, not the state side of the mall, which has the view of the state house. You're not the first ones to lose their cars here."

Mikey and I keep laughing about this over and over again the whole fifty-minute drive back to my place. Once we get there, we collapse on my bed, his face buried in my mop of hair.

"I had such a great day, Mikey," I whisper into his ear.

"Yeah. Me too, Tommy," he says, turning around and staring into my eyes.

"Thank you for being my tour guide," and I kiss him. "I won't forget this day."

We kiss on and on, passionately. My tongue gently dances behind his ears. My hand combs through his beautiful straight hair. Within a few minutes, our clothes are off and we give in to everything that had been building up since we met a few nights ago. He sweetly kisses the nape of my neck, then follows the trail of my dark hair south down my chest. He presses his lips softly against the insides of my arms, which sends tiny jolts of electric tingles throughout my body.

We roll around my bed, exploring each other's bodies, my tongue familiarizing itself with every small freckle that dots his shoulders, stomach, and legs. Every time I fondle him down there and lick his chin, his head thrusts back against my pillows. His lean body jerks up and shudders in excitement whenever I kiss that area just underneath his ear and above his neck. My stomach tightens every time I feel the touch of his lips or the grasp of his hands on any part of my body.

I get up for a second and light two vanilla candles near my bed and turn off the lights. As we kiss some more, our shadows look like one being on the wall.

"Mikey, are you a top or a bottom?" I ask, trying not to interrupt the passionate flow we've got going on here but inquiring Cuban minds wanna know certain things.

"I don't care. We can do anything you want as long as we're safe," he says.

With that green light, I pull a condom from under my bed and grab my aqua-colored bottle of lube. I gently lather some on our dicks.

We make love for hours, becoming a union, flowing as one. Our bodies writhe in sweat and each other's body heat. Whenever I sink deeper into him, he draws me closer, holding on to me as if he'll never let me go.

"I want you so much, Tommy," he says, kissing me and arching his back.

"You feel so good, Mikey," I say, almost breathless, pressing my hands on top of his. My body rubs up against his with my mouth savoring every bit of his neck.

When the moment finally comes, we both let out a collective forceful moan and just collapse in my bed side by side. My arm leans across his chest and holds him near, tightly, like a favorite stuffed doll.

"Tommy, that was hot," he softly whispers and smooches the curve of my left shoulder.

"Yeah, that was fun," I tell him. We then spoon, enjoying the lasting effects of our first time together.

He leaves at 1 A.M. because he has to be at work at 8 A.M. over in Duxbury and, well, we've had a long day, among other things. He actually ends up leaving at 1:15 A.M. because we can't separate ourselves at the door with kisses that do not seem to want to end. It's a perfect way to end a perfect day, despite the night before.

Over the next three weeks, Mikey and I spend every two or three days together, when he doesn't have a big load at school the next morning. No matter what we do, we have fun, enjoying each other's company and the warmth of each other's bodies later at night.

The following Saturday afternoon, we walk up and down Newbury Street in Boston. We visit the shops and sample the desserts in some of the swank chocolate stores until our stomachs can't take any more. Even going to the Boston Public Library one Sunday is fun. We both register and get our library cards. We play hide and seek behind the thick towering bookshelves that line this multistory library, which has the feel of an old museum. We break out in giggles whenever one of us surprises the other. For two guys in their thirties (well, almost thirty, I'm twenty-nine), we bring out each other's inner child.

So when Mikey wants to get a drink now and then, I go along with it but I can't help feeling I'm walking on eggshells. In the first month that I know him, he gets sloshed twice, and each time, the drunken duo is around. So I do my best for us to do fun things on the weekends, *away* from Club Café. And I admit, I'm not hanging out with Rico as much, something he reminds me of anytime he wants to grab a drink at Club Café.

On my third Saturday with Mikey, we decide to see the Jane Goodall movie about her life studying monkeys. It is playing on the vertigo-inducing IMAX screen at the Museum of Science by the Charles River. Mikey's a big Jane Goodall fan and recently read her autobiography. So, I surprise him with the idea of going to see her movie, but I don't realize how nauseated I'll feel sitting in those inclined theater chairs.

"Are you okay, Tommy? You look like you're gonna be sick," he says as I slump in my chair and keep my eyes locked on the screen ahead. I try not to look to my left or to my right, which makes me want to hurl. It feels like the room is spinning every time I look away from the screen.

"Yeah, I'm hanging in there," I tell him as he holds my hand and rubs the top of it gently. As the chimps swing on the trees, Mikey swings his arm around me, as if he's protecting me against something, and my nausea seems to go away.

"Just look straight ahead and you'll be fine, okay?" he says. When he gets up to go to the bathroom, he returns with a large Sprite.

"Heah, this is for you, cutie. To calm your stomach," he tells me with his trademark grin. He always seems to surprise me in some new way.

On the way back to my place that night as Mikey drives, I look out his window at the blur of trees and light posts as we speed in the Matrix along Memorial Drive. I look over at Mikey and then look up through this moon roof, watching a white moon that looks almost pregnant, or like a soft bulb in the night sky, with tiny stars that twinkle all around it. The more time Mikey and I spend together, the happier I feel and the more I find myself falling for this guy.

When we get back to my place that night, he pulls something out of his coat pocket.

"Heah, I thought it was time you had this, cutie," Mikey says as we stand near my bed. To my surprise, he hands me a Red Sox baseball cap with the letter B in red on the front.

"Oh wow, thank you, Mikey. That's so sweet of you," I tell him, giving him a nice long wet kiss.

"Yeah, now you are officially a Bahstonian. You're a membah of Red Sox Nation," he says as he puts the cap on me and pulls down on the bill so that it smushes my curly hair.

"See, now you're one of us!" he says before we hug and we hit my bed for some one-on-one physical counseling. I love the cap so much, I keep it on as we make love that night, which makes Mikey crack up every time he looks up at me.

"You're too much, Tommy," Mikey says as his naked body lies on top of mine and his hands caress my face shadowed slightly by the new cap.

"But the cap looks adorable on you. Red is your color," he says, licking my lips with his lips.

That night, as Mikey soundlessly sleeps on the left side of my bed, I look out the window and catch the moon again watching over us like a celestial guardian. I glance over to Mikey, who is soundly asleep. I tug at the bill of my new favorite cap and stare out at the moon and I smile. I think about how Mikey has awakened something inside me again that yearns to be cared for, protected, to be desired, listened to, and most of all, to be loved unconditionally. He isn't just my potential boyfriend; he is also becoming my best friend in Boston. And for the first time in my year here, Red Sox Nation is feeling a lot like home.

Chapter 8

RICO

Shit, it's that time of the month again. Gotta call Tommy to give me a hand. I fucking hate getting older and this is one reason why. I dial Tommy Boy.

"Yo, dudette. I need you to help me, with you know what. It's that time of the month, you know."

"Oh hey, Rico! No problema. It's about that time for me, too. Mikey just left to head back to Duxbury. I can be over in an hour or so. I just want to finish washing my sheets and cleaning up here. He was a little sick this morning from last night. Is that cool?" he says as a vacuum cleaner revs in the background.

"Yeah, come over whenever. Thanks, man, for doing this again."

"De nada," Tommy answers in his perpetual chipper tone even though I'm sure he's not too happy cleaning up his place right now. Sounds like his boy toy Mikey had one too many Coronas last night at Club Café, again. That's the third time this dude gets trashed in front of Tommy. That's not cool in my book but Tommy's the type of guy who'll turn the other cheek if he sees something he doesn't like. Love or a strong-like is blind sometimes.

"That's what *amigos* are for, especially the hairy ones," Tommy says, laughing. "While I'm there, you can do mine, too!" he says as the vacuum cleaner winds down.

"Yeah, we might as well do it to each other," I tell him before hanging up.

"Nos vemos," he says in Spanish. I've hung out with Tommy long enough to know that means "We'll see each other soon." In a year, I should know Spanish by osmosis because Tommy can't help but speak Spanglish at times.

I'm here in my bedroom in Savin Hill, doing a quick workout before Tommy arrives. I did 100 push-ups, 100 crunches, and now I'm doing some bicep curls. My veins bulge from underneath my tight Italian skin like they want to break free. Yeah! It's 25 degrees outside and I'm not gonna go to the gym today with this shitty weather, so fuck that. I create my own home gym for the afternoon.

An hour later, I hear Tommy's beat-up old Jeep pull up outside the house. Damn, that thing is loud, even with the howling wind. A minute later, I let him in. His cheeks are red from the whipping wind and snowflakes cake his eyebrows.

"Good to see you, man," I tell him, giving him one of my hugs.

"Dude, watch it with your hugs. You're like the Hulk. You don't know your own strength," Tommy says, recovering from my hug. "I don't need the Heimlich maneuver every time I see you. I'm fragile goods. Handle with care, *chico*," he says with a sly grin, peeling off the new black wool coat and matching scarf he bought with Mikey the other day.

We walk into my bedroom and sit on the bed.

"So you've got the stuff we need, right?" he asks.

"Yeah, come on in to the Chez Rico salon!" as I lead him into the bathroom. My roommates aren't home so nobody will see what we're doing.

The task I need Tommy's help with today, the one I dread

and hate to admit to, is back hair removal, you know, the back manscaping. Yeah, I've got some hair on my back. What's wrong with that? Nothing, if no one knows about it. I bought a new bottle of Nair and an application usually lasts me a month. I like having a nice smooth back to wear my tight white tank tops at the gym. Guys look gross when they have hair pushing up from the back of their tank tops like a forest. It's so barbaric. That's why God invented Nair and back waxing. (Nair is cheaper, by the way.)

We walk into the bathroom. I pull off my tank top and hand Tommy the light blue bottle of this stuff, which smells like burning rubber when left on for a few minutes.

"So how was your night, Tommy?" He squeezes some of the cool liquid onto his hands and smears it all over my back, especially the top part, where most of my caveman hair is. That kinda feels good, almost like a minimassage.

"It was okay," he says, almost crestfallen, as he massages the Nair into my back. I'm sitting backward on the toilet staring at the white tiles of the bathroom while we chat.

"Let me guess? Mikey had too many beers last night with his friends around and you were the designated caretaker of the night, right?" The Nair starts tingling all over my back. I turn around on the toilet to talk to Tommy face to face.

"Well . . ." Tommy says, taking a slow breath as if beginning a story he rather not write about in the *Daily*. "We had such a great weekend. We drove to Freeport, Maine, yesterday afternoon to visit all the outlet stores. We had such a fun time, just me and him and Maine's fresh air. Then his friends call as we started driving back, and before I know it, Mikey wants to hit Club Café with me to meet up with his buddies," he says, peeling off the dishwasher gloves he used to apply the Nair.

"So why don't you just say no if you don't want to go?" I grill him.

"If I don't go, he'll go without me and I'd rather be there

to catch him if he falls, if you know what I mean. Besides, he drove me to Maine and showed me around there just like he did with Providence, so if he wants to hang out with his friends, I can't complain too much. It's not that often, just once in a while. It's a compromise, Rico," Tommy says as if trying to justify the whole thing.

"But he got carried away last night with the Coronas and he got sick this morning. He barfed on the side of my bed, and well, it wasn't pretty. My poor bed."

"Tommy, I really liked the guy when you guys first met. Hey, I was the one pushing you to go over and talk to him but there are two sides of him. That really sweet guy he is to you when he's sober. And then there's his lush side, when he gets sloshed and sloppy. Do you really want to deal with that?" I ask him as the Nair feels warmer and warmer, beginning to burn a little. What's in this stuff anyway? It's like it's alive.

"This is only the third time in five weeks. I don't think he ate enough before we headed to the bar. No one is perfect, Rico, everyone has their flaws," Tommy calmly but forcefully says. I hit a nerve with him. He wets a towel in warm water to start wiping off the Nair.

"I agree with you, Tommy. No one's perfect but not everybody has a drinking problem. He should just be treating you and himself better, that's all. I am telling you this because I care dude, okay?" Tommy doesn't answer and just nods as I talk. He just digs deep into my back with the towel. "I tell it like it is. I wouldn't bullshit you."

After cleaning me up, we switch positions. It's his turn and he finally speaks again.

"Use the razor. I brought one from home. I hate that Nair stuff. It could probably eat the soap scum off my bathroom," Tommy says, taking off his shirt and revealing his thin frame, almost like a runner's. I pump the shaving cream can and plop the white stuff on his upper back. He barely has any hair but I guess he wants to be clean and groomed for Mikey and their late-night fuckathons.

"When we're done, wanna hit the BM," he says as I shave his upper back slowly.

"Yeah, that sounds good to me. I'm always hungry, Tommy. I can never say no to mac 'n' cheese from Boston Market. But before we go, let's measure each other's body fat. I've got these clippers a guy at the gym let me borrow."

I grab the clippers from the bedroom and clamp on Tommy's waist, then chest and inner thigh. It's hard to do this because there's not much to grab.

"Dude, you have 10 percent body fat. That's really good. Maybe I should call you Tommy the Twig," I tell him. Now it's my turn. I take off my shirt and hand him the clippers.

"Ouch, not so hard, Tommy." After he pinches my waist, chest, and inner thighs with the clippers, the device reads "12 percent."

"Can't be. You have less fat than me?"

"Yeah, that's what the thing says, Rico. Isn't that good, too, 12 percent?" Tommy says with a slight smirk on his face.

"But I work out so much and I even have a six-pack. See?" I tell Tommy. I figured I'd have less fat than Tommy, who doesn't have a lot of muscle mass but is superlean from the gym.

"Rico, you're in great shape. We just have different bodies. It's not like you should be on NBC's *The Biggest Loser* or anything. You have more muscles than me. I just do a lot of cardio at Bally's. I spend forty-five minutes reading my William Mann novels on the bicycle machine. That's probably why I'm leaner," he says, putting his shirt back on. "Besides, I eat the same thing every day for lunch and dinner. It's the OCD, re-member?"

"That's true, dudette. You do eat the same old thing day in

and day out. Anyway, check these out. Welcome to the gun show," I tell him, holding up both my arms and flexing my tight biceps.

"Okay, Rico, all of Boston knows you have the best biceps. Okay, all of Massachusetts and perhaps parts of Rhode Island know this, too. So can we get going to Boston Market? I'm getting hungry. I didn't eat much today watching Mikey barf up last night's liquor. I think he drained the bar of Coronas."

Twenty minutes later, we and our smooth backs are at Boston Market. Tommy gets the usual: the turkey meal with sweet potato and a Diet Coke. I get the half chicken with the two sides of mac 'n' cheese. I smelled it from the moment we walked into the place, about two miles from Savin Hill on Morrissey Boulevard.

We grab our food and sit down in the corner of the joint.

"So what are your plans for Christmas, Tommy? I'm heading to the Berkshires to hang out with my parents and my sister and her hubby. We have a big Italian celebration, with all my cousins coming in from the rest of the state. I can't wait. Lots of food and beer." I scoop up the melted glob of yellow cheeses from my plate and shove it in my mouth. Damn, this is good. Fuck the body fat index.

"I'm heading back to Miami for Christmas and New Year's. Gonna spend a week or so there to thaw out. We have a big Cuban roasted pig feast on Christmas Eve called Noche Buena. All my cousins and aunts and uncles will be there. Sounds similar to what your family is doing," Tommy says, savoring the gooey marshmallows that top his orange sweet potato side. "While I'm there, I am going to the pool party at the White Fiesta. Some old reporter friends got me a pass to go New Year's weekend. Should be fun."

"What about Mikey? Is he going with you to the MIA?"

Tommy lowers his eyes. "Nah, he's staying in Duxbury with his family. They have a big celebration, too, and he doesn't want to miss it although I really wanted him to see Miami and where I'm from. I bet if he wasn't in the closet, he would have come with me."

"That's too bad, Tommy. At least you'll have some time with your family and old friends down there. And maybe the time will give you and Mikey a little break. You guys have been inseparable since day one." As he listens, I dig into the layers of my white chicken, squeezing the juices out onto my plate. "I barely see you as much and I'm your supposed wingman, dudette. I feel like I've been flying solo lately. Goose would never do that to Maverick in *Top Gun*."

Tommy laughs back.

"Oh, come on, you've missed me, Rico, with all your on-line and CC conquests?"

"Well, let's just say we used to hang out more but I understand. You've got a boyfriend. But remember, good friends, especially the hot Italian ones, are forever. Boyfriends tend to come and go," I say, just before shoving more mac 'n' cheese into my mouth. I can't get enough of this stuff. I'm glad I worked out today and built up an appetite.

"What about you, any prospects on the Rico horizon?"

"Nah, I like the single life. I don't have to deal with what you're going through. No offense. Lots of guys out there for the Italian Stallion to fuck," I say.

"Yeah, that stallion of yours is galloping all over Btown like Paul Revere," Tommy says with a smirk. "And now he has a smooth back to keep on riding."

"I just wish I could take my stallion up to *Brokeback Mountain*. I could have showed those two cowboys a thing or two," I tell Tommy, who is biting into his fluffy cornbread.

"Yeah, I'm sure you would have given Ennis a new anus, Rico."

And with that, we both burst out laughing, spitting chunks of our food at BM.

Chapter 9

TOMMY

I see Papi and Mami's house as the American Airlines airbus begins to fly over Miami Beach. There it is, the little white house with the red shingles in the midsection of Miami Beach right by the sprawling La Gorce Country Club, sort of like the scene you quickly see in the opening montage of *The Golden Girls* on *Lifetime: Television for Women and the Pigs They Love*. It's amazing how Miami Beach's colors leap off the land. The lush green palm trees. The pastel-colored Art Deco buildings and condos that rise along the sandy white shoreline.

I am so happy to be flying back for Christmas and I can't wait to feel that familiar tropical breezy vapor greet me. Only a newly minted Bostonian can appreciate that kind of greeting this time of year. This will be my first Christmas in Miami since I moved away to Boston. We always eat the traditional roasted pig on Christmas Eve at my aunt's house. It's a Cuban thing.

I can't wait to see my buddy Brian, who always flies down from New York to meet up with me in his partner's helicopter. And of course, there's Mami and Papi, the sweetest and greatest Cuban parents on earth. I haven't seen them since Labor Day weekend but they call me every night, at 8 o'clock, on the dot, just to see how my day was. They also tell me the next day's weather forecast for New England. That's Cuban parents for you. If I don't return their calls from the two messages they leave on my answering machine, they start calling my cell. I can't complain. It's just their way of showing how much they love me so I always remind myself of that when they call and interrupt me when I'm having dinner with Mikey or driving home from the gym. Mikey doesn't understand the invisible umbilical cord that exists among Latino and Caribbean families.

The captain has announced we are about to land and to fasten our seat belts. A few minutes later, we're on the ground, taxiing to the gate. I dial Mary, my older sister, on the cell to let her know I'm finally here.

"Mary, hey, I'm still in the plane. I'm here," I tell her as fellow passengers pull down their carry-on bags from the above storage compartments.

"Great, Tomas, we're on our way, wait for us outside in the departures lane for the airline. See you soon, little brother." Mary is the only person who calls me by my real name, and when she doesn't, she attaches "little brother" to the end of her sentences. We're only three years apart but she's also a schoolteacher so she tends to stay in that disciplinarian mode 24/7. She means well, I remind myself, when she gets carried away with all her nagging suggestions on what I should wear or buy for my studio. And she's always been like this since I was born. We get along pretty well but she's adamant about living at home until she gets married while I've always told her she should move out and enjoy some independence like I did by moving to Boston. We clash on issues like this at times. It's more of my independent streak that conflicts with her traditional old-fashioned Cuban ways of wanting to be near the house to help out Papi and Mami and I understand that. But I also feel people should live their lives for themselves, not for their parents. My Cuban friends in Miami get this because usually one sibling tends to stay near the parents while the other moves away and that happened to be me in the Perez family.

I trudge through the sun-filled Miami International Airport terminal as I make my way to ground transportation. A grin plasters my face. I hear fellow passengers chitchatting in Spanish, English, and Spanglish as they wend through the terminals. It's music to my ears. I can smell the earthy aroma of rice and beans wafting in the airport from the Cuban restaurant. Nothing like being home again.

Twenty minutes later, I see Papi, Mami, and Mary pull up in the blue Honda Civic sedan, with Mary at the wheel as usual. They are all enthusiastically waving at me and smiling.

"Tomasito, estas flaco!" Mami gushes, calling me by my nickname and telling me that I am skinny as she kisses my cheek and caresses my curls in the backseat.

"Tienes el pelo muy largo," she continues, talking about how long my curly hair is getting.

Papi sits shotgun and jumps into the conversation.

"Tomas, como te fue el viaje? Tienes hambre," he says, asking about my flight and my appetite. To Cubans, you can never eat enough. Luckily, there is a lack of Cuban food in Boston. If not, my willowy frame wouldn't be so willowy. I was slightly heavier when I lived in Miami, but in Cuban families, that's a good thing. It means you're healthy.

On the eight-mile trip to Miami Beach, I sit back in the car and just take in all the palm trees that tower along the Interstate's median.

As we cross over one of the bigger bridges to the beach, a canyon of condos and hotels spike up from the shoreline like giant Lego pieces. Gloria Estefan crackles on the radio, and later Shakira, whom the deejays play often because they are both Latina singers who call Miami home.

After fourteen minutes of driving, Mary pulls us into the butter yellow house we grew up in. Ah, nothing like being back here, in my old bedroom, where Ceci, my small gray fluffy Persian cat, awaits me.

"Meow, meow," she greets me as soon as I walk in. I scoop her up and carry her like a baby.

"I've missed my Ceci so much," I tell her, coddling her as she purrs and buries her head into my hairy arms.

I'm not even home five minutes and Brian's already calling my cell.

"Tommy Boy! Are you here yet? Welcome back to Miami, *amigo*," he says.

"Hey, Brian! Yeah, I just got home. I'm about to unpack. How are you doing? What's up, *chico*?"

We talk for a few minutes about my flight, and then about his bumpy helicopter ride back to Miami from New York City. Brian is learning to fly the chopper because his partner wants him to be able to fly it in case he suddenly gets sick during one of their flights. It's also a way for them to share a common hobby. So Brian has been trying to clock as many flying hours as he can with his partner's copilot.

"I almost threw up my lunch because of all the turbulence in the chopper. Whew!" Brian tells me. "But I'm back on the beach. Can't wait to see you. Spend some time with your family and we'll hit Lincoln Road later and catch up. Talk to you later, *amigo*."

Brian is the all-American boy, brown spiked-up hair, big blue eyes, and a hunk of a guy. Women and men can't resist his magnetic pull. But he prefers those Spanish-speaking bad-boy Tony Montana types from the 1982 movie *Scarface*. While he has a partner, they have an open relationship so Brian loves to cruise with me at the bars when I'm back in town. Their arrangement has always baffled me. If you love someone, why mess around on the side? I always think of my parents' marriage as the standard of what I want in a relationship. They've been together for thirty-five years since they met at Papi's small coffee shop in Havana. They still have a way of making each other laugh. There's an endearing electricity between them, and it's obvious to anyone who spends five minutes with them.

When I have a boyfriend, I am monogamous. But many gay men, after years together, allow their partner to play on the side, to keep the fire burning in the relationship. I haven't been able to achieve a long-term relationship yet. Tell-a-Lie-Teddy lasted only a few months when I lived here, and we were always arguing about his lies. I'm hoping Mikey might be the one for me, like Papi is for Mami. But there are so many differences. I bet Mami never had to hide Papi from *Abuela* when they began dating and it seems easier when you're straight than when you're gay. Two men stand out walking in public holding hands or having dinner, especially if they're having a good time and obviously fond of one another.

"Tommy, your turkey is ready," Mami yells out to me in Spanish from the kitchen as I get off the phone with Brian.

She always heats up fresh roasted slices of turkey breast with rice and yucca and a side of salted crackers. Of course, she stocks up on a case of Diet Coke for my visits. For dessert, there's her sweet-tasting Cuban flan. It's to die for, so much so that she makes it regularly in case one of my cousins or an unannounced houseguest drops by. Mami never worked while I was growing up. She spent the day cooking and cleaning or picking me and Mary up from school while Papi worked ten-hour days as a waiter for a Cuban restaurant on the beach. Frugal but wickedly smart, he knew how to invest his money well when he and Mami first arrived in Miami from Cuba in 1968.

When I was twelve years old, he had saved enough money from his tips that he was able to put a down payment on our beautiful three-bedroom Miami Beach home in the middle section of the city. It was run-down when we first saw it. The one-story house needed some TLC but Papi saw its potential in the mid-1980s.

It's not as big as the grand majestic waterfront estates owned by JLo and Ricky Martin a few blocks away. Those are bedecked with gated fences, fancy pimpin' Escalades, flowing fountains, and maids' quarters.

But to Papi, our house is a castle. No matter how often re-altors approach him to sell, with today's hot booming Miami real estate market, he won't budge. To Papi, the house is akin to gold. But it's also an extension of our family, where we can all be together as the Perez family. Hence, he hasn't changed my old bedroom. It still has the same large wooden twin bed he bought me when I turned seven years old.

"This will always be your room, Tomasito," he has told me often. He even framed my first front-page story in *The Miami Chronicle* from a few years ago about a pack of orphaned dogs who survived days at sea on rafts during the Cuban raft crisis in the mid-1990s. They landed in Key West and eventually were adopted by new owners in Miami. They were called *los perros balseros*. Papi hung the story above my bed. "No matter where you live in this country or how old you are, you will al-ways have a home and a bedroom to come home to."

I plop down at the dinner table and start digging into my fresh turkey when Ceci strolls up, sits down beside my leg, and stares up at me with those big green eyes of hers. She always does this when I eat because she knows I will drop her some pieces of food. I love Ceci the cat.

A few hours later, after telling Papi about my latest articles in the *Daily* and how my Jeep is running, I change into my Gap blue jeans, a red Old Navy T-shirt, and head out to meet up with Brian at his beach house.

The boy has his own Miami Beach villa filled with co-conut palms, a gleaming swimming pool, and a two-car garage for a Porsche Cayenne and a Mercedes two-seater. He shares this home with Daniel for quick weekend getaways from the Big Apple. I always sit on his kitchen counter here, where I sip Diet Coke with vodka as Brian gets ready to go out. It doesn't take long. He always sports a white Polo T-shirt and a pair of Levi's blue jeans. It's almost like his uniform.

No matter how much money Brian has, he dresses very casually. But if you look closely, you'll see a gleaming Rolex on his right hand or a thick silver necklace. Brian is a laid-back kind of guy who tells it like it is, but with heart, kind of like Rico in Boston.

"So tell me about Mikey! How are things going there? Why didn't he come with you on this trip?" Brian asks me, pulling out a Marlboro light as we chat in his kitchen, which is about the size of my studio in Cambridge but with sparkling white marble floors. The kitchen alone could be the cover photo on any home and design magazine.

"Well, Mikey wanted to spend Christmas with his parents and sister. He says it's a big thing in his family, with his grandparents and cousins coming over, which I totally understand," I tell Brian, sipping my tall cool glass of DCV as I try to hide my disappointment of not having Mikey with me. "I tried to convince him to come for a quick weekend so he can see Miami, meet you and my family, but he said he wanted to stay in Boston and go skiing with his straight friends."

Brian sees I'm getting a little sad. He comes over and puts his arm around me.

"The important thing is you're here, in Miami, with your family and your friends. Don't worry about Mikey. From what you tell me, it sounds like he has some things to sort out," Brian says, not hiding what he wants to say. "He's in the closet. He likes to drink a lot on the weekends. Tommy, I know you have feelings for this guy but is that what you really want? You deserve to be with someone who won't hide you from his family and is proud to be with you! And do you really want to clean up after this guy and be his crutch whenever he drinks? Maybe you should talk to him about it when you get back to Boston."

"I know what you're saying, Brian," I say in between sips of my drink, feeling like I just had the same conversation with Rico the other afternoon. "When he doesn't drink, things are so great with us. In a way, I'm kind of relieved he didn't come with me home to Miami because it will give me a little break from him, time to sort out my feelings for him." I look out the kitchen window, which faces all the majestic cruise ships docked across the water at the Port of Miami.

"Brian, I haven't told this to anybody but I'm falling in love with Mikey. He's everything I want in a guy and we have such a great connection but I just hate it when he gets drunk."

Brian's eyes light up.

"I knew you were falling in love with him. I totally could sense it. Tommy is in looooove. Tommy is in looooove," he teases me.

"Look, it's great that you know how you feel. You have to be true to your own feelings. But he's not here right now and I am! Now, let's go to Lincoln Road, sit in the outside patio of Hombre's bar and have some drinks and watch all the hot *papitos* out here, okay? You're here to have fun, with me. Got it?"

Half an hour later, after circling South Beach for an open parking space in Brian's Porsche, we arrive on Lincoln Road, an artsy pedestrian mall in the heart of South Beach where people go to see and be seen. Once the home of struggling art galleries, the strip has exploded into a colorful shopper's paradise, with Victoria's Secret, Banana Republic, Starbucks, and chi-chi shops that have sprung up here in recent years. Basically, it's become an outdoor Main Street Mall USA like Newbury Street in Boston.

Brian and I head to the gay bar on this strip, Hombre's, which is a lot like Club Café except for its tropical location and the large number of gay Hispanic men who frequent here. Replace the Matt Damons and Ben Affleck types in Boston with tank-top-wearing Antonio Banderas and Enrique Iglesias types and that's Hombre's crowd. It's amazing how wherever there are more than a few dozen gay men, chances are, there's a gay club nearby. It's our unofficial gathering spot, a community center of sorts. And while the city might be different, it's the same type of guys, drinking, cruising, and what not. Even the music sounds the same at each bar, no matter where you are.

Brian's already on cruise control, eyeballing every Latin guy with his piercing blue eyes to get their attention. I always laugh when Brian gets into his manhunt mode. And while I see some really cute guys smile at me and walk by, I can't help but think about Mikey, wishing he were here with me tonight.

"Stop thinking about Mikey, okay?" Brian surprises me with his statement. He knows me so well.

"I can see it in your face. Help me find a hot Latino *papi,* okay? Work your Spanish for me? You know most of these guys anyways from living here for so long."

And so, I get up, walk around the bar, and become Brian's Cuban pimp for the night. But the whole time, I wish I were with Mikey celebrating Christmas with my new love.

My phone starts chirping at the bar. I pull it out and see that it reads "Mikey." A euphoric wave rolls inside me as I answer the phone.

"How's my cutie?" Mikey asks. "I can't wait 'til you get back, Tommy!"

We talk about my flight and my family and his family and all the preparations going on at his house.

"Tommy, if you can, call me right at midnight on Christmas Eve. I gotta tell you something," he says.

"Okay, we'll talk then," I tell him as Brian gestures for me to get off the phone so we can have fun.

"I miss you, cutie," Mikey says.

"I miss you, too."

I can't stop smiling for the rest of the night at Hombre's, wondering what Mikey wants to tell me but I have an idea. I can feel it, too.

It's Christmas Eve and the Perez household is abuzz with activity. The Christmas tree is all lit. Tia Caridad and Tio Bartolo are here along with my cousins Nicole, Marie, Ann, Jen, Steph, and Lora. (Can you tell I'm pretty much the only guy here?) Oh wait, my other cousins, Frank and José, are here, too, with their families. The house is bursting with people as Mami prepares the last-minute touches of her flan, and Tio Bartolo and Tia Caridad are arranging the plates and serving drinks. The rest of my female cousins are packed into Mary's bedroom, where they are all putting on makeup, watching MTV, or checking for the latest sales online. The men are crammed into the living room with Papi watching whatever sporting event is on TV. I'm not into sports but I hear cheers from the TV set so it might be football.

After we say a prayer in Spanish and dive into our portions of roasted pig, yucca, black beans and rice, and mashed potatoes, I remember to call Mikey. It's just about to turn to midnight so I step outside and feel the cool tropical breezes tickle my face under a starry night. I dial Mikey.

"Merry Christmas, Mikey!"

"Merry Christmas, Tommy. I hope you're having a great time down there with your family."

"I am but it would have been better if you were here," I say, sitting on the stoop of our porch as Ceci steps outside and rubs up against my leg. She can sense I feel a little lonely tonight even though I can't hear myself think in the house with my loud *familia*.

"So why did you want me to call you at midnight, Mikey?"

"Well, I wanted to wish you a Merry Christmas and give you your gift."

"You know I have a gift for you, too," I tell him, hoping that it's the same thing he's gonna give me or else I am gonna feel really stupid and embarrassed.

"But my gift can only be told in person or on the phone and I'd rather not wait until you get back to Boston," he says.

"Same here. So why not say it at the same time, okay?" I hope this is a good idea. Please God, let us say the same thing or I probably won't be able to show my face in Boston again. I could just move back into my old bedroom here on the Beach.

"So on the count of three, we'll both say it, okay, Tommy?"

"Okay," I answer, and close my eyes and count to three.

Here we go. One . . . two . . . three.

"I LOVE YOU, Mikey!"

"I LOVE YOU, Tommy!"

We both said it at the same time and so loudly that we weren't sure what the other said.

"Huh?" Mikey asks me.

"I didn't understand what you said. I think we said the same thing, that we love each other, right?"

"Yes, yes, I love you, Mikey. I've known for weeks."

"I love you, too, cutie. That was my gift to you. Those three words."

"Same here but there are two words that are just as great. *Te amo!*" I tell him that I love him in Spanish. I smile and look up as wind-whipped clouds temporarily cover the moon as if to give me some privacy with Mikey.

I replay the words in my mind and savor them. I love you. I love you. *Te amo!* I can't remember the exact moment I fell in love with Mikey. It's sort of like seeing the wisps of darkness forming in the sunset. Little by little, you eventually know those slices of red and orange shimmering light wane into shades of indigo and black and then suddenly night. But you don't know the precise moment the transformation occurred. One day, I just knew I loved Mikey.

   This is the best Christmas gift I ever got, definitely topping the remote control Knight Rider car from 1982. And for the rest of my stay here, whenever Mikey and I talk on the phone each night, we end our conversations with the best three words the heart ever invented. I love you! I just can't wait to say those words in person.

Chapter 10

KYLE

The morning light casts a buttery incubator glow over the city. The tropical vapor of summer—or is it fall? or winter?—flares across the 305, producing a thick haze on city streets, making winter in Boston seem so far away. Supa-dupa fly drivers with their tops down and spinning rims prowl around for any empty parking space near the Raleigh Hotel, where I'm staying. Thong-thong-thong-thonged women (and some men) whirl around on their rollerblades, showing off the goods that God gave them. The air carries a mix of coconut tanning oil and sea salt as if the light puffy clouds held some special concoction of both and unleashed them over SoBe.

Ahh, Miami Beach, my kinda town. I'm here for the White Fiesta, *the* party of all gay circuit parties, and I'm the host of the WF pool party at the Raleigh Hotel. I just got here and I'm unpacking in my Old Havana–themed room as I take in the whole lush tropical elegance from my sixth-floor view. I haven't been here in two years since I did some runway work for two designers while I was on *The Real Life*. Miami always left a good impression on me with all its diverse culture and hedonistic energy, and so did the hot Latino *papitos* here. *Que caliente!*

So it's good to be back on this all-expense-paid trip. Eric is supposed to meet me here for the party later this afternoon. Between hosting breaks, we're gonna hang poolside and catch up. I can't wait to see him. It's been at least six months since we've seen each other but we gab all the time on the phone and AIM so it's like we pick up where we left off whenever we see each other in the flesh. But before I head downstairs and prepare for my gig here, I'm gonna take a nice long hot bath in the ultrawhite bathroom and relax for a bit. I got up at 6 A.M. to catch my red-eye from Logan and my body needs a break from the jet lag. I start filling the gleaming porcelain tub with hot water. Calgon, take Kyle away.

It's 2 P.M. and the pool area has filled up pretty quickly with a shirtless sea of gay revelers in tiny Speedos and fashionable bathing suits. They lull to the electronica playing from the speakers and rustling from the thicket of palm trees and seagrapes that gently sway with the tropical breezes. The guys float on inner tubes and toss rainbow-colored beach balls to each other in this shimmering lagoon of a pool. These hunky hombres with perpetual tans are looking to be entertained for this fund-raiser and I'm just the guy to do it. Kyle, at your service, *señores*!

"Kyle, you're on," Rich, one of the party coordinators holding a clipboard, informs me as I do a last-minute check of my hair and subtle makeup in the bathroom near the curtained cabanas. The cover-up is working, cloaking that little blemish near my chin.

"I'll be there in just a second, Rich. I'm almost ready," I say as I slather globs of sunscreen all over my arms, shoulders, and chest to protect my fragile white skin from the intense sun rays here. If not, I'll look like a giant lobster. But the southern Florida sun will at least make my curls look blonder.

When he disappears, I give myself a quick pep talk in front of the mirror.

"Kyle, you are a beautiful man with a good heart who deserves the best in the world and nothing less. Now, one for the money, two for the show, three to get ready, Kyle, go go go!"

And with that self-cheer, I venture outside into the blinding sun and walk past crushes of oiled-up men who frame the pool perfectly. I step up to the stage that rims the front of the cabana area and I see before me what could easily look like a mirage, a giant orgy of gay men, a few hundred of them, splishing and splashing in the sheetlike pool. They pack the outdoor pool lounge area as the white and blue hotel towers in the background against a bright blue sky like a postcard. All their eyes are on me. This is heaven.

"*Buenos dias*, everybody! *Bienvenidos* to the White Fiesta Pool Party. I'm Kyle Andrews, your hostess with the mostess. Are you having fun this afternoon? Let me hear you, people!"

The crowd roars and cheers "YEAH" and "WHOO!" and I hear a chorus of whistles. I feel my cheeks redden but I'm not sure if it's from the searing sun or me blushing. I can stay up here all day. I just hope I don't pop a boner in my nut-hugging little blue Speedo from staring at all these ripped, bulging, sculpted hot men. The last thing I need now is a wardrobe malfunction. I want people to look at me but not all of me, you know.

"Now that's more like it. We've got a great show for you this afternoon. First up, I'd like to introduce you to one of the hottest Caribbean rappers who's gonna make your temperature rise, if you know what I mean. Besides being a hottie, he was so kind to be with us this afternoon for such a great cause that is dear to all our hearts. Let's give it up for the one and only SEAN PAUL. Whooo!"

I exit the stage and the guys go wild as Sean Paul, that handsome Jamaican rapper who was in that Beyoncé video a few years ago, emerges on the stage. He immediately starts rapping to "Temperature," one of his more popular songs from 2006, and all the guys start jumping, humping one another, and thumping their tight butts on the nearby speaker boxes and lounge chairs.

After I step down from the stage, I grab some Evian, dab my face with a hotel towel, and take a break. Sean Paul is supposed to perform two songs so I have a little downtime. No one said hosting was easy. Damn, it's so hot down here. The heat just sticks to my skin. Nothing like being back in Boston right now. I don't miss it at all.

"Oh my God, aren't you like *the* Kyle Andrews, the biggest star of reality TV?" I hear a voice shriek from behind.

This always happens to me, part of the life of a reality star, you know. It's probably some eighteen-year-old guy who just came out of the closet or something and wants an autograph or to take a picture with me. They're my fans so I'm always polite. If it wasn't for them, I wouldn't be where I am today. So I turn around and I see, to my surprise, it's Eric! He's pulling my leg as usual. Sometimes I forget how much he looks like a more rugged Ryan Seacrest from *American Idol* except Eric's hair is a darker brown spiked up and his eyes switch back and forth from green to blue, depending on his shirt. He's also taller than that twit of a host.

"Want an autograph, Eric? If you're nice, I'll give you a WF pool party T-shirt." We start laughing and he gives me a big tight hug.

"So good to see you, Kyle. You're doing a great job here. I knew you'd be perfect for this event," he says, playfully messing up my hair.

"Thanks again, Eric. You always look out for me. This has been a great little getaway from the land of Paul Revere and we get to hang, just like we used to in Oklahoma. But they're no horses here to ride for one of our chitchats."

"Yeah, but I bet there are men hung as horses trotting around here poolside. Just look at their bathing suits. You can see their manroot perfectly defined."

We talk about our flights and it turns out Eric, who flew in from San Francisco, is staying at the hotel next door.

"I gotta get back onstage. My break is almost over and Sean Paul seems like he's winding down. Be back in a few, Eric."

"No problem, Kyle. Do your thing. Work that microphone," Eric says, patting me on the back as he disappears into the crowd of shirtless built men. He's one of them and looking more pumped up than usual. He must be using a new routine or something at the gym because his chest is as big as the hot gardener from ABC's *Desperate Housewives*.

After Sean Paul bows and thanks everyone, I give a speech about the importance of raising money for AIDS research and attending events like this. The men quiet down as I talk. It's nice having a captive audience all to myself and I feel honored they're really listening to what I have to say. I then introduce one of the bigger local drag queens, Mia Mi, who looks like a flashier and more diva-esque exaggerated version of local Conga queen Gloria Estefan. I love Mia Mi's name, it's basically the word "Miami" split into two and it shows how much she loves her hometown. She gets the crowd going with her rendition of "Turn the Beat Around," followed by "Everlasting Love" and "Always Tomorrow," which gives me a nice fifteen-minute break or so.

I mingle in the crowd and talk to some of the guys by the bar. I'm swimming in this vibrant mix of men and just loving it, flirting with the locals and out-of-towners. They're all telling me I'm doing a great job and asking me about *The Real Life* and how real was it. Three guys slip me their room numbers on scraps of paper, which I squeeze into the side of my blue bikini. They'll come in handy for later.

I then head to the front of the beach bar to grab an icy cocktail and look for Eric when I notice a very familiar bush of dark brown curly hair in front of me. No way, it can't be.

"Tommy Perez?"

The curly-haired guy turns around and breaks out into his wide happy-go-lucky smile.

"Hey, Kyle! Welcome to Miami! That is so funny that we're both here."

"Yeah, I'm hosting the pool party, in case you haven't noticed. What brings you down here, working on a travel story for the *Daily*? Oh wait, a story about *moi* perhaps?"

"Nah, just here visiting *la familia*. You know, I grew up here in South Beach. It's my hometown and I wouldn't miss this pool party for anything, especially with the extra ticket I got from my friends at *The Miami Chronicle*, my old paper. I spend Christmas and New Year's here. I head back to Boston tomorrow night."

I notice Mikey's not here with him. Hmmm. I smell some *Queer as Folk* drama.

"Where's your boyfriend? Is he here?"

Tommy's eyes light up and he flashes an even bigger smile that stands out against his tanned skin. He definitely got some color by being back home. He's the pale Cuban in Boston.

"He's back in Duxbury with his family. He's picking me up at the airport. I can't wait to see him. It's been almost two weeks."

His eyes twinkle as he talks. It sounds like things are going pretty well with him and Mikey. I guess he doesn't know that I saw Mikey with his drunken pals getting trashed at Club Café Thursday night and making total asses of themselves just before I came down here. Or maybe he does know and Tommy's okay with it. Well, that's *his* issue.

"It's great seeing you, Tommy. I hope you have fun this afternoon here. I gotta get back to the stage. Looks like Mia

Mi is about to wrap up her final song. She just threw her Gloria Estefan wig into the crowd so she's gonna finish any minute now."

"Yeah, good seeing you, too, Kyle. Great job this afternoon. You're a natural onstage."

We hug and air-kiss and I start maneuvering through this logjam of men back to the stage. I see Eric by the front, nodding up to me with his bottled water and cheering me on. I guess he doesn't want to drink today, which is odd, because he usually loves his Rolling Rock beers when he's out and about. But it's very hot, so water is better to stay hydrated. It's better for the skin and the kidneys, you know.

"Let's all hear it for Miami's own Mia Mi," I shout to the partiers, whose applause and cheers could probably be heard miles away by the real Gloria in her Star Island home.

"Our last performer is a very special guest, someone who inspired me when I was just a boy growing up in Oklahoma with big stars in my eyes, and she's always had a special place in our community. Let's hear it for one of the first ladies of country, the grand dame of Dollywood, Mrs. Dolly Parton!"

Again, the guys go wild and Mrs. Parton strolls onto the stage and gives me a sweet kiss and a hug. I feel so honored being in the presence of such a country legend. She's always so chipper and never with a hair out of place. She has this amazing peacefulness about her, as if she's super comfortable with who she is. Nothing seems to knock her down.

"How y'all doing on this gorgeous Sunday afternoon? What a way to start the new year. I was down here for a concert in Fort Lauderdale last night and just had to extend my stay here to drop in on your lovely party. It's such a good cause and I wanted to donate my time and some dimes . . ."

I stand from the side of the stage in complete awe of how Dolly Parton commands an audience with her childlike voice and timeless beauty, and yes, her bazooka breasts. All the guys stop playing around in the pool and hang on to her every word and cheer her on. Mrs. Steel Magnolia is in the house and it's as if we are her honored guests but she's really our honored guest. She's so humble and yet uplifting and full of positive and good energy. You can't help but giggle when she giggles, which is like every other minute. After she gives her speech and sings her famous "I Will Always Love You" a capella, which gives everyone goose bumps including yours truly, the show is over and everyone lingers around for the rest of the afternoon.

Dolly has signed some autographs backstage near the cabanas that overlook the beach and the Atlantic Ocean, and she comes up to me and gives me a big hug.

"Hey, Kyle. You were so sweet up there. Thank you for your kind words. May the Lord bless ya," she says, before being pulled away by her publicist and bodyguard. In a few minutes, she's out of sight and probably heading back to Miami International Airport and back to the Smokey Mountains of east Tennessee.

Eric finds me at the side of the stage and we decide to break out of here and get some good Cuban food and some one-on-one time.

We walk over to a cute little Cuban restaurant called Puerto Havana on Collins Avenue. We sit on blue stools at the counter as Shakira plays "Whenever Wherever" in the background on the radio and I feel refreshed from the cool air-conditioning. After looking over the menus, whose covers feature an old fisherman reeling in a giant marlin, very *Old Man and the Sea,* we order. Eric orders the *media noche* sandwich and a bottled water. I order a croquette sandwich and a strawberry milkshake from the friendly older salt-and-peppered waiter named Pepe.

"Coming rrright up," Pepe says in his Spanish accent. I guess he likes to roll his *r*'s in English.

"So how are things going in San Fran?" I ask Eric as Pepe

brings us a red basket of fresh hot Cuban bread rolls. I grab one and smear butter all over it and pop it in my mouth. Deeelicious!

"Things are going great, Kyle. I've been getting a steady flow of work. I'm an ER computer doc. The clients scream and cry or they carry on about how important their work is and how badly they need to be back up and running again ASAP. It's as if their computer was a life support system or something. I shut 'em up by fixing whatever problem they have and then they purr like kittens, all happy and shit. It's all good and it teaches you to deal with your own stress by seeing how they freak out day in and day out. Hell, I don't want to ever look like that," he says.

"Well, you look great. Look at your chest. I've never seen you so built. Did you change your routine or something?"

Eric sips some of his water and turns to me.

"I decided a few months ago that it was time I start taking better care of myself. Less Sonic burgers and Mickey Dees and more chicken breasts and vegetables and more water. You've only got one life to live and you might as well be as healthy as you can. When you're healthy on the inside, you look great on the outside, and vice versa. You should know that. You're a model."

He keeps using the word *healthy*. The Eric I know ate everything in sight without a care about how bad the food was. We used to always order Domino's in OK City. Don't get me wrong, he always had a nice body from running, but now, he's like an Adonis, just like one of these muscle boys here in South Beach.

"Eric, is everything okay? Is there something you're not telling me? You know, you can tell me anything. Remember the pact we made years ago while riding Mustache and Pokey Joe on your uncle's dude ranch. No matter what stupid things we do or what bad mistakes we make in life, we will love each other unconditionally and not judge. Remember that, okay?" I tell him as Pepe dashes out of the kitchen with our plates of sandwiches and my super pink shake.

"Kyle, it's all good. I'm thirty now and my metabolism isn't as fast as it used to be so I have to work out more, that's it. You overworry about everything just like you did on the show and back home. So what's going on with you? Any potential love interests in Beantown?"

He sinks his teeth into the *media noche* sandwich. I can smell the mixture of pickles, cheese, mustard, ham, and pork from here. Damn, that looks good but my sandwich is good, too. Besides, I have to watch my figure for tonight's big White Fiesta fiesta.

"Nah, I haven't met anyone I liked up there. You know me, I go with the flow. I really loved José but the faggot just used me because of the show. It's amazing how many guys just want to talk to me because of the show and not because of me. They just want bragging rights to say 'Guess who I hooked up with?' It gets tired after a while. I don't know how mega celebs are able to date anyone these days. It's so hard, Eric. I'd rather be single for now and just have fun and play butt-pirate."

"I hear ya, Kyle, and that's what this weekend's about. You, me, and all the hotties in Miami Beach. We have a lot to pick from, judging by the guys at the pool party."

We start laughing as we chow down our delicious Cuban food. Whenever Pepe delivers an order from the kitchen, I notice him glancing at my shirt, which says BOSTON RED SOX in big red, blue, and white letters. Maybe he's a fan.

"Are jou from Boston?" he asks me on his way back to the kitchen.

"Well, I live in Boston but I'm originally from Oklahoma."

"Ah, mi son works en Boston. He's *un reportero*. Maybe jou know him or read his *articulos*."

"Maybe I do. I know lots of people in Boston, Pepe. What's his name?"

"Tommy Perrrez! He is *un cubanito* and writes for de *Boston Daily*."

Oh my gosh, this is Tommy's waiter father. He even looks like him with the dark brown eyes, thick eyebrows, almost like a sixty-year-old version of Tommy sans all the curly hair. At least his father grooms it and keeps it slicked back. What a small Cuban world.

"Mr. Perez, I know you're son. He is *buena gente*, as you say in *español*. I'm hoping he will write a story about me *un dia*," I tell him in my broken Spanish.

He smiles back at us.

"*Bueno,* welcome to Miami Beesh."

"*Gracias*, Pepe," I say.

"Thanks, Pepe," Eric pipes in as we finish our late lunch in this city of guilt-free cocktailing and clubbing. Eric looks to his side and gazes out the restaurant's windows.

"Check out the nipples on that guy walking by with the beach chair, I love when a man's nipples are wide and tan like that, not too dark and hanging just high enough on his pecs," Eric says, with a big old grin on his sunburned face. "I loves me some nipples."

"Me, too. These Miami men are too much, Eric. I'm glad we're here enjoying this together," I say, sipping my shake.

"Anytime, Kyle!"

Chapter 11

TOMMY

"I just landed, Mikey. I'll be right at the gate, by the escalators for American Airlines."

"Okay, cutie, see ya in a few," he says before hanging up.

I'm back in Boston. It's been two weeks and I can't wait to see Mikey who is sweet enough to pick me up tonight from Logan even though he lives some thirty miles way-out-of-the-way-south.

Ever since we exchanged I-love-yous over the phone on Christmas Eve, I've been dying to get back up here to say it in person. The pilot announces it's 25 degrees here as the plane taxis to the gate. A few minutes later, I emerge from the plane, walk through the chilly connector corridor, and I'm greeted by Logan's bright fluorescent lights. Fellow passengers put on their coats and scamper around with their bags toward the GROUND TRANSPORTATION signs.

After walking what seems like forever to the terminal's entrance, I pass the security machines and I see Mikey in the distance staring up at the arrival monitors. He then spots me and waves up. I rush toward him and softly kiss him right here in the middle of Terminal B.

"I missed you so much," I whisper into his ear and tightly hug him.

"It feels so good to see you, cutie," he says, returning the powerful embrace. "Let me take that for you. You must be tired from your trip."

"Thanks, Mikey. I appreciate that but it's a heavy bag."

"What are you trying to say, that I can't lug this bag around? I've got some muscles around here somewhere," he says, throwing my backpack around his back, which makes him stumble a little.

"Oh yeah, where? Let me grab my magnifying glass so I can find them because I've never seen them before, not that it matters." I start laughing at my own joke. Hey, it was funny, no?

"On second thought, maybe you should carry your own bag," he teases back and we both laugh. I love the way he teases me. It makes me giggle. He teases because he loves me. He can tease me all he wants.

For the twenty-minute drive back to my place in Cambridge, Mikey holds my hand, plays with my fingers, and asks me about my flight and my family. Along Storrow Drive, the streetlights flare like sunbursts in the night, highlighting all the white snow that saturates both sides of the Charles River. I lean my head against the side window and feel the chilly glass. I think about how a little while ago, I was in sunny Miami, soothed by the warmth of the sun and my family and friends. Now I'm here, in my other life, without my family but with someone I love as well.

A few minutes later, Mikey pulls in front of my building along the snow-caked sidewalk, grabs my bag, and we walk up the three flights to my studio. The minute we get there, he tosses my bag on the sofa and we start kissing, soft, slow, deep kisses, the kind your mouth and your heart sink into.

"I love you, Mikey."

"I love you, too, Tommy."

It feels so wonderful not just to hear him say those words but to see the intensity and the sincerity in his eyes as he does. He really does mean it, from the bottom of his heart. He's not just saying it to echo what I am saying. He loves me despite my eccentricities (ordering the same food all the time, repeating myself, and telling cheesy jokes). He loves me despite my fanatical love for Gloria Estefan's music, which I make him listen to a lot. He accepts me unconditionally for who and what I am and loves me for it and I the same of him, despite his occasional bouts with booze. When you love someone, you love him for good and bad, as long as the bad doesn't get worse so that it endangers your life or lands you on *The Maury Povich Show*.

We walk over to the bed and collapse into each other's arms. My head snuggles into his neck, where I smell the sweet scent of his baby-powder cologne. I don't unpack. We spend the rest of the night in bed, cuddling, kissing, spooning, and tickling one another. My squeals resonate in the studio and probably down the hallway as he grabs me and tickles my stomach but I don't care. I'm happy right where I am.

"I love you, Tommy Boy," Mikey whispers.

"I love you, too," I whisper back. "Mikey, um, can I ask you something?"

"Sure, fire away, Tommy."

"Okay, why are you whispering?"

"I don't know," he whispers. "Why are you?"

We break out in giggles and I kiss him on the cheek and forehead.

"Seriously, though. What do you love about me?" I ask as we stare face to face with our heads on the pillows.

"Well, if you really want to know. Let's see . . . You live in your skin, Tommy Perez. You feel everything and you're not afraid to show it, especially how sensitive you are. That and your compassion come through in your writing, your concern about other people and wanting to help them. You're not afraid to be who you are at work, or in life. You're such a good person with such a warm heart. I know I can trust you with anything and know you will always be there. And even though you can be goofy at times or tell bad jokes, you enjoy life. You're a happy spirit and that inspires me to want to be a bettah person, Tommy."

"I tell bad jokes?" I say, feigning offense.

"Yeah, sometimes but you're so cute, I have to laugh. Your smile is contagious. See, you're doing it right now and the world is a better place when you smile."

"Aww, thank you, Mikey. I love you, too. That was so sweet of you. No one has ever said anything like that to me," I say, reminding myself to chronicle this later or tomorrow in my journal.

As I marvel at his face, the moonlight reflecting in the blue of his eyes, I can't help but cherish this moment. Mikey is such a special person who loves me, Tommy Perez, all of me.

"So, Tommy, now it's your turn, what do you love about me, cutie?"

I caress the side of his face with my hand and I begin.

"For one, you've got a big heart, one that makes room for anyone you think needs help, especially the students who seek your guidance. You are one of those rare selfless people who want to genuinely help people and that quality comes out whenever you talk about your work, your family, or your friends. You are super smart and I love hearing about your love of books, especially the ones about Jane Goodall. You have this beautiful spirit about you, an adventurous energy that likes to surf, ski, or go out and have a good time. You have this joie de vivre that one can't bottle up and that has opened up a whole new world for me in Boston. You have helped me feel at home in my adopted city and have shown me the way to love. Besides, you are super cute to boot."

Mikey smiles the whole time he listens to me and then plops

a nice gentle kiss on me. We fall asleep holding each other as the wind blows soft powdery snow against my window overlooking Concord Avenue below. I don't want to be anywhere else right now, not even under the roiling South Florida sun.

It's Valentine's Day, and it happens to land on a super sunny yet chilly Sunday. The temperature is hovering around the mid-thirties. I can't wait to give Mikey the gift I bought in Miami and saved for this occasion. I'm not a big Valentine lover since I never actually had one. I think you can be romantic anytime of the year or do a sweet gesture. When something is a surprise, it feels more special rather than the commercialism of a day like today. But I couldn't help but watch with envy as everyone exchanged roses and sweet candy with one another in high school, college, and at *The Miami Chronicle*, where a lot of couples worked. I dated Tell-a-Lie Teddy in the summer through the end of fall so no Valentine there. And my boyfriend before him, Ren the South Beach model, was in the winter and lasted only three months because he was never around that much. You can't build a relationship on a domestic and international-trotting model from Kansas who is in South Beach for three days, then Milan for a week, and then New York for a few days, only to come back to South Beach two or three weeks later for a few days. If you add up all the days we saw one another, it would have been two full weeks. Not enough in my book, although he was bigger than life and wildly fun. He now lives in Los Angeles trying to be an actor. Last I heard, he was trying out for CBS's *Survivor*.

Come to think of it, I've never had a boyfriend during my birthday either, since it's so close to Valentine's Day. Maybe that's why I want to enjoy this Valentine's Day as much as I can because I've never had someone to share it with. I bought a box of chocolates for Mikey and a pink rose to greet him with when he comes over at noon. But the main gift is the Key West conch, the beautiful giant seashell I picked up for Mikey on a day trip to Margaritaville when I was in Miami for those two weeks. When I lived in Miami, I would drive three hours south to get away from the city and the *Chronicle* with my Jeep's top down, surrounded by the colorful blue hues as the Atlantic Ocean intersects with the Gulf of Mexico. I had the words *Mikey, te amo, Tommy* inscribed on the back of the shell. I bought it at a shop on tourist-busy Duval Street. The shell is so exquisite, shiny, and pink that it almost looks like a gleaming expensive ceramic good. If you listen closely, you hear the wind.

Just before noon, the buzzer to my studio goes off. I buzz Mikey up. When I open the door, I see him standing in the doorway with a bouquet of pink and white carnations. He has a soft smile on his freshly shaved face, which makes him look more boyish than usual. He looks so handsome, wearing a blue chambray shirt, a black belt, and brown baggy Abercrombie jeans.

"Happy Valentine's Day, cutie. Heah, these are for you," he says, kissing me and then handing me the beautiful flowers.

"Thank you, Mikey. I love them. I'm gonna go put them in some water in the kitchen."

After doing that, I sit down with Mikey on the sofa to give him his gifts.

"These are for you, Mikey. I hope you like them."

First, I hand him the pink rose. Then, the box of chocolates, which makes me feel like Forrest Gump. And then finally the seashell, which I wrapped in a red box.

"Awww, cutie. You shouldn't have. I love the rose and the chocolates. I've never seen a pink rose. But what's in this box? It feels heavy."

"Open it and you'll see. It came a long way."

As we sit on my blue sofa, Mikey opens up the box and he

looks surprised when his eyes meet the shell's shiny surface. He takes it out and admires it from all sides.

"Look on the back. There's a message," I tell him.

" 'Mikey, te amo. Tommy,' " he reads out loud. "I know what that means. *Te amo*, too cutie. I know *mi* some *español*, thanks to you," he says, kissing me again on the lips.

He studies the seashell, turns it upside, holds it up to his ear.

"Where did you get this? I've nevah seen anything like this. It's so big."

"It's from Key West or, as we say in Miami, *Cayo Hueso*. Just a little something from my trip to Miami."

"This is beautiful, just like you, Tommy. Thanks. I'm gonna put it by my window in my bedroom. I know the perfect spot for it."

After we passionately make out a bit, Mikey takes me to a special lunch in Providence. We eat at a small Italian restaurant on Washington Street, where other couples are eating and holding each other's hands across the tables with red tablecloths and roses in the middle. After we share some lasagna and chicken with pasta, we then share a delicious chocolate tart for dessert, using the same spoon and feeding one another. I accidentally miss and smear some chocolate frosting on Mikey's mouth.

"Can't take you anywhere, Tommy," he says, cleaning himself up.

"You moved! I almost made it in your mouth." We exchange playful smirks.

After we drive back to Boston in his Matrix, we take a romantic stroll through my west Cambridge neighborhood and admire the McMansions. Later on, we head back up to my apartment, where we watch *Brokeback Mountain* on DVD. The whole time as we listen to the mournful strum of the guitar, my head rests on Mikey's lap as he sits on the carpet. Every now and then when Ennis and Jack exchange their seductive

glances on the mountain, I feel Mikey's hands run through my
curly hair. When there's an intimate scene between the lovers,
be it a tender kiss or a strong embrace, I look up at Mikey and
he smiles down back at me as if reading my mind.

"Tommy, I can't quit you," he playfully says at the end of the
DVD as the brooding music continues playing over the credits.

"I can't quit you either, cowboy."

By the time dusk arrives, we make tender love under the
watchful glow of the white vanilla-scented candles that sit on
my windowsill near my bed. We lie in bed for an hour, our
bodies recovering from the sexual fireworks. When Mikey and
the giant seashell leave at 9 P.M. to head back home, I thank
Cupid silently for helping make this my first and best Valentine
ever. I turn on *Desperate Housewives* on ABC and dial Rico and
tell him the play-by-play of the entire day even though I am
somewhat pooped out from the whole day.

"That's great, Tommy. I'm happy for you," Rico says.
"Sounds like Mikey came through for you and made it a Valen-
tine you'll always remember. I'm sure he liked the seashell.
That was really creative of you."

"Thanks. The day was so romantical. I wanted to give him
something no one else has, something to remember me by. I'm
so happy. What did you do for V day?" I ask Rico as I blow out
the candles in my apartment and straighten up my bed while
Susan, Edie, Lynette, Bree, and Gabby play poker on Wisteria
Lane.

"Ah, nothing. I just banged a cute guy I met online. I shot
my arrow right into his ass," Rico says, laughing. "You should
have seen this guy. He was five feet seven, perfect height for
fucking. He couldn't get enough of me. I made him eat my
candy. That was my Valentine. No big wup."

"I'd love to see you with someone you care about and who
cares about you deeply. I just want you to feel what I'm feeling
now."

"Maybe one day, Tommy. For now, it's all good."

"Well, Rico, I know we're not boyfriends or anything, but Cupid left you a little something here in Cambridge for Valentine's Day. I guess he figured I'd know how to best get it to you."

"No way, something for me? Thanks, Tommy, but you really shouldn't have. Valentine's doesn't mean that much to me. It's a commercialized holiday. But thank you anyway. I'll get home from the gym by 9:30 A.M. tomorrow in case you want to drop it off on your way to the *Daily*?"

"Sounds good, Rico."

It's 9:45 A.M. Monday and traffic has been smooth on I-93. I guess all the lovebirds are calling in sick today from last night. I exit at Columbia Road and drive down Morrissey Boulevard, past the *Daily* to Savin Hill. I pull up to Rico's place near the top of the hill with my gift in hand. I ring the doorbell. Rico opens the door and he appears in a tight white tank top and boxer shorts. As much as I try to force myself to look away, I can't help but notice how hot Rico looks in the shirt, his muscles tight and pumping adrenaline, blood, and sex appeal. I can see his abs defined through the shirt. He looks like he just did his morning workout or just walked out of a Hanes ad. Tommy, focus! I'm here to give him a gift, not to eyeball the hell out of his hot body. It's not like I haven't seen it before from our back hair removal sessions. Focus!

"Hey, dudette. C'mon on in!" he greets me with one of his big bear hugs. We make our way to his bedroom in the back of the house, where we sit down.

"Hi, Rico. Here, this is what I wanted to give you. Everyone deserves something on Valentine's, even if they're not dating anyone." I hand him a small box.

I watch as Rico opens the box, pulls out a small plane, and reads the card.

The plane is really an Air Force–type jet with two dark-haired toy male pilots sitting in the cockpit. The pair could easily be us. Attached is a bag of pink jelly beans and a card that reads "Happy Valentine's Day, Rico, from someone who will always care. Don't give up on love. Your wingman, Tommy Boy!"

A warm smile slowly spreads across his face and he looks up at me with his big green eyes, which look a little watery. He's obviously touched by what I wrote because he starts to stumble over his words, something I've never seen him do before.

"Oh wow, Tommy. Um, this is so sweet. I'm so, ah, touched, dudette," he says, giving me a big hug that lifts me off my feet, as usual. He strongly pats me hard on the back with both hands like a pair of bongos.

"It was nothing. I saw the jet plane and I thought of us, flying out on a Thursday night to Club Café. I know I haven't been around as much but that doesn't mean I don't care. Anyway, I gotta get going to work. I have a phone interview at ten-thirty with this Cambridge young woman who is homeless but chronicles her life on the street on a blog, which has become her cyberhome, so to speak. I already know what the headline's gonna be: HOMELESS.COM. Have a good day, Rico." I start to walk out of the house and back to the Jeep.

"You, too, Tommy. You, too," he says from the entrance of his doorway.

"Wake up, wake up, Tommy! It's your thirtieth birthday." Brian's voice echoes in my studio from the answering machine. He then starts belting out "Happy Birthday" in his Josh Groban–type voice, which sounds like a birthday version of "You Raise Me Up." Brian is a baritenor, in between a baritone and a tenor. He's got some powerful pipes.

"Happy Birthdaaay, deeear Tommmy . . ." he croons on the

machine. I pick up the phone because he's gonna wake up my entire building.

"Hi, Brian! Thank you for the sweet phone call."

"Hey, Tommy. *Feliz cumpleaños.* You're the big thirty even if you don't look a day over twenty-seven. What are your plans for the day? Are you going to Friday's like every year? I have the photo of us from last year in my pad in New York, of us sitting in the red-and-white-striped booth at the Friday's in Coral Gables."

"Yeah, I told Mikey that TGIF has become a birthday tradition for me. And Rico is gonna be there, too, so it should be fun. That's later tonight," I tell Brian as I lie in my bed, the sun pouncing through my window. I have to work today, this March 8, but tonight should be fun.

"Well, I'll let you get ready for work. Happy Birthday, *amigo*! And I'll take you out the next time you're in Miami."

"Thanks for the call, Brian. You totally beat my parents this year."

"Happy Birrrrthdaaay, deeear Tommm-ayyyy," Brian sings one more time before hanging up. You'd think he was auditioning for *American Idol* or something. He loves to sing, and it shows.

I'm thirty and yet I don't feel it at all. It'll hit me when I go to Bally's and I have to punch in "30" when it asks for my age on the elliptical machine. Threeeee zeroooo. Three decades of life. Thirty, half of sixty. I can't believe ten years ago I was twenty, and twenty years ago, I was in the fourth grade at North Beach Elementary, with the same head of curls I have now. Wow, thirty, *trenta,* as we say in Spanish. Just as I start thinking about how in ten years I will be forty and how in twenty years I will be fifty, my phone rings again. The machine grabs it on the second ring.

"Feliz cumpleaños a ti . . . Feliz cumpleaños a ti . . ." It's Papi

and Mami singing me "Happy Birthday" in Spanish and laughing the whole way through the song. They are so funny.

"Yonito, wake up! Pepe, maybe he is *durmiendo*." I hear
Mami talking to Papi.

"No, he should be *en casa*. He works today. Maybe he went
to de gym," Papi says.

"Or maybe he went to work early," Mami says and they
start having an entire conversation on my answering machine.
I give in and pick up the phone because, if I don't, they'll use
up my entire answering machine's recording time.

"Hola, Mami y Papi," I say after picking up the phone.

"Feliz cumpleaños a ti." They start singing all over again. I
love my parents no matter how wacky they can be at times.

Their phone call is followed by one from Mary, calling
from her classroom at Miami Beach High, and then from my
gazillion cousins, my aunts and uncles, Rico, and then finally
Mikey.

"You're line has been busy, cutie," he says. "I couldn't get
through. Happy Birthday, old man," he says, calling from his
office at school.

"Thanks, Mikey. I can't wait for tonight."

"I'll pick you up at 7 P.M. Your friend Rico said he'd meet
us at the Friday's in Back Bay on Newbury Street. I love you,
Tommy, and have a great day!"

"Thanks, Mikey. I love you too. See you later."

It's 7:15 P.M. and Mikey and I walk into Friday's, which is
below street level, on this dreary winter night. Spring is around
the corner so it shouldn't be much more of these cold days.
Rico waves to us from a booth in the back. I wave back and
we make our way toward him.

"Happy Birthday, dudette," Rico greets me with his Hulk
hug.

"Thanks, Rico. I appreciate you guys coming out to dinner here at Friday's. I know it's not the fanciest place but it's been one of my favorite places to celebrate my birthday ever since I was sixteen. It's simple, cute, and fun, with good food. You can't go wrong."

"Anything for you," Mikey says as he unwraps his black scarf from his neck. "This is your day after all."

We sit and scan the menus and order.

The waiter, an OC college student type probably working here to help pay his college tuition, comes and takes our order. Rico orders a Sam Adams light and the chicken tender strips and fries. Mikey orders the sampler and a Corona. I get the usual, a club sandwich and a Diet Coke with Vodka.

Rico grabs his beer and makes a toast.

"To Tommy Boy. May this be one of your best birthdays, dudette." He holds up his bottle to mine and Mikey's.

"To the cutest guy here," Mikey declares.

Our glasses all clink and we take big gulps and Rico excuses himself to go to the bathroom. He probably wants to check out his hair and biceps.

After dinner and two more rounds of drinks, we sit back and let our food rest.

"So what are you guys doing afterwards?" Rico asks, slouching into the back of his side of the booth with his hands resting on his full stomach.

"I'm taking him to Club Café. I have some friends who want to wish Tommy a Happy Birthday. It'll be fun. Come join us," Mikey invites Rico.

"Yeah, that sounds cool," Rico says, giving me a look that hints that may not be such a great idea.

"Yeah, we can stop by Club Café for a little while," I say, finishing up my drink and putting my arm around Mikey. "But I don't want to be there all night long."

Rico looks downward as if in disapproval. When Mikey

looks away, Rico mouths to me "Not a good idea" and raises his eyebrows to emphasize the point.

I'm guessing he thinks Mikey will get trashed on my birthday. He's been good lately. He wouldn't do that on my birthday. It's been a few weeks since anything has happened but I appreciate Rico looking out for me. I mouth back to him, "It will be okay," while Mikey seems to be looking around the restaurant.

"We'll be there for a little while and then we'll head back to your place and I'll give you the best birthday massage you ever got, Tommy," Mikey says.

"Sounds yummy, Mikey. I can't wait," I say.

As I look over the dessert menu, I suddenly hear a roar of clapping and singing. Oh no, a conga line of waiters and bartenders marching toward our table with a candle-lit chocolate cake oozing with hot fudge.

"Happy Birthday to you . . ." they sing. I'm so embarrassed. Okay, secretly, I love it. It's one of the reasons I like coming here on my birthday. The waiters make me stand on my chair and make me blow out the candle and the whole restaurant wishes me a Happy Birthday.

Rico and Mikey pat me on the back when I get down and Rico snaps a photo of me and then of me and Mikey with my Walgreens $9.99 camera. I have Mikey take a picture of me and Rico, *mano a mano*.

Half an hour later, the three of us start to walk over to Club Café, a few blocks away in the South End. I do my best to keep the conversation going but there's this awkwardness between Rico and Mikey because Rico doesn't really try to talk to Mikey. Mikey tries to make conversation with Rico but it seems to be a one-way street, like much of the narrow public alleys we pass on Boylston and Clarendon Streets. As we walk, I see Rico mouthing silently to me again, "He's gonna get drunk. That's not cool."

I mouth back, "It'll be fine. Now stop it!" and I glare at him. All I hear is the crunching of the snow as we stroll to CC. I see the steam rising like plumes from the manholes on the city streets, and every now and then, I hear the slight hiss from some of the flickering gas lamps along the side streets. Yeah, Boston still has vintage gas lamps working, if you look close enough.

Fifteen minutes later, we arrive at Club Café. Mikey's friends Patrick and Will greet us at the entrance and they both give me big hugs and wet cheek kisses. They hand me a Vodka with Diet Coke and Mikey a Corona. They're already buzzed. I can tell by their slurred speech and overenthusiastic demeanor. Rico orders a Sam Adams light, as usual. We all make our way deep into the back video bar, where the veejay plays, for the fifty-millionth time, Madonna's "Hung Up," which is so 2005 but it still sounds good because of the ABBA hook.

I keep hearing someone singing the lyrics very loudly. I look through the crowd of men and I see the source of this wanna-be audition. It's Kyle, grooving his hand left and right and being his dramatic self. He then spots me and makes his way toward us.

"Hey, Tommy. Happy Birthday. A few little birds told me it's your big thirty," he says, giving me a hug and two air kisses. "You look fabulous for thirty."

"Thanks, Kyle. It's been a fun night so far."

"What did you guys do for your birthday? What fancy place did you take him to, Mikey?" Kyle says, standing over us and taking a sip of his Cosmo.

"We went to TGIF. It's Tommy's favorite place to go on his birthday," Mikey says.

"Oh," Kyle deadpans. "That's so, um, nice. Anyhoo, have a fabulous birthday. I'm gonna make some rounds here, people," and he wanders off back into the crowd, singing out loud the

next song on the monitor, "Since You've Been Gone" by Kelly
Clarkson. I guess the veejay wants to play the best hits of 2005
or something.

I stand in the corner here with Mikey, where we're holding
each other and kissing. Mikey then downs the rest of his drink.

"Hey, guys, I'm gonna take a lap around the bar. Be back in
a few," Rico says.

"We'll be right here. Don't be too long," I tell him. "I
wanna hang with you on my birthday."

Over the next hour, Mikey drinks two more Coronas and
I stop with one more Diet Coke with Vodka. Patrick and Will
are pretty much wasted and hanging off one another in the
corner of the bar and bumping into people. Rico comes back
for a bit and then says he's going to make another bar lap. It's
his way of saying how much he disapproves of all this.

Before he leaves, he whispers in my ear in a serious but
concerned tone, "Dude, this is your birthday. If anyone should
be getting wasted, it should be you. Not them! This is not
right. Get Mikey out of here, pronto!"

"We're leaving in a few," I tell him.

But we don't. Mikey sees me talking to Rico, and as he
leaves our group, Mikey turns to me.

"What's up with your friend? He's been giving me and my
friends attitude the whole night. What an asshole!" Mikey says,
his words flowing as one fast long sentence.

"Hey, that's my friend. He's just looking out for me, that's
all."

"Well, I think your friend is a little too protective of you,
Tommy. He's not acting like a friend but a jealous boyfriend. I
think he wants some Cuban in him," Mikey says in a bitchy
tone.

"You're wrong. He's my friend looking out for me on my
birthday. I think we should get going. You're a bit buzzed. I

don't want you to get sick." I grab Mikey's beer, which is half full, and put it on the bar counter.

"Come on, ten more minutes. They're playing Justin Timberlake now," he says, grooving to the music as Justin dances on the monitor. Mikey pulls me over to the lip of the small stage and starts dancing with me and slobbering all over my neck as he drinks the beer behind me.

"Happy Birthday to my Tommy. Happy Birthday to my cutie," he starts singing loudly.

I'm feeling really uncomfortable now. I hate it when he gets like this. I've lost the sweet and sober Mikey tonight. Rico was right and he removed himself from the situation. I don't blame him. As much as I try to get Mikey to leave, he doesn't want to budge. I try to ease the situation, and fifteen minutes later, we're back to the original conversation.

"Hey, let's get going, Mikey. I want to get back to my place and have you all to myself for my birthday. It's getting late," I say, as Ricky Martin's "I Don't Care" blares on the video monitors.

"Fine!" he shouts. "You can be a party POOPer sometimes." He downs the rest of the beer and wipes his mouth with the sleeve of his shirt as all the other guys in the bar look our way to see what the commotion is all about.

"Yo, Patrick, Will! We're leaving. Do you guys need a ride?" Mikey motions to them.

"Yeah," Will says, spitting out the word.

"Cool!" Patrick says, his eyelids barely open.

I interrupt the conversation. There's no way in hell Mikey's driving. I squeeze my way through the wall of men at the bar to order a bottle of water from the pony-haired bartender and I start drinking it. I'm not even buzzed. I guess I ate too much.

"Mikey, give me your keys. I'm driving tonight," I tell him and he slams the keys to the Matrix into my hand. I get Jose

Cuervo and Johnnie Walker out of the bar along with Mikey. I end up having to drive them home. I lost Rico. I don't know where he went. I'll talk to him tomorrow. He probably met a guy and took off.

During the whole drive to Charlestown to drop off Will at Patrick's condo, I am silent, grinding my teeth and rubbing my forehead with my left hand. This is not how I wanted to end my birthday, chauffeuring these guys home. Mikey has passed out in the passenger side, his head bopping against the glass. The other two probably don't even know who is taking them home.

An hour later, I pull up to my condo, and help Mikey up the stairs to my place. When we get to my front door, he throws up.

"Well Happy Birthday to me, too," I tell Mikey. "Thanks for a night I'll never forget."

"Tommy, I'm sorry," he says. "I overdid it." He then passes out on my sofa. I clean things up and get ready for bed. Mikey has this way of opening up my heart and then breaking it. I liked being twenty-nine much better.

Chapter 12

RICO

It's about friggin' time the cold began to go away. It's the first Saturday in April, and Boston seems to be waking up from winter hibernation. Everyone's running outside again here in Stab N' Kill, I mean, Savin Hill. Kids ride their bikes up and down the hilly streets, play street ball or basketball kinda like I used to back in the Berkshires.

I can finally jump rope in my yard that overlooks *The Boston Daily*. Shorts are finally wearable again.

It's 65 degrees outside on this cool afternoon but to us Bostonians, it's h-h-h-hot.

Perfect weather to walk along the Charles River, get some eye candy and grab some sun rays for my night out later on at Club Café. This will be a nice cheap way to spend the afternoon.

After hopping on the T and getting off at the Park Street stop at the Boston Common, I dial Tommy Boy on my cell to see if he wants to hang out this afternoon.

"Tommy, yo! What's up with you? It's Rico." I'm walking under a canopy of trees in the Common toward the Charles River, where bushy squirrels run around and hop from tree branch to tree branch.

"Hey Rico! Waassup, *amigo?*" Tommy responds in his usual chipper voice. That guy is always happy, so positive. I've never met anyone who laughs and giggles as much as he does. If there were a blizzard today, he would probably say, "Isn't it poetic?"

As I walk, the sun filters through the trees, casting shadowy spots on the pavement and my Nikes. This is probably the greenest part of Boston, which is mostly red and brown from all the brick buildings and brownstones.

"Hey, I'm walking along the Charles River and checking out the scene and the guys. You're welcome to join me. I can meet you on the Esplanade by the Hatch Shell stage. *Capisce?*" I tell him, as I spot a marginally cute guy with a nice firm chest in a tight green tank top (Yum!) that outlines his tight nipples (Double yum!). I'm eye-fucking the dude as Tommy talks.

"That sounds great," Tommy says. "It's so pretty outside today. I'm not meeting up with Mikey until later so I'm free this afternoon. I was gonna go running but this is just as good. I'll be there in half an hour, in the spot where everyone sunbathes and cruises along the shore. See ya in a few!"

About half an hour later, Tommy shows up, wearing his favorite red Nautica hood, black shorts, and a beige *Boston Daily* baseball cap. His curls push out from under his cap, making him look more boyish than his actual age.

I have to admit, he looks really cute. I've always thought Tommy was a cute guy even though I think he needs a haircut. Those curls can get out of control, almost chaotic, but they work for him. I'm so jealous. I've got my thinning hair so I have to keep my hair short and cropped so that the gaps aren't as obvious. What I wouldn't do to have my former thick black hair back spiked up again.

Tommy and I gel pretty well, and deep down inside, part of me has always wondered what it would have been like to date him. When we met last September at Club Café, we instantly clicked. We both shared a funny moment, waiting for the fugly bartender to come our way to take our drink orders. I couldn't help but laugh along with Tommy, who kept busting out whenever the bartender missed us in his back-and-forth trips because the bar was so crazy that night. Every time we opened our mouths to get his attention, he whisked by us in a blur. That's when Tommy and I started talking. A friendship was born.

I couldn't commit to anyone then or right now. I don't want to date again for a long time. No way! I have a brick wall around my heart, guarding it from lying and cheating assholes like Jeff and my boyfriend before him, Steve, who had a girlfriend the whole time we dated for six months. Jesus! It's the stuff of country songs or a typical *Jerry Springer* episode. I caught Steve fucking his girlfriend in his apartment, in the bed we fucked in that morning, when I decided to come home early from the university when my economics class was canceled. I bitched her out and whacked him in the face. The dude deserved it. The girl ran out screaming. I was so much hotter than her, and still, he wanted to go fishing. Yuck!

I don't put up with bullshit. Then a few months later, there was Jeff, with his floppy straight black hair and hazel eyes, who was a real estate broker and part-time model, doing those catalogs for Filene's and Sears. The dude needed so much attention, that should have been a red flag from the start, but he was hot, what can I say, and a great lay. After dating a few weeks, I moved into his place and I thought things were going well. For our anniversary, he helped me buy my Ford Explorer as a gift. Then I find out he was screwing another guy behind my back when I accidentally intercepted an e-mail from his lover on the computer.

"Let's meet tonight at 8 P.M. while your boyfriend has night class," the e-mail stated. Jeff's response: "Meet you at your place. Can't wait to suck you off! Rico won't be around. He doesn't know a thing." Fucker!

That's two lying, cheating dudes in a row. I was always faithful to the relationships. Stupid me. You trust someone and they stomp all over your heart. Assholes!

I don't understand why guys can't be honest with each other if they say they love one another. If you don't want to be monogamous, at least be honest, and maybe that'll work. I need time to let my emotional scars heal. My heart has a scab around it and it's not ready to be scraped off. I haven't given up on love, though. I'm just not there yet and I haven't met any guy who can open me up to love again, someone I feel I can trust again. It's gonna take a while. It's kind of scary to let someone in and then they wreck up your heart, your feelings. I'm too good for that.

Cindy, my little sister, seems to have found true love. She's been married to her high school sweetheart Robby for five years and they're planning on having a little bambino next year. Mom and Pop are really excited about being a *nonno* and *nonna* and I can't wait to be Uncle Rico. (My real name is Ricardo, after my grandfather on my pop's side whose lineage traces back to Napoli. But everyone calls me Rico. It may sound Latino but it's definitely an Italian name. *Capisce?* If you tell anyone my real name, I'll get my uncles Louie, Tony, and Joey in Revere to rough you up!)

When I think of my ideal relationship, I think of Cindy and Robby, and Mom and Pop, open, loving, and yes, sometimes loud. But whenever they fight and hurl their insults the same way Manny Ramirez pitches his balls at a Red Sox game, it's just my parents' way of showing how much they love each other. They always make up by bedtime. It's in our Italian DNA to be loud and I've got that gene along with these green eyes. I just haven't found the right guy to share that true kind of romance with. Maybe one day I will. In the meantime, fucking is great. Good cardio, too. Did you know that your heart rate reaches 160 beats a minute when you cum! I read that in a dirty magazine once.

Anyway, when I met Tommy Boy, I had a gut feeling he could be a cool bud here, someone to hang with and check out guys and get the occasional beer. We were both sort of new in town and we're both close with our families. My parents call me twice a week, not like his, who call him daily at 8 P.M. That's way too much. He seemed like a good-hearted guy. So while we have a lot of common ground, nothing ever happened between us, which is rare for gay guy friends because we're such horny fuckers that we all mess around with one another. Guys seem to think we've dated or sense there is something between us but there's not. It's just a cool friendship. Let people think what they want. I don't care. It's a free friggin' country.

"So how are things with Mikey? It's been a few months since you guys have been dating. When I see you out at Club Café, you seem so preoccupied with Mikey, keeping an eye on him like a hawk," I tell Tommy, as runners and bladers breeze by us on the concrete trail along the water's edge.

"Yeah, things have been going smoothly. I'm in love with the guy, Rico. It's such a great feeling, so powerful. He calls me each night before he goes to bed to chat a little about how our workday went. Before we hang up, when his voice begins to trail away in sleepiness, he'll say, 'Tommy! You know I love you, cutie!' and my heart is just tickled. Did I tell you about the first time he told me he loved me?"

Oh God! Here Tommy goes again, talking about the first I-love-you exchanged between him and Mikey. He's told me this story like three times since January and he will recite it with the same exact details and enthusiasm as the first time. He even text-messaged the story, too, and sucked up a lot of the texting time on my cell.

I'll be a good sport and entertain his request because I haven't seen Tommy Boy in two weeks and he did come out here to hang out with me.

"Yeah, you told me already, but knowing you, you're going to tell me again. So go for it." As he talks, we walk along the lagoon, where swans bob up and down in the murky water and sailboats from Boston University dot the water like paper boats. Too bad the hot shirtless rowers are too far away. I can't see their ripped bodies.

"And so on Christmas Eve, I sat outside of my parents' house and dialed him and he said he had a gift to give me over the phone and so I told him I had something to tell him, too . . ." Tommy continues telling his story, lost in his own gay romance novel that should probably be called *My Boyfriend Loves Jose Cuervo More Than Me.*

As he babbles, I notice along the grass that some tulips have begun to burst through the ground the same way my Italian dick bulges through my boxer shorts every morning, or when I get a dirty thought, which is like every other minute. Wow, spring is da bomb in Boston. No wonder everyone is outside today.

"Rico . . . Rico . . . RICO!! Are you still listening to me?" I hear Tommy talking to me after I briefly drifted into a daydream that could have been a kinky wet dream. I was imagining what I would do to that hottie in the green tank top who I saw earlier.

"Yeah, Tommy, I heard you LOUD and CLEAR," I tell him, feeling slightly annoyed by the story. I wasn't really listening but I could recite his love story by heart.

"I'm glad you're happy and that things are going your way. How is the drinking?" I fire back, to snap the sap-tastic story back to reality.

"Well, Mikey hasn't been drunk in three weeks, since my birthday, so I guess that's a good thing, no?" Tommy tells me as if he's looking for some reassurance that it's okay for someone to get drunk and majorly hung over every few weeks like Mr. Corona does.

I can't seem to get through to Tommy that his "love" has a problem. He's gonna have to learn the hard way that Mikey's in denial and now Tommy seems like he's in denial about Mikey being in denial. Geez!

I have to get through to Tommy Boy one more time.

"Dudette, you're my friend and I've told you this before and I'm gonna tell you again. This guy is an a-l-c-o-h-o-l-i-c. Hello!" I tell him as we sit on a green city bench facing the Cambridge side of the Charles River. "I will never forget last month, the night of your birthday, how sloshed he was. He was bumping into people and raising his voice to you and there you were, holding him and trying to take care of him. And dude, it was your thirtieth birthday. The night was supposed to be about you and it wasn't even about you at the bar. It was about you taking care of him and driving around his drunken duo pals afterward. I was so disgusted with his behavior and how you were enabling it that I left Club Café that night. We barely got to hang out on your birthday, besides the Friday's dinner."

Tommy's eyes pool now. Darn it, what I just said really got to him. Good! Maybe it will sink in this time.

"He just overdrank. Besides, we had a wonderful dinner on my birthday. I just wish we could have had more fun at the club."

Tommy looks frustrated now. You can tell because his thick eyebrows furrow in and his arms are folded like a little boy who is mad. I put my arm around his neck, like an older brother would, even though the dude is older than me.

"Look, Rico, I appreciate you looking out for me but I think I've got things under control. Mikey is a guidance counselor and very stressed out, and every now and then, he overdoes it with the liquor. I've talked to him about it and he says that's how everyone is here in Boston, which I somewhat agree with," Tommy tells me, almost selling me on his point. Not! He's just making excuses for the guy because he cares about him, but if he really cared about him, he would make him go to an AA meeting or see a counselor to help him get a handle on his drinking.

"If Boston wasn't a drinking city, then Club Café and all these other bars, straight and gay, wouldn't be so packed all the time. This city is one drunk town. It's like part of the culture or something. Alcohol is in the air. The most historic tourist spots here are the bars!" Tommy explains to me.

Uh-oh, I hear a "Back in Miami" comparison coming up, which Tommy does all the time.

"Back in Miami," Tommy begins, "guys drink but they tend to drown themselves more in suntan oil and Cuban coffee. Hey, that's funny, no?"

Yeah, one of Tommy's cheezy jokes, but because he laughs at his own jokes, you have to laugh with him. It's contagious. So we're both laughing on this bench as all these couples walk by with their dogs and some gay guys I like to call Tonya Hardings are skating backward so that everyone can check out their asses as they glide and twirl like Olympic ice queens.

Up ahead, in the distance, we see a tall guy spinning and twirling on his skates like a big show-off. As he comes into focus, we realize it's the KY, *Real Life* has-been Kyle.

Figures he would use the great weather to go out and parade around town like he's the mayor. That guy thinks he is the star of his own reality show called *Kyle's World*.

I wish I could switch channels but this guy always seems to be around everywhere I go in Boston. This really is a small town.

"Heeeeeeeeeeey, fellas!" Kyle tells us as he turns around and skates in reverse alongside Tommy and me. "Isn't this such a fabulous day. Whew! I haven't seen weather like this since I was in Miami for the White Fiesta. I just had to come out today and skate up and down the river. What are you guys up to?"

I just nod and give Kyle one of my fake smiles, which look real, according to people. Tommy, the more diplomatic one, actually talks to the fucker.

"Hi, Kyle. We're enjoying the weather, just like you, walking around and savoring the sun. How was the rest of the White Fiesta? I lost you after Dolly Parton performed," Tommy says and Kyle continues to skate around us in circles.

"It was great. I saw Sean Paul perform and I got a hug from Dolly Parton. I could have sworn I saw Bette Midler but it could have also been a drag look-alike. I was standing far away. Cher made a surprise appearance at the Vizcaya party and I got to meet her. *'Do you believe in love after love'* . . . Cher was there!" Kyle tells us, dripping with enthusiasm as if this were the most important event on the planet. It was just a stupid, overpriced circuit party. You could have probably seen all the same guys for free at one of the bars later on that night.

"I was one of the emcees and I ended up featured in some of the celeb rags in New York and L.A. This emcee job landed me another hosting gig for Provincetown this summer for the Fourth of July at the Crown and Anchor Hotel. Are you guys going there for the Fourth? So, Tommy, when are you going to do a story on me in the *Daily*?"

Kyle has asked Tommy the dreaded question, one he hates, when people who know him socially hit him up for a story in the paper.

But Tommy, ever so polite, responds, "Well, I've been thinking about doing an article about life after reality TV but I haven't pitched it to the Living/Arts editor yet. I'm still flirting with the idea, the concept may be something like 'Life After Reality TV: Fame or Lame?' "

Kyle's eyes flicker with excitement.

"Oh my gosh!! I am so your story, Tommy, at least the fame aspect. You have my card so call me when you talk to your editor. It could be an in-depth profile on how well I've done since *The Real Life Boston!*"

Damn it! I wish this guy would just go away but he's one of those butterflies that hover all around you and you just can't seem to escape. I came here to check out the cute guys, not the attention-grabbing drama queens on friggin' wheels. I'm not even making eye contact with Kyle, and yet the dude doesn't get the hint that I don't like him or want him around.

"Let me get back to you, Kyle, but I think it would be an interesting story. Take it easy and talk to you soon," Tommy tells him.

Kyle begins to skate away and says, "Fabulous! Toodles!" as he waves his hand goodbye and disappears into the distance.

Tommy and I continue trekking along the bike/jogging trail and he picks up where we left off before the KY interrupted our conversation.

"Rico, I am very well aware that Mikey's drinking can sometimes get out of control. I promised myself that if he overdoes it one more time, I'm gonna have a long talk with him and tell him that he either gets help or—another boyfriend," Tommy tells me, with a little attitude in his voice.

"The last time he got trashed, which was my birthday, he threw up by my front door. I was so pissed. I don't work hard all week to clean up his vomit on the weekends. I mean, we're not in college anymore. We're in our thirties now."

I'm glad to hear him talk like this. He needs to toughen up a bit in his relationship.

"Good for you, Tommy Boy! Don't let him charm you and sweet-talk you like he always does by doing nice things for you. You fall for that so easily, bro. Stick to your guns and tell him how you feel. If he really loves you—and himself—he'll realize he has a problem." We continue strolling along the river toward downtown among the masses of people enjoying this beautiful spring day.

"So what are you doing later, Tommy?" I ask him while scanning the grassy areas for any other cute guys. Besides that guy with the green shirt I saw earlier, I'm just seeing trolls and Frankenstein faces here. Where are all the sexy Harvard rowers this afternoon? I want to plow them the same way they plow the Charles River.

Tommy's babbling has just snapped me out of those dirty momentary daydreams.

"Mikey and I are having dinner in the North End tonight but he said he wanted to meet up with his friends Patrick and Will at Club Café, which I'm not too excited about. But they are his friends and he doesn't see them as much as he used to since we've gotten so much closer since the new year."

I think Tommy's gonna have that serious talk with Mikey sooner than later.

"Hey, I'll be there, too. I'm really horny today, so hopefully, I'll find a young cute guy there to play with since this afternoon is lacking in them," I tell Tommy. "If you wanna take a break from Mikey and his drunk friends tonight at the bar, look for me at CC. I'll be there."

As we walk on the pedestrian ramp over to the shops in Back Bay, where throngs of people fill every space of the sidewalk to window-shop and lunch in the outdoor cafés, I can't help but think tonight's gonna be another disaster for Tommy.

Oh wow, another shirtless hottie in sight running on Newbury Street. I love Boston in springtime.

Chapter 13

TOMMY

The thunderous buzzer in my studio rudely goes off. Mikey is here and he's early. I just got home an hour ago from walking around the city with Rico and I am beat. I'm barely done with my hot shower. I leap out of the tub, buzz Mikey up, and start drying myself quickly.

I dab some Aveda curling gel into my hair before he makes the three-story trip up to my studio.

We're having dinner at one of his favorite restaurants, La Dolce Vita in the city's North End. After a while, Mikey got tired of Bertucci's and Boston Market and all the other chain places I like. I never tire of them. But hey, change is good, I always say, even though I don't necessarily apply that to my eating habits. I mean, there is nothing wrong with eating lunch at Boston Market every day. You at least know what you get. Besides, the Brazilian server there, Celestina, always gives me extra turkey whenever I pull up. She likes to practice her Spanish with me.

Tonight marks my four-month-aversary with Mikey. It feels like yesterday that we met at Club Café. We've done so much in such a short time, and tonight, we're having a special dinner. It was Mikey's idea and I'm all for it. The only thing that can ruin this is what happens after dinner, us meeting up with Patrick and Will, whom I like to call (but never out loud) Drunk and Drunker. Mikey could easily be the third party. I'd call him "Drunkest." Oh, what awaits me! Hopefully, things will go smoothly and not be a rerun of my birthday night. If I could just get Mikey out of Club Café sooner than later, then we'll be okay. But ever since we've been together, I've been a failure at that and I'm just about at my breaking point.

There's a saying I heard on *The Oprah Winfrey Show* that I keep in mind often. It goes something like this: If you want to know where a situation is going, look back to the beginning, because all the signs are there whether you choose to see them or not. I hate to admit this, but alcohol and Club Café were both elements from the moment we met. It's like Corona has been a third party in our relationship and it just won't go away.

"Hey, cutie!" Mikey greets me with a kiss and a hug as I let him in. He's all dapper in his Abercrombie blue polo shirt and baggy blue jeans while I stand dripping in a brown towel with a mop of wet gelled hair.

"How you doin', Tommy?"

"Oh, I'm not ready. You're a little early, Mikey. I wasn't expecting you for another half hour." As happy as I am to see him, I'm also slightly annoyed that I have to rush now to get ready. But I think my annoyance stems from the fact that we are going to the CC later tonight.

I head back to the bathroom, dry myself off, and change into my clothes, a new pair of denim Gap blue jeans, a long-sleeved V neck brown shirt, a black belt, and black loafers.

"There was no traffic coming from the South Shore so I got heah fastah tonight," Mikey says, opening my refrigerator door and grabbing his first Corona for the night. "Tommy, I can't wait to eat. The food at this place is sooo wicked good."

"I know. I'm starving, too." I bend down by my bar counter and I begin to lace up my shoes. "I worked up an appetite walking with Rico through the city. It was such a beautiful day."

I grab my olive windbreaker because the mercury is expected to drop a few degrees for a nice cool breezy night and we head out the door. We walk a half mile, passing the guarded decayed tombstones of the Cambridge cemetery as we head toward the Harvard Square T stop. There's no parking in the North End so we're better off taking the subway to the restaurant.

After two transfers, from the red line to the green line by Government Center downtown, we continue walking, passing city hall and bustling Quincy Market. Then we cross over the former Central Artery and make our way to the North End just on the lip of downtown Boston and the wharf. The streets here are rife with small four- to five-story brick buildings crouched on narrow streets that call to mind any neighborhood in New York City. No matter what block we walk on, we're hit with the aroma of boiling pasta and tasty sweets in the one-mile-long neighborhood, which has always been predominantly old-school Italian but is quickly becoming a magnet for yuppies. (I know this because I recently wrote an article about it.) I can see the appeal: You can't beat the panoramic views of downtown's thicket of skyscrapers and the water here.

We finally arrive at La Dolce Vita and we squeeze our way through the crowd inside. Mikey tells the host, who is really the enthusiastic owner with a thick black mustache and potbelly, our names and he quickly matches Mikey's name on the reservation list. A few minutes later, we're seated in a corner that is dimly lit by a flickering candle, very romantic, like a quaint restaurant in Torino or small village in the real Italy. We have some privacy here. I order penne with chunks of grilled chicken in a cream sauce and a Diet Coke. Mikey gets the meat lasagna and another Corona beer. He really loves that beer. For dessert, we share a chocolate torte from the same fork.

"Tommy, the last few months have been great. I really love you." Mikey holds up his second Corona beer to toast my glass of Diet Coke. "I know I'm a pain in the ass when I get trashed and you always take care of me. I feel safe with you, Tommy. I trust you. I love you, my *cubanito*!"

My eyes dampen a bit, and I smile back and look down at the soft candle. I love this guy so much, if only he didn't drink so much. Why can't he always be like this, the sweetest lover, the kindest person.

"I love you, too, Mikey." I lean over the table and gently kiss him, so lightly that it tickles. Underneath the table, our feet play footsy.

"Do we really have to go to Club Café tonight? I know you want to meet up with your friends but it would be so nice to walk around the North End, and then back to Cambridge and climb into bed, no?" I tell him, sounding as convincing as a good used car salesman. I'd really rather just go home and have Mikey all to myself and watch *Saturday Night Live* or *Mad TV.* I want to spoon against the curve of his back and nuzzle my nose into his neck.

"Tommy, I already said yes to Patrick and Will," he says, doing that thing he does where he bites down on his tongue and smiles. "It will be quick. An hour at the most. I promise. Then you're all mine! Let's have a few drinks there and enjoy the music and my friends."

"Remember my birthday? You said the same thing that night, too, and it was my birthday!" I stroke the top of his right hand.

"I've apologized for that, Tommy. I got carried away. That won't happen again. I won't let you down, cutie," he says, taking my hand into his hand and fiddling with my index finger. I get aroused from his sweet touch.

"I can't deal with you getting trashed again. I'm serious. It's not healthy for you or for me."

"It'll be fun. Just for a little bit, Tommy, okay?" he says, his brows pleading with me to go along with him. Who knows, maybe he has a surprise planned for us tonight at the CC. The thought excites me.

So I give in, silently praying the night will unfold as I hope. I'm such a wus but I know we are not going to be there "just an hour." Knowing Mikey, we'll probably shut down the place but part of me feels I have to let the night take its course even if I may regret it and trust Mikey this one last time. I am putting my trust in fate. Whatever happens, happens.

After dessert, we take a romantic stroll along the Boston wharf at Christopher Columbus Park. We gaze at the water, where the lights from the buildings shimmer off the harbor like tiny diamonds in the night. We take the T to the Back Bay Station stop because it borders the South End. Half an hour later, we're walking two blocks on this cool night holding hands as we approach Club Café.

A bevy of guys smoke outside the bar since smoking has been banned inside Boston bars. We walk through a cloud of smoke and pass them on our way in.

We pass the coat check dude and head into the main bar. Drunk and Drunker are already buzzing like inebriated bees. And they have Mikey's Corona with a lime ready for him. They also have a Diet Coke and Vodka for me, which is nice of them. Bostonians will go out of their way to make sure you have a drink in hand, at all times, from what I've observed in my short year here. Glasses and beer bottles are never empty for too long.

"Hey, guys! Good to see you two," Patrick says in a high-pitched chipper tone. He hugs us while holding the drinks in his hands behind us. His speech is already slurred. I need subtitles to understand what he's saying. Will, the redhead, is no better off.

"Heeeey, guys, happy four-month-aversary," Will greets us, also mobbing us with hugs and drinks. This is going to be a *long* night.

We grab a small table over in the front lounge, where it's not as crowded as in the main salon and there's more space to move around and talk.

Over the course of an hour we've listened to the first American Idol, former Destiny's Child, and the Pussycat Dolls purr on the video monitors. Mikey has had three Coronas, which makes five in total for the night so far. I've stuck with my lone DCV. I wish we were back in the North End. I know where tonight is headed already. This is not La Dolce Vita. It's just the opposite.

"Yo, Tommy, have another drink. Catch up to me, will ya," Mikey dares me. I flash him one of my I-am-so-annoyed, stop-drinking looks. "I'm feeling as good as you look, Tommy," he says, trying to butter me up and laughing back as Drunk and Drunker join in the revelry.

"Mikey, slow down. You've had three drinks one after the other. Maybe you should chill down with the beer," I assert in a serious tone.

"Oh c'mon, TB, we're celebrating our four months to-gethah. Chill out or I am gonna call Fidel Castro and have you and your family deported," he says, thinking he's funny while Drunker declares, "Two points for Mikey. Zero for Tommy Boy. Your turn, Tommy."

What is this, an insult-you contest? I'm not playing this stupid game, which reminds me of those "your momma's so fat" jokes.

"Mikey, stop it! You get so obnoxious when you drink. My parents fled their home country to the United States without even knowing the language because of that dictator and you make a joke out of it. Dude, I was born in Miami Beach, re-member?" I snap at him. Roiling flames of anger flare inside me and his cute expressions or blue eyes are not going to tame them. It's as if he slapped my parents in the face right now. "Can we go home now? You are really pissing the fuck out of me."

Mikey takes a big slug of his Corona, finishing every last drop of the bottle, as if to spite me.

"You're too sensitive, Tommy. Geez. I was just joking and you get all worked up like a little bitch, just like my two ex-fiancées."

Oh no, he did not just call me a little bitch! No way. And he did not just compare me to a girl. Oh no! First he insults my family and now he is calling me a woman?

I can't deal with this shit anymore. I want to be with someone who appreciates me and who can handle their liquor, not lose control of themselves like Sandra Bullock's character in the 2000 movie *28 Days*.

I mentally count to 10 to calm down and tell Mikey, "Let's go. NOW! You've had too many drinks and we have to take a taxi back to Cambridge." I get up and shove my chair back under the table.

Drunk and Drunker are in complete shock, their mouths wide open after witnessing the exchange between Mikey and me. They have never seen us fight. I never lose my cool. Never. I've always been a paragon of patience but Mikey has pushed me to my limit. Mami and Papi would be so proud of me right now, standing up for myself and defending not just me but them, our *familia*.

"Hey, Tommy, Mikey . . . guys, calm down. Have fun, relax," Drunker Will tells us.

"Tommy, it was a slip of the lip. His bad," Patrick jumps in, trying to calm down the situation. The women at two other tables are all staring at us. How embarrassing.

"Nah, I think we should get going before things get out of hand tonight. Are you coming, Mikey?"

He looks at me as if he's possessed by another spirit with that glassy look in his eyes. I can't seem to reach the Mikey I love. His beautiful blue eyes seem empty.

"Dude, I don't want to leave. I'm here with my friends. You can go if you want. I want to hang out with my friends. Go back to Cuba or to Miami or wherever you came from," Mikey shouts at me in his slurred speech and flings his hand as if dismissing me.

"Fine! I'm not dealing with you like this, right here. I'm heading back to Cambridge. Do me a favor? Don't call me when you're drunk off your ass and throwing up like a college student and need a place to stay tonight!" I fire back. I storm out of Club Café. I am hoping Mikey will follow me to apologize. He doesn't.

I stand outside the club amid the smokers to gather my thoughts. I pace back and forth as cars zip by on Columbus Avenue. I'm infuriated, waves of anger swelling inside me like a tsunami, drowning out the hurt but pushing my disappointment, my frustration to the surface. I feel my cheeks redden from the internal heat and my heart drumming inside like a wild bongo player.

Mikey would rather be drunk with his friends tonight than with me. He should take a stroll with Johnnie Walker or sail away with Captain Morgan or date Corona Beer's company president.

I stare up at the distant skyscrapers that lord over Chinatown and I feel a familiar hand on my shoulder. That has to be Mikey coming to apologize for his behavior.

I turn around. To my surprise, it's Rico.

"Hey, dudette! Why are you alone out here?" he says. "You look really upset. What's wrong? Oh, let me guess, the alchy is drunk again, right?"

I look at Rico and stare into his soothing green eyes and I hold back my tears. I don't want him to see me like this. He can read me like a book, though. I'm embarrassed to admit the whole thing and Rico has been warning me about Mikey from the start. The ironic thing is that it was Rico who pointed Mikey out to me that night back in November.

"Yeah, we just got into a fight," and I rehash the details of tonight's bar drama.

"I can't believe he said that about me and being deported. Absolutely no respect. If he had met my dad on my trip down to Miami in December and saw what a sweet gentle man he is, Mikey would feel like such a lowlife right now."

Rico offers to give me a ride home since tonight he actually drove his Ford pickup truck for once.

Twenty minutes later, Rico pulls off Storrow Drive and into Harvard Square to drop me off. I keep staring out the window, jabbing my fist into the paneling of the door. Then my cell phone vibrates, buzzing in my right pocket.

"I bet you that's Mikey," Rico says as he rounds the rotary by the Cambridge Common. It's just past 1 A.M. "Wanna make a bet? He's wasted, feels bad, and is now calling the one guy he knows who will take him in—that's you, my friend."

It is Mikey but I don't want to pick it up in front of Rico. I want to be strong or at least appear strong to Rico, and most of all, myself.

"Aren't you gonna answer it?" He finally pulls up to my building on Concord Avenue.

"Rico, thanks for the ride and for listening. I'm so fuckin' mad. Damn it! I just want to be alone for a bit," I say, holding open the passenger door.

"Dude, I know you're hurting. It's fucked up when the one person you love treats you like shit. But you have to respect yourself. Never compromise who you are because, no matter what, you're the only person you'll have to face in the mirror every day. Listen, gimme a call if you need anything, and whatever you do, DO NOT LET HIM IN, *capisce?*"

"I won't. Thanks, Rico." He gives me one of his tight big hugs, which feels so good right about now. I need his strength, physically and emotionally. I wish he can hold me for the rest of the night and make this all go away.

"Let's have breakfast tomorrow at McKenna's, okay? My treat," Rico offers. "I'll call ya tomorrow. Take it easy, Tommy

Boy! Just go to sleep, and tomorrow, you'll feel better. You're not alone in this. Remember that! Your Italian brother has your back."

A few minutes later, I'm in my bathroom, washing my face and cooling some of my anger with cold water but it doesn't really help. The water just cloaks my tears.

My cell phone begins to vibrate like a jackhammer on my desk.

It's Mikey but I don't want to answer it. He needs to learn his lesson. I can't deal with this crap anymore. I love him sober. I hate him drunk. I hate myself for always giving in to him. I would love not to deal with this anymore but I love him.

About twenty minutes later after drinking my lemon-lime Gatorade and plopping myself on my sofa to watch a rerun of NBC's *Providence* on Channel 4, I try to digest why Mikey can't seem to stop drinking after one or two drinks. Why can't he stop drinking? Why does his personality do a 360? How can someone be so incredibly sweet and then become a total jerk as if someone flipped him on and off like a light switch? The buzzer to my unit goes off.

"Hello! Who's there?" I talk into the wall intercom.

"Tommy! It's Mikey downstairs. I love you, cutie. I'm so, so, so sorry. I took a taxi here. Let me up so we can talk," his slurred voice echoes from the intercom.

"No, Mikey. Go away!"

"Pleeeeeassee. I need you, cutie. I'm so, so sorry," he says. Then I hear him crying on the intercom, followed by some upchucking. Great, my neighbors are gonna love to see what's in the lobby tomorrow morning.

Against my better judgment, I buzz him up.

Once inside my studio, I help Mikey to the bathroom. I clean up the barf on his shirt, wipe his mouth with a wet hand towel, and give him a T-shirt to sleep in and boxer shorts to put on. I hand him a glass of water and some aspirin.

"Tommy, I'm so sorry," he keeps repeating.

"Shhh, Mikey. Just drink this water and get into bed. We'll talk tomorrow."

"I love you, cutie. You're so good to me," he says, his blood-shot eyes fiery red.

"Just get into bed and sleep it off." I tuck him into my bed and he passes out, looking like a lifeless puppet waiting for someone to hold him up and resurrect him. I grab my extra yellow sheets and pillow and sleep on my sofa. I don't want to be next to Mikey tonight. I know what I have to do.

I wake up at 10 A.M. to the sounds of Mikey barfing in my bathroom and then coughing. There goes last night's special dinner and dessert. He stumbles out looking like hell, rubbing his stomach.

"I feel so horrible," he says, getting back into my bed. He passes out again. Rico calls me on my cell a few minutes later and I take the call in the brightness of my beige-tiled bathroom.

"How's noon for a nice fattening delicious breakfast? I've been working out every day so I can cheat today," he says.

"Um, Rico. I can meet you at 2 P.M. I have something to take care of."

"Don't you mean, someone to take care? I can hear it in your voice. Mikey's there, isn't he?" Rico says.

"Yeah, he's here but I'm kicking him out by noon. Don't worry. I know what I'm doing. I'll see you at 2 P.M. at McKenna's. Got it?"

"Sure. As long as you're okay, Tommy."

"I am. Thanks," I say, matter-of-factly. "I have everything under control."

At noon, I wake up Mikey, whose left arm dangles along the side of my bed and swings back and forth like a pendulum.

"I'm so sorry, Tommy. I have such a wicked headache," he

says, knuckling his eyes and then rubbing his temples. I give him a glass of Gatorade.

"We're not going to talk about this now. Here's an aspirin to wash down with the Gatorade. I need to be somewhere in a little while. You need to get going back to Duxbury," I tell him, sitting on the edge of the bed. He looks so pathetic with his hangover.

"I can't believe I got this sick," he says in between gulps of the drink. "Whoa, what a night, huh, Tommy? I don't remember all of it."

"Yeah, it was a night all right, but I want to talk about it when you're feeling better and alert. Whatever I say to you now won't register. You need to get going. I have a lot to do."

"Okay, cutie. I'm gonna take a quick showah and head on back home. I'm sorry again."

"I know you are, Mikey. I just want you to be better."

At 2 P.M., I pull up to McKenna's in Savin Hill, right next to the subway stop. I love this little coffee/breakfast shop, which serves breakfast all day. I walk in and I see Rico sitting in one of the booths. He waves to me and I nod back and make my way over to the wooden booth. He gets up and gives me one of his hugs. It feels so good right now. I need all the support I can get.

"I hope you don't mind but I ordered you some strawberry pancakes—your favorite—and a Diet Coke," Rico says. He always knows what I want. He's such a great *amigo*.

"Thanks, Rico," I say, my eyes watering up again. I do my best to hold back my tears but they overpower me and start staining my face. I put my hand over my forehead so no one can see.

"Hey, hey . . . take it easy. B-r-e-a-t-h-e. I'm here. Talk."

I explain to him the rest of the night as a dozen or so customers sit near us and chow down on their eggs, turkey, and grilled sandwiches in this small eatery. The smell of succulent toasted bread perfumes the whole place. The crowd is a mix of local gay guys who have moved to Dorchester in recent years for more affordable housing (translation: gentrification), local old-school Irish families wearing their Sunday best after mass, and some Cape Verdean couples who also call Dorchester home. Gays are calling Dorchester the *South* South End because of the rainbow migration. (I also wrote a story about that, too.)

"I can't take this anymore. It's too much. He confuses me. He hurts me when he drinks. I don't understand any of this, Rico," I tell him as the young waitress, who looks just like Reese Witherspoon but with a Boston accent, serves us our meals on the teardrop-shaped dishes. Rico ordered French toast, which he drowns in syrup, a side of crispy bacon strips, and a cup of black steaming coffee. He wasn't joking about pigging out today.

"Tommy, I know you love this guy but he needs help. When you think you are helping him, all you're doing is enabling him. You're hurting him and yourself as well. You've got to have a serious talk with him and tell him he needs to go to AA or see a therapist. I don't think this dude can give up alcohol without some professional help. He can't do it for you. He's gotta do it for himself, dudette."

We both dig into our meals. I smear butter all over my stack of golden thick pancakes. They're so scrumptious. I deserve to indulge after putting up with Mikey last night. Rico shoves chunks of his French toast into his mouth and *Mmm*s every now and then.

"I know. You're right, Rico. I am taking a few days off from Mikey this week so I can gather my thoughts and have a sit-down with him. This has gone on long enough. *No mas*, as we say in Spanish, which means, 'No more.' I just love him so much but this is not the kind of relationship I want, Rico. I don't want to compete with alcohol. My mom and dad and uncles never had to deal with stuff like this."

"I know but this is affecting you and you don't need this. You're a great guy who deserves the best in this world and you've done so well for yourself. Mikey has some things to work out on his own. You can't do that for him," Rico says, reaching out to pat my shoulder and giving me a sympathetic look.

"Rico, thank you for being my friend and putting up with hearing all this. I don't know what I would have done if you weren't my friend in Boston. I don't have any other close friends here."

"That's what friends are for. Even the ones who are super stubborn Cubans with out-of-control hair like you," he teases with a wink.

Rico and the delicious pancakes help me feel much better, at least for the moment.

Chapter 14

KYLE

One . . . two. . . . three   PUSH!   One . . . two. . . . three . . .
PUSH! Ugh. I hate doing squats. Can't I just take a pill that
would firm up my whole body instead of lifting weights and
exercising?

I need to firm up my ass for this upcoming bathing suit
modeling job. There's a local clothing designer here in Boston
who asked me to model his new line of bathing suits for gay
men and metrosexuals who can easily pass for one another
these days. It's hard to tell who is who, with the throng of Euro-
peans and well-dressed, coiffed men in Boston, especially inside a gym.

Is he or isn't he, is what I constantly ask myself whenever I
see a handsome groomed man here at the gym below the club.
The gym is technically underground, basement level, because
you can see the stampede of legs from all the pedestrians and
office workers and residents dashing back and forth on
Columbus Avenue.

While I have a nice Oklahoman white ass, enough to land
me this modeling job, I want it to be tighter and harder so that
my buns appear bubbly and rounded like two basketballs.

So here I am at the gym on a spring weekday afternoon

working out and working it. I've been indulging in one too
many Frappuccinos at Starbucks lately and those delicious
espresso brownies. Just having the coffee and the brownie
serves as my breakfast and lunch but they're fattening. Time to
burn those suckers off. Damn it!

So many cute guys here, but again, I can't tell who is who.
My gaydar, my gay Spidey sense, has been getting static lately.
And I thought that only happened with lesbians.

I am here wearing my iPod player blasting Missy "Mis-
demeanor" Elliott. (For the record, she's more of a fashion
felony with the way she dresses sometimes.)

*"Is it worth it, let me work it . . . I put my thang down, flip it
and reverse it,"* she sings before breaking into the part that
sounds backward. I think she can easily be saying something
like *"Is your feminine napkin wet yet? Is your feminine napkin wet
yet?"*

Well, at least that's what I hear.

The gym is not that much different from Club Café upstairs. Instead of A&F shirts and jeans, everyone here wears
small shorts and A&F tank tops. They walk around in their
Reeboks or Nike sneakers. They wear baseball caps to look
younger and butch.

It's the same kind of cruising that goes on upstairs but you
have a significant influx of straight guys who happen to live in
Back Bay and who work out here, too. So these added metrosexuals are jamming my gaydar.

After my last squat, I throw myself on the carpeted ab area
and get down and do some crunches. I hate crunches, but
since I am naturally lean, it doesn't take much to get my cuts to
surface.

"Is it worth it, let me work it," Missy raps inside my head.

And yes, this is worth it so I am gonna work it.

The modeling jobs have begun to trickle in again this

spring. Ever since I appeared at the White Fiesta, where I was a hit, I've gotten some renewed momentum in my career. Also, they keep re-airing my *Real Life Battle of the Genders* challenge, where I walked away (okay, more like limped away) with $45,000 by being on the winning alpha male team during the final mission. We pushed a car uphill in the California desert and I got $7,500 as my share. Cha-ching!

Who would have thunk that a Toyota Celica weighed so much, even with six guys pushing it. So all in all, spring really is about rebirth—in my career and my pocketbook.

I never did hear back from the trio of scouts for the Papito Clothes line that had a casting call back in December. I was really desperate then for some work, any work, so much so that I was trying to pull off a Latino clothing line. Hello! That's like asking an Asian guy to promote an all-American Chevrolet.

But since I've secured some more money in the bank thanks to the *Battle of the Genders* and a few modeling gigs here and there, I am doing just fine. I've cultivated 20 minutes out of my 15 minutes of fame and I am working toward 22 minutes of fame. Take that Tommy Boy at *The Boston Daily,* who still hasn't written a decent story on me. Besides Mayor Tom Menino, Governor Mitt Romney, and Senator Ted Kennedy, I am probably the other most famous Bostonian. Where's my ink?

One . . . two . . . three . . . crunch . . . Whew! These are hard. My abs are screaming. They're on fire. Keep going, I tell myself. No pain, no gain, no work, no fame.

"Hey, Kyle. How's it going down there," a voice beckons above me. I look up and it's Tommy.

"Oh hi, Tommy, how have you been?" He's wearing khaki pants from Old Navy, a sky blue chambray buttoned-down shirt and his *Boston Daily* press pass around his neck. Looks like he's working on a story.

"What brings you to this gym? Don't you work out in Cambridge at Bally's?" I ask Tommy, who is holding a reporter's notepad in his hands.

"Yes, I do. But I'm actually working, not working out here this afternoon. I'm doing a story on how everyone uses their lunch hour to run errands rather than eat lunch and how the lunch hour is being gobbled up because of our harried work lives. So I'm interviewing office workers who use their lunch hour to work out," Tommy explains to me, in his professional reporter's tone. He is actually being serious now, not the giggling guy I usually bump into around town. "You wouldn't happen to be here on your lunch break, would you, Kyle?" he asks as I get off my back and stand up, lording over Tommy and his bouquet of curly hair.

"Nah, you know me, Curly Sue. I don't have a regular nine-to-five job. I'm here now because there aren't as many people in the afternoon as there are at night so I can work out without being rushed." As I talk, I stretch my arms sideways and form the letter T (as in top model) with my body.

"Ah, okay. Totally understandable," Tommy says, looking a little sad in the eyes. He has one of the most readable faces. His face speaks before his mouth does.

"Are you okay, Tommy? Everything okay with your boyfriend Mikey?" I ask him.

"Oh yeah, things are fine. Nothing's wrong. Don't worry. Gotta get back to work," Tommy says curtly.

I must have struck a nerve. I'm not surprised. Everyone in town knows his boyfriend has a drinking problem. That's why the two other guys dumped Mikey before Tommy came along. I've always wanted to tell Tommy that but it should be noted that (a) it's none of my business, and (b) I don't want to piss Tommy off and have that ruin any chances of me getting an article in the newspaper. The *Daily* has such credibility and a story in there would really establish me to regional and national readers that I am the real thing.

I can see why guys fall for Mikey. He has that boyish Ethan Hawke/Mark McGrath look and a very outgoing personality. He's a guidance counselor at an elementary school, which translates as good guy.

But anyone who has lived here long enough knows the guy has a drinking *problema*. It's obvious to anyone who goes to Club Café and watches him drink up the entire bar. And it should have been obvious to Mr. Big Time *Boston Daily* reporter, but apparently, he is a better reporter than a judge of boyfriend material. Meow! Okay, that sounds harsh but the truth hurts, baby.

After a while, the drinking and the hangovers can really wear someone down. Tommy's been in this for the long haul so far. He's probably getting sick of it all already. I wouldn't blame him since he is always sober and his boyfriend isn't when they're out, upstairs on Thursday or Saturday nights.

"Okay, Tommy. Remember, I'm still looking for my front-page story in *The Boston Daily*." I wink at him and he cracks a small smile and looks downward for a moment.

"Yeah, keep me posted," Tommy says as he walks away toward some guys over on the treadmills. He should have that line copyrighted since he says it to me so often.

As I get back on the mat to do some leg-ups, my cell starts to ring.

I grab the phone out of my fanny bag and I don't recognize the number. It's from New York. Great, maybe it's another job!

It's one of the producers from *The Real Life*, who want *moi* to host the casting special episode for the next season of *The Real Life: Key West*. Of course, I say YES! It's a free weekend in Margaritaville, all expenses paid, and all I have to do is sit in the new *Real Life* digs and give an on-camera tour for the show, which will be called *Kyle's Couching Casting Call: Key West.* They are going to pay me $5,000 for the hosting duty. Can life get any better? It would be if this stupid zit on my chin would just go away. The producers are sending me some footage of the first episode, to air later this June, so that I can have the inside track on the cast to be better informed for my camera close-up. I also get to chat about my season and what made it such good television. Well, if you lived in a former firehouse with six other unstable people in the toniest and most conservative neighborhood in Boston (home to Senator John Kerry, people), shit is gonna happen. Producers are flying me in next weekend. I can't wait. Move over, Jimmy Buffett, here comes Kyle Andrews.

"Helllooo to all of you in TV land! Welcome to the casting special of *The Real Life: Key West.* You might remember me from the Boston season. I'm Kyle Andrews and I'm going to be your guide to what's in store this season," I talk into Camera 2 inside this spacious and brightly lit two-story house. My voice echoes as I talk because there's no one here besides me, two cameras guys, a sound guy, and Kathy, one of the show's producers. It's so quiet in here, you can hear the electric hum from the central AC.

"Are we going to have peacemakers or troublemakers this season? We shall see. Let's take a look-see," I continue, gabbing into the camera.

This oceanfront butter yellow mansion sits just on the outskirts of Key West off US 1. It's a three-story, four-bedroom house with red Spanish roof tiles and lush orange and yellow hibiscus flowers lacing the front yard like a necklace on a Hawaiian dancer. There's a fabulous deck that overlooks the tranquil water, an indoor Jacuzzi (a prerequisite to any *Real*

Life digs), a pool table, a tennis court, and a pool. Bright fluorescent lights hang in every room of the house, for the gazillion tiny cameras. I took a quick tour of the place before
sitting down on the plush red Ikea sofa in the living room to
do my monologue for the show so I know what I'd be gabbing
about. The producers have me reading the cue cards about the
cast and what to expect. I can't help but ad-lib a bit here and
there to punch up the script. I want to appear as au naturel as
possible, none of this scripted show stuff. It makes my intro on
The Real Life well, unreal. Tsk.

"Here is the Jacuzzi where many a hookup took place this
new season. When you've got the South Florida heat and seven
hot bodies, things are gonna happen in the tub, if you know
what I mean. Rub a dub dub, two hoes in a tub." I wink to the
cameras as I continue walking throughout the house with a
cameraman in tow. At this point, producers show slices of this
season's debauchery, which has the girls and boys getting it on,
then the girls and the girls getting it on, and then two boys
smooching. Oh my! They never have two gay guys on the
same season. Hmm. I smell a supersize serving of drama.
Yowza! Someone call *OUT* magazine to cover this or LOGO,
the gay cable network. I wouldn't be surprised if the producers
spiked their beer in the freezer with a little something something. Besides, all the beds are twins except the big double bed
in the spare room. I guess the producers hope that some of the
roomies will get their groove on together. From the brief clips
I saw, this season is all sex and boobs and beers. They should
have called it *The Real Life: Viagra*. At least my season had real
people with real stories, about class distinctions and race issues.
Our project was to work with an after-school program in predominantly Hispanic East Boston and help kids with their
homework and arts and crafts. Whatever happened to showing
The Real Life of today's youth and not just the drunken spokes-
people for it? This season's project: opening up a tanning

salon. How . . . un-interesting! How South Beach of the producers. Just an excuse to show a lot of hot bronzed skin.

"Well, that's all, folks. I hope you enjoyed this home tour as
much as I did. I'm done here. See you next time on *The Real
Life*. Don't be good. Be bad. Buh-bye," I talk into the camera,
standing outside the front of the house, and closing the front
door as if I lived here.

"Kyle, thanks again for doing this. Enjoy the rest of your
time here in Key West," Kathy tells me as she removes my al-
most-invisible microphone from my back. "There's a driver
outside to take you back to your hotel on Duval Street. Take
care, Kyle."

"Oh, it was my pleasure. I always have fun doing these
types of segments," I tell her, unloosening my figure-fitting
button-downed red shirt to get more comfortable. It's 85 degrees outside and it's only 4 P.M. I want to go out on the town
and enjoy my short time here. I leave tomorrow afternoon.

After heading back to the gay bed-and-breakfast, the La Te
Da, and slipping into a pair of jean shorts and a tank top and a
pair of blue Dolce and Gabana flip-flops, I hit the town. On
my way to South Street, I almost step on a brown hen. It
comes out of nowhere.

"Shoo, go away, Big Bird," I order it as it scampers away. I
almost fell right on top of chicken little. Where did this come
from? It starts to follow me. Oh well, it can't hurt. Walking the
streets, you hear Spanish spoken, smell the aroma of Cuban coffee from sandwich shops, even hear the "cock-a-doodle-doos"
of roosters, apparently a beloved pet back in Cuba and here in
Key West, according to the brochure I read on my short flight
from Miami.

I follow the human traffic of flip-flops and tank tops and
start at the southernmost point, here on South Street. Key West
feels a lot like a mini–South Beach but the heat is muggier

here and there's less traffic. You can also walk everywhere. I see a line of tourists fifteen feet deep waiting to be photographed here with a giant buoy that marks ninety miles to Fidel Castro's house. The visitors ask me to pose with them, and of course, I oblige. I ask one of them to use my digital camera to snap a photo of me with the buoy. I put my arms around it and smile. Say Kyle!

I walk back on Duval Street, the main drag here rife with bars, stores, and T-shirt shops, and I hear a chorus of cock-a-doodling. I look ahead and see why. It's The Chicken Store, a haven for neglected birds. There's Kiwi, Bubba, and one named Kyle. How funny. He's the loudest of them all and, may I add, the prettiest.

Wow, the island charms with a laid-back appeal and airline-ad lushness. I hear the slight hiss of the tropical breeze blow through the palm trees. The city wears the salt scent of the ocean like a natural aftershave.

Things are in slow motion here, no rush to get anywhere and do anything. Even the mopeds zip along slowly as if the drivers had all the time in the world. I spend the rest of the afternoon absorbing the sun rays, touring Papa Hemingway's classic house and his gazillion six-toed cats there. I rest at the pier and admire the giant colossal cruise ships docked in their berths. Sitting back on a wooden bench there as the water sparkles ahead, I close my eyes and feel the sun warm my face, making me see red spots through my eyelids. I wonder what it would be like to live here, away from the ruthless cold of Boston. I can get used to this. Key West agrees with The Kyle. Then I feel something stabbing at my feet. It's another wandering chicken. I wasn't joking when I said they're everywhere here.

"Shoo, go away!" It then flies up on the bench and sits next to me, looking up at me with its big black eyes.

"I'm Kyle. What's your name, little fella?" I ask it. The bird just looks up at me and crows, reminding me of the chickens on Eric's family's dude ranch back in OK.

"Well, nice to meet you, too."

We sit until dusk, side by side, watching as slices of salmon cut into the Key West sky, creating swirls of sherbet over the city and above the sailboats bobbing in the distance. The street performers come out and start juggling and playing music as part of the night sunset festival, and me and Mr. Chicken sit here and enjoy the view.

Chapter 15

TOMMY

It's about 9 A.M. on a Wednesday morning and I am on my way to the Boston municipal courthouse. It's an old gray hulk of a building in the heart of the city's financial district that has inspired many a David E. Kelley TV legal drama such as *Ally McBeal* and *The Practice*. The latest show to be set here is yet another David E. Kelley show, *Boston Legal*, starring Captain Kirk. Talk about going where the law has never gone before.

My next story brings me here, to write a profile of a gay judge named Jack McGlame. He's the state's first openly gay judge and he is quite a character, championing gay causes in the legal community. He is old-school Irish, having been born in hard-knocks, Irish-Catholic South Boston, and he has fought many social and cultural battles in his day. He still does.

But that's all old news. The focus of this article is that he writes short stories based on the colorful characters that appear before him in court and on the street. Writing is a hobby for him and he's had four of his short stories published in local literary magazines. So he's making another name for himself, as a writer. His stories have been making the rounds among Boston-area judges, which is how I heard about his judicial prose.

Work has always been therapeutic for me. No matter what goes on in my life, interviewing people and writing about their issues and their stories always take my mind off whatever is bothering me, or help me reexamine my own issues. After my fallout Saturday night with Mikey with his latest drunken episode and his sloppy hangover, I've been throwing myself into my work. Earlier in the week, I wrote about how today's lunch hour is being gobbled up by errands and now I am working on my profile on Judge McGlame. I haven't sat down and talked to Mikey about the drinking yet and how he doesn't remember most of what he told me Saturday night. I'm still steamed about the whole thing. I want to talk to him when he is levelheaded and so am I.

I saunter into the marble-floored courthouse and approach the walk-through security monitors. I empty my wallet, my keys, my reporter's pad, my handheld tape recorder, and my cell phone into the white plastic tub and hand over my *Boston Daily* black messenger bag to the officer.

As he waves an electric wand up and down my front and back, and the green light clears me of any dangerous or hazardous materials, I pass through and head to the judge's chambers on the sixth floor.

"Are you the *Daily* reporter Tommy Perez?" the judge's secretary asks me as soon as I approach her desk midway through the hallway. The press pass that hangs around my neck and my reporter's pad in hand always give me away.

"Hi, yes, that's me. I have an interview with Judge McGlame for nine-thirty," I tell her with a smile.

The secretary shakes my hand and says, "I'll show you to his chambers. He's been waiting for you."

As we walk down this long hallway, the sunlight gleaming against the marble floors creates a blinding sheen and causes my eyes to painfully squint. The secretary's shoes echo with each step, breaking up any silence that existed a few minutes before.

She knocks on McGlame's wooden door, which bears his name.

"Come on in," a thick and thunderous voice declares from behind the door.

I hate interviewing judges, detectives, or policemen. They get nervous about what they say and what you write. So on these occasions, I bring a tape recorder to assure them that they won't be misquoted and so they can be more candid with their words. They tend to open up more if they feel comfortable with the reporter.

Law officials tend to be distrusting of reporters, who in general have a bad rap for turning on their sources for a good scoop or that flashy front-page story. But for every one of these newshound pit bull reporters that give us a bad name, there's one of me, someone who enjoys writing about everyday people doing extraordinary things or extraordinary people doing everyday things. I'm more of a puppy than a pit bull. I'm happy writing a story that offers some sort of revelation about a Boston neighborhood or ethnic community. I want people here to know what goes on in their own backyard so they may feel empowered in their lives and enriched about their city.

The judge's story is one of those quirky profiles that many people may find entertaining as well as intriguing. How often do judges write about the people who appear before them? More so, how many judges out there are openly gay and flaunt it like a rainbow-colored robe?

"Judge McGlame, I'm Tommy Perez from the *Daily*, nice to meet you." I greet him with a strong handshake. McGlame and his black robe suddenly rise from behind the mahogany-wooden desk like a curtain at a play.

The judge is about sixty-one years old with short straight

white hair slicked back and blue eyes that look like two small marbles. He is a tall man, about six-feet-one with a slight belly. He could easily pass as Mikey's grandfather, if I ever meet any of his relatives. McGlame's cheeks blush rosy. He looks like a sweet man with a tough voice and intimidating job.

"Good to meet you, Mr. Perez. I read your articles in the *Daily's City* section. I loved the one you wrote about Santeria and the difference between a Latino and a Hispanic. You're a good writer with fresh ideas. That's why I allowed you to interview me. I've heard some nice things about you," McGlame tells me as we sit down on a small plush sofa in his chambers. "Besides, I'm a sucker for Latinos, especially *los cubanos*," he adds with a chuckle and a wink.

Um, okay. On that note, I ease myself into the sofa and right into the interview.

McGlame had sent me some of his stories before our interview. One of them was a humorous story about a flasher who appeared before him in court for loitering in locker rooms and health clubs—including the judge's gym in Back Bay. Another story chronicled a clothing store employee who had a five finger discount and was caught stealing suits from a Harvard Square store. Weeks later, the judge bumped into the gentleman in Harvard Square, hitting him up for a good deal on Prada wallets and Armani shirts in Downtown Crossing. And then there was the story of a dapper panhandler who told McGlame he was an attorney and how he was mistaken for a panhandler because he was soliciting money from passersby in the Boston Common for gas money. Weeks later, the same man approached McGlame on the street without recognizing him and asked him for money to catch the bus.

"Could you believe that, Tommy?" McGlame says as his laughter creates tiny ripples all over his robe. "I see these people in court for a range of petty crimes and then I bump into them in public doing the same thing. There was so much comedy in these slices of life. I had to write these things down on my laptop after they happened. Over time, they grew into these hilarious tales about wacky Boston people that I had to share them with fellow judges. Call me the accidental writer," he says with another wink.

As I keep tabs on my tape recorder and jot down some notes, I fire away—nicely—with my next question.

"Judge, what are you most proud of? Being an openly gay judge, an aspiring writer, a gay activist?" I ask him in my serious but friendly tone.

McGlame looks at me, then looks down and smiles.

"You know, Tommy, I'm proud of all my accomplishments. But the one I am truly most proud of is being sober for twenty-eight years," he deadpans with his hypnotic blue eyes without a hint of the previous smile or chuckle. "I go to meetings three times a week and I share my story with anyone who will listen. I'm a recovering alcoholic. It wasn't easy at first, but as they say, you have to take it one day at a time. That's what I am most proud of."

I'm speechless. I didn't see that coming. News of him being an alcoholic didn't appear in any of the background stories I had researched. He then begins to tell about his struggles with alcohol in his twenties and early thirties, about his late-night rowdy escapades at Club Café, which was called Chaps in his time, and his chronic blackouts after leaving the bars. The more Jack spoke, the more I thought of Mikey.

"You had blackouts, Judge McGlame?' I ask him, intrigued not just for my story but for Mikey.

"Oh yeah, I used to wake up in some guy's bed and didn't know how I got there from the night before," he says, leaning forward to me. "I was pretty wild as a young lawyer in this town. You can't do that today with all the diseases floating out there. Another time, my Ford Pinto was found parked in the middle of Columbus Avenue in the South End. I didn't even realize it was there until the police called me the next day. How embarrassing! I couldn't go a day without three or more drinks at night. It got to the point where I had to stop. It was taking over my life, my career, my sanity, Tommy."

As I scribble some notes and digest what he has told me, I already have the lead of the story baking in my head. An hour later, after chatting with McGlame and walking away with more insight into alcoholism than I ever imagined, I realize I must talk to Mikey.

"Tommy, you seem really intrigued with my alcoholism. Do I remind you of someone in your family or in your life?" McGlame asks, putting his soft wrinkled hand on my right shoulder as if to comfort me. He senses that I recognize what he is talking about, very well.

"Um, no. You just caught me off-guard, that's all," I tell him, trying to mask my facial expressions, which often speak before I do. "I'm sure a lot of people out there will be touched by what you've told me this morning. It seems to be an issue that affects everyone in some way, shape, or form. I'm pretty much set so I'll let you enjoy the solitude of your chambers. I have to get back to the *Daily* and start writing my story. You gave me a lot to think about."

McGlame again rises from his sofa, smiles, and escorts me back to the hallway.

"If you have any questions about the story, or if you just need to talk, give me a call. Here's my home number, Tommy," McGlame says, firmly shaking my hand with both of his. "And call me Jack, no Judge McGlame or Mr. McGlame. I'm here if you need me."

As I exit the grand hallways of the courthouse and walk out into the bustling street filled with pedestrians going in all directions like ants on the run, I head toward the T stop and think, Mikey really needs help and I'm going to get it for him.

Chapter 16

RICO

I've got a fucking new job. I couldn't stand working in a windowless space at the firm, compiling stock prices for our international clients. The minutes inched by like Sunday mass back home in the Berkshires.

The workday seemed like it would never end. But hey, this was the first job I landed after graduation last year so I took what I could get. So I quit two weeks ago after I saw this ad in the *Daily* looking to hire rental associates in Boston. The pay wasn't that much different from what I'm making but at least I can play dress-up. I'm a tie-wearing guy these days and I get to interact with people and not just numbers. I feel important.

I am now a rental agent in Boston, working for a real estate company called Boston Rents. I help newcomers to the city, mostly employees recruited to work here, find immediate housing. It's a personable job and I really got to work my people skills. My smile and Italian charm come in handy here. Rico DiMio at your service. Plus, I get out of the office and meet people all-da-time.

While I work here, the company is helping me pay to get my real estate license certification so that I can later sell properties for them. My first real estate class is next Wednesday night at the Boston Center for Adult Education. It's a six-week course with a state test at the end.

With Boston's hot market, I could make a hefty commission. That's where the dough is. Who-hoo! So this has all been a great learning experience, full of eye candy. Some of the guys I've helped this past week find an apartment have been kind of hot, and so far, this is only my first week on the job.

Today is Thursday and I don't mind. Work has been fun. I feel energized. Forget Club Café. This is another great way of meeting guys.

Today I'm showing this new reporter for Channel 7 some of the one-bedroom rentals around the Back Bay and parts of the South End. We drove around in my Ford and I was his host with the most on this city tour.

His name is Josh, a former Miami weatherman at one of the TV stations down there. He meets me at our office on Newbury Street at 10 A.M. on this sunny breezy spring day. When he walks in, my eyes are feasting on this gorgeous creature. So far, the forecast today is hot, thanks to Josh.

He's a tall dude with blondish spiked-up hair, green eyes similar to mine, and white-as-pearl teeth. Just really yummy. Our eyes keep locking. He carries a slight Miami accent but this guy is whiter than me. He has nice vanilla-fair skin. Slurp! Turns out the dude is a Jewish Cuban. Hey, maybe he knows Tommy, who used to be a reporter in Miami.

"So you're from Miami? What brings you to our wonderful city, Josh?" I ask him as we walk into a vacant one-bedroom rental off Commonwealth Avenue in Back Bay. It's the second unit we've seen in the last hour.

"My job. I was hired as a weekend weatherman for Channel 7. In Miami, the weather is all sunny or hurricanes. Boston has wild wicked weather and this is one of the bigger TV markets," he says as he scans the high ceilings of this 700-square-foot unit. It's going for $1,700, not bad for this area.

I could just imagine what he looks like underneath his chambray dress shirt and khaki pants. A few light brown hairs poke out from his chest through an unbuttoned opening in his shirt. He looks like he just walked out of a catalog for Macy's department store. His shoulders are broad and it V's down to a small waist, a size 31, I suspect. I check out Josh's bum as he explores the rest of the unit.

"Well, welcome to Boston. You picked the right time to move up here," I tell him as we stand shoulder to shoulder in the white-tiled bathroom with vintage faucets. We're cramped in here but I don't mind the close quarters with this Miami hunk. I'm beginning to like Miami more and more now.

"You'll have a gradual deep freeze over the next eight months. This place goes for $1,700," I tell him with a blinkless hard intense stare.

He flashes an electric smile that tickles my Italian heart— and cock.

I do the mental math here. A weatherman. No ring on his finger. Too groomed to be straight. He's definitely a fag.

"So what are some good places to go tonight?" he asks, leaning in close to me as we stand by the grand windows that overlook the street where shoppers scurry along Newbury Street. "This is a house-hunting trip so I head back to Miami tomorrow. I start work in two weeks."

I turn to face him head-on as he gazes out the window to make sure he gazes into my eyes, and perhaps, senses what I'm thinking right now. I call it dick telepathy.

"Well, there's this place called Club Café a few blocks from here on Columbus Avenue. Lots of guys go there to chill, grab a drink, and hang out. It gets good after 10 P.M., especially on Thursdays," I explain to him, clutching my organizer full of listings tightly against my hard chest. "I'm heading there tonight. Probably meeting my friend Tommy, who's Cuban, too, and a fellow reporter. You're welcome to come along. We hang out by the front bar. At least you'll have two new friends in the city."

Josh breaks out into a smile that feels as warm and bright as the sun pouring into the window. Whoa, this dude is hot.

"Yes, that sounds great. I'll make it a point to be there," he says. "Wait a minute, there's another Cuban here? I thought I'd be the only one," he says with a laugh.

"Yeah, Tommy Perez, my bar buddy here. He has a boyfriend that he's in love with," I quickly mention to dispel any possible hookup between him and Tommy. "You'll meet him, if his boyfriend's not drunk or anything. Oops, did I just say that? You'll quickly learn that dudes here like to drink."

As we walk out of the unit and make our way down the two flights of narrow stairs, Josh adds, "By the way, I want to take this place, today."

I look at him, thinking, I'd like to take him, too.

Chapter 17

TOMMY

"Mikey, can you meet me at the Barnes and Noble tonight in Braintree about 7 P.M.? We need to talk." I'm leaving a message on Mikey's voice mail in the middle of my workday at the *Daily* as I finish up writing my story on Judge McGlame. Mikey is probably taking a nap from his long day at school. "It's important. I'll come straight from work and meet you there. Talk to you later, Mikey."

The time has come to say what I have been wanting to say about Mikey's drinking. I've talked to him here and there about the binge drinking and the every-other-weekend hangovers at my place but it has to stop. He has a problem. He needs to address it. I need to address it. Someone who can't stop drinking after five, six, make that seven drinks needs to get a sobering wake-up call.

At what point does your body say "Enough!" Well, I'm saying enough. If he can't admit he has a problem, I can't be his boyfriend. You can't sit back and watch someone you love self-destruct. It's toxic to you and the person. Mikey has a disease he needs to treat.

My heartbeat races as I walk out of the *Daily*'s brick fortress of a building and hop into my Jeep Wrangler. The sun begins to dim in the magenta sky and my cell phone buzzes "New message." It's from Mikey. I have horrible reception on my cell here at work so my calls go straight to voice mail.

"Hey, cutie! I got your message. I was sleeping. Sure, I'll meet you at the bookstore by the coffee area at 7 P.M. I hope you're having a great day. See ya soon."

I press Delete, toss the phone in my black *Daily* messenger bag, and hop on Interstate 93 to Braintree to the South Shore Plaza, this giant suburban super mall full of minivan moms and bored iPod-toting teens. The bookstore is down the street perched on a hill and it's about halfway between the *Daily* and Mikey's house in Duxbury. Sometimes, during the week, we meet up there because we both have to get up early on weekdays.

The whole ride, I agonize about what I am going to say. I think about all the articles I researched online at work about alcoholism and how alcoholics can't help drinking. One article explained that alcoholism has a genetic disposition. Another stated that alcoholism is the disease of denial. It tells the person he doesn't have a problem when he really does. For others, it's a social lubricant. They depend on alcohol to come out of their shell and loosen up. In my back pocket, I have some notes I scribbled down to say to Mikey.

"A normal person doesn't drink until he gets sick," reads one line on the folded-up piece of paper.

"You are thirty-three. You are not in college anymore. You are a school counselor. You can't handle alcohol. You have a disease," reads another.

"You become a different person when you drink, someone I don't like," another line states.

"Whenever I am around you and in a bar, I feel like a bomb is going to go off. You need to stop!" reads the back page.

"You hurt me with your words when you drink," states another line.

I rehearsed this at lunch, sitting in the Boston Market parking lot, reading this out loud to myself in the Jeep as folks drove away with their turkey carver sandwiches and chicken.

I want Mikey to hear me loud and clear. I know there is a strong chance he may not be ready to hear what I have to say. I know there's an even stronger chance I may lose him. But I can't take this anymore. If he really loves me—more importantly, if he really loves himself—he will stop and get some kind of help.

The veins in my head pulse like the bang-bang-bang drumbeats of a marching band, pumping from all the adrenaline coursing in me. I'm so nervous. I'm scared. I can interview police chiefs, celebrities, and criminals for my job and be a cool mellow guy. But when it comes to Mikey and confrontations of the heart, I'm a wimp. That may explain why this drinking—at least my enabling of it—has continued for so long. Enough!

Before I know it, I pull into the Barnes and Noble parking lot and I notice Mikey's car already there. I walk in and he waves from the café area with a big smile. He is just so cute in his blue hood but I need to focus. Focus, Tommy! I wave back and walk inside, where he greets me with a steaming cup of chamomile tea and an ultimate chocolate chip brownie, my favorites here.

"So what's up, cutie!" he says, sipping his mocha latte. He gives me a quick pop kiss and flashes that sweet smile of his. "Why the long face? Did ya have a bad day at work? Too many questions on your latest edit?"

I sit down and take a gulp of my hot tea, which burns my lips and the roof of my mouth. I dread what I am about to say because it's going to burn just as bad.

I reach out my right hand to hold his and I steel myself for what I am about to say.

My heart starts speaking.

"Mikey, I love you but I don't like you when you drink. I think you have a problem and you need to address it," I say, willing myself to keep going, to get out the words that I rehearsed earlier. "You are a DUI waiting to happen. You are alcohol poisoning waiting to happen. I can't watch you drink your life away. I won't be part of it."

Mikey's thin eyebrows furrow and he sits back into his seat.

He deadpans, "Dude, you don't know what you're talking about. I don't have a problem! There's nothing wrong with having a few drinks heah and theah. That's how I grew up on the South Shore. That's how my friends are," he says, his tone becoming superdefensive. "If anyone has a problem, it's you, Tommy! You check the lock on the door five times before you go to bed. You mention the dates of movies and songs whenever you talk, like you're in court or something. You order the same thing all the time. You are like that dude Monk, on that USA show. That's not normal."

Okay, this is not going well. I struck a big nerve with him. I can't believe he's deflecting what I'm saying and boomeranging this back to me. I fire back to maintain the focus on him.

"Mikey, this is about *you*, not about me. You can't stop drinking after your first drink. You need to be honest with me but, more importantly, with yourself. You have issues with alcohol. You blackout sometimes. You forget conversations we've had after you've drank a couple and the nasty things you've said to me. You turn from Dr. Jekyll into Mr. Hyde. My mild obsessiveness to check the doors before I go to sleep or to order the same foods at the same restaurants is not dangerous. You can't get a hangover or pulled over by the cops for eating turkey every day. You've got a problem and I'm just bringing it to your attention once and for all," I tell him assertively as other book lovers eat their muffins and sip tea or their lattes. They are oblivious to the drinking drama taking place at our table in the corner of the café. The irony is that we are sitting an aisle away from the self-help section.

Mikey looks away and then glances back at me, like I'm an alien from another planet speaking a whole other language.

"Dude, you don't know what you are talking about! C'mon, I don't have a problem but I am going to have a problem with you if you keep accusing me of being an alcoholic. I'm a counselor, for God's sake. I have a master's degree in education. I know who has a drinking problem and who doesn't and I don't," he says, hammering his index finger into the wooden café table.

I'm not getting through to him. One of the articles I read said that this kind of confrontation would most likely fail.

I feel like I'm running in place, not going anywhere. The news is not registering with Mikey. I need to keep chipping away at him so this will all sink in. I won't back down this time, no matter what.

"I wouldn't be saying this if I didn't care but I think you need to get some help," I tell him, caressing his hand.

He immediately retracts his hand away as if my touch scalded him like hot water. He gives me an icy glare. I recognize this look. It's the same expression he has when he over-drinks, like he is possessed by another spirit, but the difference is, he's sober right now.

"Tommy, I think we need a break. I'm not even sure if I love you. I've been meaning to tell you that but I haven't found the right moment. Look, I like hanging out with you. You're a good kid but I need some space," he says, drinking his coffee. "I don't need this crap! You don't know what you're talking about."

"Mikey, please, listen . . . I came here to talk about your drinking problem. I'm just trying to help, but instead of acknowledging the real issue here, you're running away from it, dodging it by breaking up with me." Tears begin to pool in my lower eyelids and I will my voice not to break. It's a good thing I have my back turned away from the rest of the coffee drinkers and book browsers so no one can see how much this hurts me.

"Look, Tommy, it was great while it lasted. But we need a break. I don't need your nagging. Take it easy." He gets up from the table and switches moods with his internal on-and-off button. He leaves me there reeling from what he just said, his words hitting me with an invisible physical force. I'm too stunned to say anything. I can't believe he's dumping me because I don't approve of his drinking. Is this crazy or what? Was he in love with me all this time or was I just a convenience for him, someone to cuddle with in bed, someone who would let him crash at his place when he got trashed? Oh my gosh! Rico was right all along.

The next thing I know, Mikey pats me on the shoulder and walks away, exiting the store with a confident stride. He strolls to the black-paved parking lot as if nothing had happened.

Under the bright artificial light of the bookstore, I sit alone quietly crying in the corner, wondering, how did all this go wrong? I cup my face with my hands so no one can see me. I wipe away the tears to compose myself. I look to my right and I see the reflection of Mikey's Matrix pulling away from the store, and from my life. I can't stay here so I walk outside to get some fresh air. The sunset smears its purple and orange ink all over the New England sky and I breathe and take in the calming daily color display. But the tears keep coming and my throat constricts as if a ball were crammed in there. I desperately try to gasp for air. An older woman in her fifties with flowing gray locks and kind eyes sees me and stops.

"Honey, are you okay? You look upset. Would you like for me to call someone?" she asks.

"Thank you for asking but I'll be fine. I just got some bad news." My voice cracks. I give her a tight smile. She nods and ventures inside the store.

I hop back in my Jeep and stare at myself in the rearview mirror. The view appears blurry, as if I were looking into an aquarium, because of all the tears floating in my eyes. I drive on Interstate 93 North back to the city and toward Cambridge and my mind instantly replays his words. "I'm not even sure if I love you," and "I don't need this crap!" Crap? He couldn't have meant what he said if he really cared about me. I've only been good to him. I opened my heart to him and let him in. I cleaned up after him when he got sick. I opened up my studio and shared it with him as if it were our home. I was so proud to call him my boyfriend, and when I show concern about his well-being and his problem, he slams the door in my face and walks away. But he said he loved me, over and over these past few weeks, and now suddenly, those feelings evaporate like the colors in this sunset?

Twenty minutes later, I pull onto Storrow Drive and emerge from the bright underground lights of the Big Dig tunnel. I drive in silence with the radio off. I can't help my mind alternate from anger to frustration to confusion and then back to sadness. There are all these warring thoughts and emotions inside me trying to make sense of it all. He didn't even fight to stay with me. He just gave up when I tried to make him face his problem. I lost Mikey to his mistress, the seductive Corona. More tears come and I start whimpering. I dry them and my red nose with a Boston Market napkin I grabbed from my glove compartment.

Fifteen minutes later, I pull into my building and sluggishly make my way upstairs into my studio as if my internal batteries were draining. Once inside, I see slumped on my bar stool the wool coat he helped me pick out in Providence. On my freezer door, I see a happy photo of us, arms around each other, in front of the Abercrombie store after we shopped in Freeport, Maine. The Red Sox cap he gave me a few months ago sits on my desktop computer waiting for me to wear it again. So many of my firsts in Boston were with Mikey and all the good memories of the things he did for me flood back to me in an emotional rush.

I grab my phone and dial Rico, hoping that he'll help me understand what went wrong or what I did wrong. I just need someone to talk to.

I rehash the whole scene, word for word, for Rico.

"I'm so sorry, Tommy. He doesn't deserve a good guy like you," Rico says. "Be glad that you got out of this now rather than five months or a year from now. The guy is all jumbled up inside his head. He doesn't know what he wants. He's unsure of himself. He still lives at home and he's thirty-three. Geez, this guy has some major issues. Look at the positive side of this. You can start to heal and learn from the experience sooner than later."

"I know, Rico, but I love this guy so much. All I want is for him to be well and he didn't even appreciate my concern. He tossed me out like yesterday's news. Maybe he didn't love me after all," I say, sitting on my blue sofa with my legs folded and my head tilted and leaning on my right fist.

"Tommy, how can he love you if he doesn't love himself? You did the best you could and you gave it your all. You can't do anything else. The next few days will be hard for you but you'll feel better, I promise. *Capisce?*" Rico says.

"*Gracias.* Work will be good for me and us hanging out. I just have to find a routine again, without Mikey. He's not a healthy person. I just have to remember that."

"This is not the end of the world, Tommy. You will survive this and come out stronger for it. I'll help you. Get some rest and walk with your head held up high tomorrow morning. You have so much going for you. You stood up for yourself and you should be proud. Don't let this screw anything you've worked so hard for, okay?"

I begin to feel better already. Rico has that effect on me.

"Thanks again. I think I'm gonna go wash up and get ready for bed."

"Anytime, Tommy. Remember, you're not alone in this. Nite!"

"Good night, chico!"

After washing my face, brushing my teeth, gargling with minty Scope, and changing into my white Bugs Bunny T-shirt and red boxer shorts, I slip into the warmth under my covers and turn off the lights. For a little while, I stare at my ceiling in the darkness, my arms by my side and legs perfectly straight as if I were in a coffin. I think about all the good times I had with Mikey. Then I start to think about all the times he got tanked, sick, hung over, and obnoxious. Why didn't I get a handle on this beforehand? The signs were there all along, but I kept looking the other way because I thought Mikey was such a good guy and so sweet. Then there was that nasty side of him. Rico is right, I don't deserve to be treated like that. I want someone who is healthy—mentally, spiritually, and emotionally—someone who is proud to introduce me to his parents and invite me over to dinner. I imagine myself with someone like that and a smile forms across my face. One day, I will meet that right guy. Mikey was not him. I can't help but still wish he were by my side right now, holding me and telling me he's going to get some help and that he loves me for caring about him so much. I pass out, drained from the entire day.

Chapter 18

KYLE

•

It's Fourth of July weekend and I'm one of the fireworks here in Provincetown. This is my first Fourth in Ptown and I *love* it! The population here year round is about 2,400 residents, but during summer, this is one hotbed of steroid-pumped-up men, 20,000 of them to be exact. You can smell the musty stench of sex, their Angel cologne and Clinique moisturizers in the air. They say Ptown is the fist of the Cape, which looks like a flexing arm on a map. But another kind of fisting goes on here, if you know what I mean. That's another story, though, for later.

Just like the White Fiesta, I am again the hostess with the mostess. I am headlining the Fourth's Fireworks Bonanza at the Crown and Anchor Hotel, off Commercial Street, the main drag where all the drag queens with their come-hither looks flag down all the guys with fliers about their shows this weekend. One of those shows belongs to yours truly. I won't be in drag (never!) but I will be as patriotic as I can. Stars and stripes thong, check. Red, white, and blue beaded necklace, check. Cowboy hat, check. Dolce blue flip-flops, check. I'm ready for my close-up, *Cover Girl*.

Hard to believe I'm really making a living of being a *Real*

Life star. I recently hosted *Kyle's Key West Casting Couch* for *The Real Life: Key West*, where I gabbed about all the behind-the-scenes unseen trysts. You know like were the two frat boys really getting it on when they thought the cameras weren't on. Or how some of the shy girls weren't so camera-shy when the infrared, nighttime cameras clicked on. Between that, my *Real Life* reruns, the White Fiesta, and the editorial work in magazines, I seem to have carved a full-fledged career of being *moi*. I am definitely self-employed, my own cottage industry. Eric is supposed to be here this weekend so we're gonna hang tonight after my show and have us some fun. I can't wait to see my best pal.

Whew! It's a steaming 85 degrees on this golden Fourth of July afternoon, so hot that you see the vapor rising on the street from a distance. The sky is cloudless yet a perfect blue, like my thong. I'm sauntering up and down Commercial Street, to see who else is here this weekend. Behind my new Ray-Ban sunglasses, I see some closeted TV reporters and weather guys, um girls. (Honey, we know you're gay if you work at Channel 7 in Boston. The big 7 might as well be in pink because of the high concentration of gays there.) Oh, there's Randy, from the GCC, the Gay Community Center, who hired me last month as a guest speaker for the gay youth pride parade at the Boston Common. There's that local celebrity of a judge, Jack McGlame, whom Tommy wrote a great profile on in the *Daily*'s Sunday paper. (Folks, can you believe I am still waiting for my story! Hello!)

The rosy-cheeked judge is cycling on his three-wheeler bike, with his white bulldog Squeak lounging in the front basket. If only the criminals he has sentenced in Boston courtrooms could see him now wearing a loose Hawaiian top, khakis, and sandals. He's ringing his bicycle's bell so people will shoo out of his way. Miss Thing looks like a gay Jimmy Buffett. He sure likes to ring that bell.

And oh, coming up near the renovated library is Tommy with Rico, the bosom bar boys. They've been hanging out more these past few weeks since Tommy and Mikey broke up at a Barnes and Noble in April. Everyone heard all about the breakup. Of all places to break up, a bookstore? I could understand if it were an adult bookstore and you caught your boyfriend blowing another guy in a stall but at a Barnes and Noble? Please! I think it happened in the romance section or maybe it was in self-help. Well, I guess that's what you get when you put a writer and a counselor together.

"Tommy, how are you doing?" I say, stopping him and Rico in their tracks, in front of a funky art gallery. Hmmm. It smells a lot like pot here. The gallery owner burns an incense to mimic the pot smell, to lure visitors to his hole-in-the-wall gallery. How *clever*!

"Doing well, Kyle. I hear you're the host of tonight's show at the Crown and Anchor." He nods and smiles, the sun highlighting his bush of curls. In this light, Tommy looks a lot like Ethan, the $1 million winner on CBS's *Survivor* a few years back. I just want to sink my hands in his bed of curls.

As he takes a big lick from his chocolate ice cream, which makes me hungry and a bit horny, he says, "You've been doing well for yourself lately. I see you on TV. I see you at some event in Boston and now you're here. You're everywhere, Kyle! It's like we travel together," he says with a boyish grin.

I look at him and beam. "Why, thank you, Tommy! I appreciate that. You have to come to the show. It will be the bomb! Anyways, I gotta keep doing my rounds here on Commercial Street. It's all about public relations," I tell him as Rico's eyes wander elsewhere, ever so rudely. He's eyeballing all the other tight tank-top-wearing muscle guys. He never makes eye contact with me. Whatever with the Rocky wannabe. He's no Italian stallion. More like an Italian jackass. "Hope you guys have fun here. Buh-bye!" I say.

And they walk off, mixing into the crowd of men and cyclists, just like another night at Club Café back in Boston. Commercial Street is like the outdoor version of it.

As I wave and sign some more autographs from fans of *The Real Life*, I spot a booth outside the Ptown monument a block away. The monument juts into the skyline like a spire in downtown Boston or like a big erect penis. Yes, I've been horny lately but wouldn't you be if you were in a zip code of total testosterone. Word is that this monument was used as a beacon for the early explorers. Now it's used as a late-night beacon for guys looking to explore one another's bodies when they have failed at the bars or online for some quick primal anonymous sex.

Outside the monument, a flowing poster that looks like it could be a colorful Gap ad reads, "Know your status. You have HIV or you don't. Knowing is powerful." The poster features a hunky Hispanic guy à la Adam Rodriguez from *CSI: Miami* hugging a black guy à la Taye Diggs, whose chocolate arm is marked by a cloverleaf-shaped Band-Aid, as if blood had been drawn out from underneath it.

There's a small platoon of volunteers here, from the local gay clinic as well as from Massachusetts Regional Hospital in Boston's West End. They're all dressed in white and red with HIV ribbons pinned on their T-shirts. As the flood of men stream by, they hand out packets of condoms and lube and say, "Get tested today! Free HIV testing. Be safe. Be careful. Be good."

Randy is there, talking to the guys, when he sees me.

"Kyle, hey! It would be great PR if you got tested. It might inspire some of the younger guys to get tested while they're down here and remind them to have safe sex," he says, the sun shining off his bald head like a bowling ball. I'm glad I have my sunglasses on. "I was going to ask you earlier when I saw you but you were talking to some guys. I didn't want to interrupt.

It would be a great community service if people saw you doing this."

I look at his big green eyes, like two small emeralds, and tell him, "Do you have to take blood out? I mean, I don't want to walk around with a Band-Aid or anything. I have a show tonight," as I step into the booth for a small respite from the roiling sun.

"Kyle, you'll only feel a pinch. It'll take a minute or so," Randy says, holding a clipboard as some guys nearby pick up the condom and lube packs and stuff them in their back pockets. "It would be completely anonymous, of course. We wouldn't use your name. Just a code so you can get your results in a week or so. But your participation would speak volumes to the greater gay community."

I know I've been safe. I always use a rubber when I do the horizontal samba and, well, come to think of it, vertical, too. I tested negative over a year ago. I don't let anyone ejaculate in my mouth. I might as well put my fame to good use. If I really thought I was poz, I wouldn't be doing such a public display of testing. Here I go. What the hell. It's a good deed. The price of fame, you know.

"Okay, Randy. Just this once here in public, for you," I tell him. "Where do you poke me with the needle again?"

He laughs back and says, "Where do you want to be poked, Mr. KY?"

We laugh as he leads me to a booth where a doctor named Jared Goldstein was waiting for the next tester. He immediately begins to barrage me with questions that make me rosy. Dr. Goldstein is apparently spending a few hours on this holiday helping out the local clinic, even though he works in the Infectious Diseases Department at Mass Regional Hospital. My back is visible to the parade of men and visitors but no one can hear what we're saying.

"Have you had unprotected sex since your last test?" is the first question.

"Do you perform oral sex on other men? Do they perform oral sex on you?" he asks, and the questions keep coming like the men disembarking today from the fleet of Boston ferries.

Within a few minutes, Dr. Needle pokes me in my right arm, the thinness of the needle piercing me with a sharp pain. Ouch! It's a quick sting. A dark red stream of blood, almost like wine, snakes through the syringe and into a vial for the test. A few seconds later, he pulls it out quickly, caps the vial, and applies a small white cotton ball to the point of entry, and then an itty-bitty Band-Aid.

"This is your bar code and number to call us in a week or so," he says. "We take the results to get tested at the lab back at the hospital in Boston. You can get the results there in downtown Boston or if you are still here in Provincetown, you can get them here. Our main testing facility is at MRH so I am guessing that might be easier for you," Dr. Goldstein tells me in a clinical but friendly voice. He looks about early thirties and he wears designer black-framed eyeglasses. He looks like the interior designer guy for *Queer Eye for the Straight Guy*. "Have fun today and be safe," he says as I get up.

I look at the skin-colored Band-Aid, grab the information card, and bid him farewell.

"Thanks for the poking. Call you in two weeks," I tell him as I walk away and back into the crowds. Note to self: Do this in private next time, at a doc's office.

As I venture back into the sea of men, who look like Terminators with their massive torsos and arms and jiggling nipple rings, I begin to wonder, was this such a good idea? When nobody looks, I rip the Band-Aid off and I head back to my hotel room, to prepare for tonight's show and to see Eric.

★   ★   ★

"Now, go out and let's have fun. It's Independence Day. Let's celebrate, people. Work it, girls!" I announce to the crowd from the lip of the small stage as I loom over the crowd of guys drinking and dancing at the Crown and Anchor pier party. They're everywhere, lining the deck as it overlooks the calm Provincetown water. The guys frame the rim of the pool as if they're posing for *Genre* magazine. They're perched over the second-floor balcony that overlooks the pool area. The deejay, known as Johnny D., is cranking up Madonna and Mariah. The dark blue waters of the northern Atlantic Ocean lap against the shore behind the pier.

"It's our party. Our founding fathers would be so proud. Give them something to talk about. The fireworks display will commence in just a few. So grab your cameras, grab your partners, or someone else's, and enjoy the show," I shout out to the crowd.

With that, I step down from the elevated pool area and work my way through the crowd.

"Yo, Kyle! Over here," I hear from behind me. I turn around and see Eric, shirtless, bronzed, and sweaty from all the dancing, sort of like a superbuilt Ryan Seacrest from *American Idol*.

"Wassup, boyee?" Eric greets me with a hug, which gets me all wet from his sweat. I'm in a white tank top and small blue shorts, make that a wet white tank top and small blue shorts.

"I'm so glad you're here, Eric. I've missed you even though we talk on the phone but it's not the same as seeing you in person, you know. Haven't seen you since Miami. I love how we can meet up in the most fun places," I say, walking over with him to the elevated deck. We squeeze ourselves through the traffic of men so we can position ourselves for the fireworks show.

"I wouldn't miss Ptown on the Fourth or seeing you. It's the busiest time here, from what the guys in San Francisco have told me," he says, sipping his green bottle of Sprite.

We stand at the deck and wait for the fireworks, looking out at the black water and the low-hanging moon, which happens to look like a backward giant letter C.

We ask the guys next to us to snap a photo of us against the night sky with Eric's digital camera. I wrap my arm around him, tilt my head, and we smile. I know exactly where to put this photo, right by my window next to the framed photo of us back in high school in Oklahoma on top of Eric's blue 1980s Honda Accord.

"Did you hear that? It sounded like an explosion," Eric says, looking all around.

"Oh, that's just the first firework going off. Here we go, Eric!" We lean forward over the wooden deck and peer out as if we're in the balcony seats of a Broadway show in New York.

One by one, the fireworks launch into the sky, like poetic missiles. At first, they look like shooting stars, straight out of Disney's *Fantasia* animated feature. The fireworks illuminate the sky, highlighting the silhouettes of the small sailboats in the harbor.

"Look at that one," Eric points out to another firework that now looks like a bright cloud floating in the sky.

"It's like an explosion of color. This is so beautiful," I say, snapping away with the digital camera.

With rapid pace, the fireworks transform into vibrant palm trees, bursting planets, and waterfalls spewing light. They're a collage of images, real-life paintings hung in the sky. The guys leaning against the pier "oooh" and "awww," as the gentle summer breezes brush our faces and blow my blondish curls. Couples or guys who've just met kiss under the twilight display. Others toast their beer and cheer "Happy Fourth of July!" in their revelry as if they're in a block party.

I glance at Eric a couple of times and we both smile, enjoying this moment and thrilled to be sharing it together. We're the same guys from our childhood in a different setting and just a little older, but still adding fun memories to our collection of shared experiences.

After half an hour, the fireworks die down, leaving smoking trails smeared across the sky. We head down to the pizza place on Commercial Street, which is clogged with men walking in groups of friends along the closed art stores and small tourist shops. We grab two slices of really greasy pizza and we squat on the front steps of the pizza shop. We watch the carnival of guys strolling back and forth tonight, cruising to their left and flexing their arms to their right. There are so many guys I want to hook up with tonight but it's not every day that I get to see a buddy in my neck of the woods. The guys can wait for tonight.

Eric and I sit shoulder-to-shoulder chowing down on our food. We toast our bottled drinks.

"Happy Fourth, Kyle!"

"Happy Fourth, Eric!"

I hold the camera and point it toward us in a slanted manner for another Ptown shot.

"Say Kyle!" I tell Eric.

"KYLE!" we both shout and the camera captures this beautiful Ptown moment.

Chapter 19

TOMMY

It's a sizzling yet humid 90 degrees in Boston and I am having flashbacks to Miami. Who would have thought it could get so hot up here? This is not good for my curly, curly hair. The humidity, like that in Miami, makes my hair frizz up. Ugh!

I am jogging along the Charles River near M.I.T. with a parade of other runners, cyclists, and in-line skaters. It's like an outdoor workout video and everyone is welcome except those pesky Canadian brown geese that are getting in everyone's way. Even with my headphones on, listening to Gloria Estefan's *Greatest Hits* CD, I still catch myself thinking about Mikey. The pumping music doesn't tune out Mikey from my thoughts, or my heart.

We used to run together along the river on the weekends. He would sleep over Friday nights and we'd wake up, have breakfast in Harvard Square, and later on, go for a walk or head to the mall. Why did he have to walk away from me that night at the Barnes and Noble and not get help? I would have fought harder to stay with him if he had gotten help with his drinking but he wasn't willing to go there. So I didn't go there.

But with this new season, I move into another chapter of my life. Since Mikey and I broke up, I have found myself heading back to Club Café with Rico to try and not think about Mikey. But then Mr. Blue Eyes shows up there every Thursday with his Corona beer in hand, make that five by the end of the night. He nods up from a distance to say hello and breaks out into his oh-so-cute smile. Ugh! I just nod up from a distance and look away. I try to leave each time without seeing him because I don't want to see him trashed with his buddies. It really does break my heart. There have been a few times when he has seen me talk to a cute guy, and as I am ready to leave, Mikey calls my cell, slurring his words.

"Tommy! I miss you. Can I stay at your place tanight?" were the typical voice mail messages from Mikey.

The first time he did this, calling me after seeing me leave with a guy, was a week after we broke up in April. I was stupid enough to answer the phone, in front of a cute Irish guy named Kelly I was talking to outside Club Café.

"Mikey, hi. What's up," I told him as this guy was looking down at the brick-paved sidewalk, waiting for me to get off the phone.

"Tommy, can I crash at your place? Please? I'm sorry I walked out on you last week. I just need a place to stay," Mikey said that night, in his raspy Boston-accented voice.

"Mikey, I'm here talking to a guy. This is rude. We are not together anymore. I can't talk now," I fired back as Kelly watched me, in frustration. We were on our way to get a bite to eat at the 24-hour diner next to Chinatown so we could talk in a quieter setting. Kelly was a political strategist who worked mostly out of DC but he lives in South Boston.

"You're not leaving with that little dude I saw you talking to earlier? That guy has nothing on me. You can do so much better, like me, Tommy Boy! Do you have to bend down to kiss him?"

I remember how emotionally caught up I felt, like a tide swaying back and forth in my head with all these conflicting feelings. I have this supercute guy, with big green eyes and a crew cut—okay, he was shorter than me by three inches and he did have a girl's name—but he wanted to hang out with me and listen to my stories about being Cuban in Boston. Then I have my ex-boyfriend on the phone, pleading to see me. But Mikey was drunk. I knew that. He knew that. And I wasn't his boyfriend anymore, something he seemed to have forgotten.

"Mikey, I gotta go. I'm being rude to my friend," I told him as Kelly began looking up at the clear sky. I had told him about my whole recent breakup with Mikey earlier in the evening by the front bar of the club.

"Tommy, I'm gonna wait for you at your place downstairs. I really want to talk to you," Mikey said, his voice slurring more with each new sentence.

"Mikey, no! You can't drive. You're drunk."

"Tommy Boy, cutie, I will call you lattah," and the call ended there.

I tried to put the whole thing out of my mind as I began walking with Kelly along Columbus Avenue to the 24-hour diner on this breezy summer night. But I couldn't help but worry about Mikey. He's drunk. He may drive. He did look pretty sloshed at the bar before I left with Kelly.

"I guess you and your ex are still pretty tight, right?" Kelly told me, sharing a similar Boston accent with Mikey.

"We just broke up last week and I still love him. That doesn't go away overnight," I told Kelly as he looked crestfallen at the mention of the words "love him."

I went with my gut and told Kelly something that seemed to hit him like a punch in the stomach.

"Kelly, you seem like a really nice guy but I feel like I have to help my ex-boyfriend out. I'm so sorry. I just want to be honest with you. He's drunk and he may drive and I don't want to think of what could happen to him. I feel like I need to help him, this one last time."

Kelly looked at me like his puppy had died or as if he were a balloon that had lost its air. I popped his balloon of hope, of whatever could have been tonight.

"Look, do what you have to do. Here's my number. I'm heading to DC tomorrow night but I will be back on Wednesday. Call me, Tommy!"

And with that, I gave Kelly a hug, apologized again, and dashed back to CC.

I sprinted hard on Columbus Avenue, just as I am doing this summer afternoon along the river.

Once I arrived at the bar a few minutes later, I saw Mikey, barely standing up near the coat check. There were still some guys at the bar, all scrambling to find someone to go home with. It was getting close to last call and the pressure was on for these guys to harbor a soul for a night. It's the same scene every week at this time.

When Mikey saw me, he flashed that sweet smile of his. He was off-balance and his friends were nowhere to be found.

"Tommy! I knew you'd come back, cutie!" Mikey told me, his slurring now even worse than before. He gave me a big hug and said, "Let's go back to your place. I've missed you, my Cuban boy."

I put my arm around Mikey, like I always have when he has had too much to drink, to comfort him and make him feel safe. We walked back to his car. I grabbed his keys and drove him to my place. His head leaned on my shoulder the whole way as Justin Timberlake—his favorite—rapped in the background on his car stereo.

"Mikey, you have a problem. I'm helping you this one last time but I can't do this again. It's not right," I told him once I got him into my studio and fetched him a glass of water and an aspirin.

He ended up sleeping in my bed that night and passed out right away, the smell of Corona stenching my yellow pillowcases.

His sandy brown hair spiked up in the back of his head from turning so many times.

The following morning, he acted like nothing had happened, like everything was okay.

When he woke up, I gave him a glass of lemon–lime Gatorade and sat next to him, on the edge of the bed. I spoke sternly and tried to be as serious as I felt. I wanted him to hear me, loud and clear, once and for all.

"I'm not your boyfriend anymore. Don't call me like this again," I told him as he downed the tall glass of the glowing liquid. Inside, though, I desperately wished he were still my boyfriend. I loved him so much. "This is the first and last time I will let you interrupt my evening with another guy. I ditched that guy to help you and that's not fair to him or to me."

In between gulps, he said, "Tommy, I just needed a friend last night. Thanks." His blue eyes were crowded by the bags underneath them. "Besides, I was doing you a favah. That guy was a midget!" he said with a mischievous smile.

By noon, Mikey was gone and on his way back to Duxbury.

After that night, whenever Mikey saw me out at Club Café on a Thursday night or a Saturday night, he would walk by and say hi. Rico would steer me away from him so as not to ruin my night or his. On some of those outings, Mikey would call me about 1:30 A.M. just as I was leaving the bar with Rico or another cute guy. But after that first night, I learned to ignore his calls. I'm not a hotel and Mikey wasn't my responsibility anymore. He needed to be responsible for his own actions, even if that meant him possibly getting a DUI. I had to move on. I had to stick to my guns or else this would be a never-ending emotional roller coaster.

It's been almost three months since we broke up and yet I am still in love with him and it hurts. My heart stings. I miss my boyfriend, my best friend for all these months, my hangout buddy. As my feet pound the pavement during my run, Gloria

Estefan's "Everlasting Love" comes up as the next song. *"Real love will last forever . . ."* she sings. I believe it, too, as beads of sweat fill my face and as I labor in breathing from running with each beat of the song. What I may have had with Mikey wasn't the real love I was looking for. When people find that real love, they will do what they can to maintain it, even overcome a drinking problem. Mikey did no such thing. He doesn't love himself enough.

It took a while to adjust to not being with Mikey every weekend. I felt lost those two first weekends because I had become so used to spending them with him. Now, I keep busy with my errands (laundry, cleaning, the gym, talking to Papi and Mami each night about the weather and my articles) as well as my reading. I have also begun looking at real estate.

Because interest rates are so low and my rent in Cambridge is bound to go up again, I've been looking into buying a condo. It's a good investment. Look at Papi and Mami's house back in Miami Beach. They bought it for $80,000 when I was in junior high during *Miami Vice*'s heyday and now our house is worth half a million dollars.

Papi will never sell it, though. Things are going well for me at work. The *Daily* asked me to help recruit other young Hispanic reporters at the upcoming Hispanic Journalism Conference in Washington, D.C., this August. The *Daily* is paying my way. They also have me featured as the first smiling face in a diversity ad for the paper. I am one of four Hispanic reporters out of 300 *Daily* reporters so we need to get our Hispanic numbers up.

I feel I have a bright future here and I don't see myself moving back to Miami anytime soon. I feel at home here, and a lot of that has to do, unfortunately, with Mikey. Whether he realized it or not, Mikey helped me find my comfort zone in the city by helping me see this town from a native's point of view. Now I am on my own and in search of finding a small one-bedroom here in Cambridge to call my own. It's a way to reward myself for all my hard work and to invest in my future. Ironically, I always thought I'd buy a place in Miami, my hometown. The fact that I am looking in Boston makes me realize, this is really my home now. Miami is never far from my heart or my thoughts, though.

But first, I have to finish this four-mile run on this glorious Saturday afternoon, without running over one of these geese.

Gloria Estefan's 1994 song "Reach" comes on and it motivates me to run faster. It inspires me to move on to bigger and better things in life.

"If I could reach, higher . . ." Gloria sings.

Chapter 20

RICO

Shit, this beer is good. Sam Adams, low-carb, of course. Gotta keep my abs in check for the rest of the fuckin' summer for my trips to Ptown and shirtless runs in the city along the river. It's another Thursday summer night at Club Café. Why am I here again? Oh yeah, to get laid. I've been so horny lately. The heat must have something to do with it. Or working out more. I hear the more you work out your muscles, the more you want to work out your love muscle, and I've been hitting the gym pretty hard every morning before work. It's a great way to start the day, get the heart pumping, the blood flowing. So I'm here waiting to perform another kind of cardio for later tonight.

I'm sitting at the front bar, watching the guys pour into the place from Columbus Avenue. It's just half past ten and the place is picking up. I have a front-row seat for my pickings. Tommy said he'd be here later but I won't hold my breath. He's been running late lately from condo hunting in Cambridge. The guy uses his lunch hour and his time after work to meet with his realtor. I haven't seen him as much but that's cool.

His goal is to have a place by summer's end, but from what he's been telling me, he can't find a one-bedroom in his price range. I wish I could buy a place but I can't right now, not with all my debt. For now, my room in Savin Hill is home, whether I like it or not.

I see the regular-regulars walking in with their sleeveless shirts and Diesel jeans. The twinks are here with their Izod polo shirts with raised collars and butt-grabbing jeans. The older guys are here and you can tell, because they look like they could have fathered the twinks. Same old, same old. So what else is new. But you never know what tourist or new face might pop up here, some new ass to pound. Yeah.

Speaking of a new ass . . . there's that Channel 7 weather guy Josh I met a few weeks back. He's walking in, sees me across the bar, smiles, and waves. I hold up my beer to salute him from my bar stool. I hope he doesn't come over here. I'm not in a superchatty mood. He was so yum! I helped him find his new apartment in Back Bay. Once he moved here two weeks later, I fucked him like a tornado. I'm sure he didn't see that coming on his Doppler radar. It was the first time I hooked up in a unit I rented but I'm sure it won't be the last. Talk about a hot commission.

Cute guy, fun in bed, but dating's not my thing. Besides, he seemed like one of those needy emotional guys, almost like a parasite, a clinger. You know them, the guys who want a relationship as fast as instant coffee. This beer is working its magic. *Burp!*

The weather girl wanted to spend the whole morning with me and then meet up again that night. Nah. Fuck that. We hook up now and then when he sees me online. He knows I am not looking for anything more. I just have to remind him each time because he'll want to go on a date or something. No way.

Beyoncé's on the monitors again. How did that girl get all that straight hair? Maybe she could give me some to fill the little missing gaps near my forehead. Every four songs is Beyoncé or Britney. Shit, I want to hear some Cher.

I'm done with the beer and I order another. It's already 11 P.M. and the place is filling up with guys like a Madonna concert. Who will come home with me and Oscar?

Not Kyle, Mr. KY, who I see prancing in like he owns the place. He heads straight to the back bar. A few guys behind him is Mikey, Tommy's ex, with his new boyfriend in tow. Poor guy. He has no idea what's in store for him with that alcoholic. I never liked that dude.

As the bartender with the ponytail and wife-beater shirt fetches me another beer, I notice a figure in the corner of my eye.

"Hey, can I get a Vodka Tonic. Thanks," the voice next to me tells the bartender. It's a deep masculine voice. I'm horny from just listening to it.

I turn to my left and look him up and down as my arms flex my biceps on the bar counter. I gotta show off the goods.

He's got a shaved head, big hazel eyes, thick eyebrows, chiseled jaw, big red lips, and a slightly beak-type nose kind of like Ashley Simpson's. He's wearing a white T-shirt with the sleeves rolled up on his bicep. A vein there bulges like a piece of rope. Yum. Put him in a pilot uniform and he could be one of the dudes from *Top Gun*.

I flash him my smile. It works every time.

"Yo, what's up tonight?" I say to him, keeping my eyes locked on his, and taking a swig of my beer.

"Just hanging. This is my first time here. I'm David," he says, pulling out his hand to shake mine.

"Rico here. Welcome to CC, Club Café."

I can take this guy right here, throw him over the stool, and plug that tight-looking ass of his.

"Are you new in town?" I ask him, slowly sipping my beer

and maintaining constant eye contact. He pays the $5 for his drink, takes a sip, sits on the stool next to me, and faces me.

"I guess you can say that. I just sailed in and dropped anchor," he says, now stretching his arms up, making his chest pop out. He's nice and lean and muscular, just the way I like them. A gay GI Joe.

"Dude, you sound like Captain Stubing or a sailor. Not many people here drop anchor," I say to him.

"But I am a captain, of my own boat. It's docked in East Boston at the marina there, with all the other liveaboards," he says, eyes lighting up as soon as he mentions the words boat and marina. "I live on my boat. Home is where I hang my life-jacket," he says with a sweet laugh.

"You're shitting me? You live on a boat? Is your name Captain Morgan?" I tell him, laughing at my own joke, something Tommy would totally do. The guy laughs back and he continues to explain that liveaboards are people who live year-round on their boats. He sailed his 29-foot boat from Key West, where he was working as a painter for some hotels.

The job lasted five months this winter. He's a drifter, as he puts it, traveling around the country in his boat, finding odd jobs and living the simple life. No nine-to-five job. No boss. No hassles. He tells me how he used to be a web programmer at a dot-com in New York City that went bust with the whole dot-com bubble. He lost his shares and his job. With whatever money he had left in the bank, he bought this old sailboat, which he named *Goliath* and he's gone from job to job on his boat ever since. That's cool. I know what it's like to break away from the world and be the captain of your destiny. But for all the fun it was, it drowned me in heavy credit card debt.

"I'm here for the summer. I thought this would be a good place to chill and maybe take some trips to the Cape or Newport," he says as he continues drinking his Vodka Tonic.

"A friend promised me some work here to paint his house

in Dorchester and two of his friends' town houses. So that should keep me busy for a few weeks," he explains.

"Oh, I live in Dorchester! In Savin Hill," I tell him, a little bit too enthusiastically. I need to simmer down. I don't want him to know how cool and hot I think he is.

"My friends are in Pope's Hill and Lower Mills. Is that near you?" he asks as we lean closer to talk. Our faces are inches from one another's. I can feel his breath and smell the vodka.

"Yeah, I'm in Savin Hill. Dorchester is a big neighborhood of hilly microneighborhoods. Pope's Hill and the other one are pretty close. They're pretty similar—triple-deckers and Victorian homes, with lots of families and single professionals. Working-class folk. Like little suburbs in the ci-tay."

He smiles and then offers, "Wanna show me?" I'm taken by surprise. I'm usually the one who makes the first move and controls the seduction.

"Sure, I'm parked outside," I tell him.

We put our drinks down and we head outside. I eye him the whole time we walk to my truck on Dartmouth.

All I'm thinking is, I wanna rock David's boat.

Chapter 21

KYLE

I'm back in the South End. It feels so good to be back on my Macy's bed. I spent two weeks in Provincetown. I was such a hit during the Fourth of July Fireworks Bonanza that I was also asked to stay there for additional emcee gigs at other bars on and off Commercial Street like the Paramount and The A-House.

And of course, I obliged. How can you turn down opportunities like that, especially during the summer when Ptown is *the* place to be. I met so many people from San Francisco, New York, and Chicago. Many of those boys remembered me from my pool party event at the White Fiesta in Miami earlier this year. Yowza.

I'm unpacking, neatly laying out all my wrinkled Calvin Klein, Abercrombie, and Hollister shirts and shorts to be washed. My thongs need a washing, too. Luckily, I was able to get by being shirtless most of the time, wearing jean shorts or my Speedo blue and red bathing suits and Dolce sandals. *Time to wash all the stains right outta my clothes.*

As I remove items from my Prada bag, something falls out and drops onto my hardwood floors. I bend over and pick it up. It's the card with my code to call for my HIV results. Oh, I totally forgot about that.

It's been two weeks so my results should be in. I know I am fine. I just dread the part where you get the results. It's a total mental masturbation. It really plays tricks with your head. Am I negative? Am I positive? Did I slip up one night when I had too many Cosmos?

I've always come out negative, but still, there is always that lingering, nagging voice in the back of your head that whispers, "What if . . . I was positive?"

I don't want to even go there. When you are young and gay, getting tested becomes a right of passage. You have to do it at least once a year, like a woman does with mammograms. I would take a mammogram, hey even a Pap smear, any day over an HIV test. Now comes the hard part.

I pull the card out and dial the number on my Cingular cell phone, with the radiant red cover. A friendly woman on the other end answers and asks for my code number. When I read the numbers back to her, she answers, "Your results are in. When would you like to come in to meet the doctor? You can either do it here at Mass Regional Hospital or in Provincetown. Which would you prefer?" she says.

"Boston, thank you very much," I tell her. She then gives me an appointment for this Wednesday at 1 P.M. at the hospital with Dr. Goldstein.

That's the same doctor I met in Ptown, who gave me the test. So that's a good sign. I already know him. He seemed sincere and on the up and up back in Ptown. He was cute in a Doogie Howser, M.D., kind of way.

Before she hangs up, I ask her, "Um, can you tell me what the results are over the phone? It would save me a trip and some time. I'd rather just get this over with."

In a tone that I can't tell whether is good or bad, she says, "Sir, state policy dictates that results, no matter what they are, must be given in person. I apologize but that's the way it is. Please understand."

I thank her and agree to the Wednesday appointment. She's just doing her job. Even if I am negative, which I know I am, I still have to see the doctor. Darn it! No sweat. I'm sure I am fine. I just need to put this out of my head until then. No sense in getting bent out of shape like a pretzel. I will go to the gym, do some crunches, work out my obliques, rework my face shots, and just stay busy for the next two days. I've been here and done that before when it comes to HIV test results. What a drag, like those queens on Commercial Street in Ptown.

It's Wednesday morning and I'm sitting in the waiting room of the Infectious Diseases Ward on the eighth floor at Massachusetts Regional Hospital. What a gloomy place. To get up here, you have to take a side custodial-like elevator, not the traditional brightly lit elevators at the end of the hospital.

Outside the elevator, the scene is even drabbier. We need some bright colors here, people! The walls are off-white. The chairs are gray and hard to sit in comfortably. The rug is worn out. Total negative energy here.

The only bright spot about this place is *The Ellen Show*, playing on a small television set in the corner of the waiting room. People here look so sad, with their long faces. There's a mix of people, older men, gay, I suspect. Younger men in their twenties and, luckily, no one that I recognize so I think they're hetero.

There are some women who look like they are immigrants from South America or Haiti. I can't believe the nurse made me sit here to wait for Dr. Goldstein. If you are in this ward, chances are, you've got an infectious disease or you are waiting for the results to see if you have an STD. I wore a blue Abercrombie baseball cap and my reading glasses so I wouldn't stand out as much. Just when I thought this couldn't get any worse, the friendly young black receptionist with straightened hair like Naomi Campbell steps into the room and calls out my name: "Kyle Andrews, Dr. Goldstein is ready to see you. Come with me, please."

Just great! Now everyone in Boston will know that I was here and think I am positive or something. Why did I agree to do this again? Oh yeah, because supernice Randy from the community center asked me to get tested to inspire younger guys to do so as well.

Out of the waiting room, I walk down the polished, shiny floors of the ward and step into an examining room, which is just as depressing as the waiting area except there is a grand view of the Charles River and Cambridge from up here. Dr. Goldstein waits inside and greets me.

"Kyle, good to see you," he says, shaking my hand. He sits down and types in some figures into the computer and pulls up my test results with my code.

"Hi, Dr. Goldstein. I don't mean to be a pest but can we hurry this up. I kinda want to get out of here. So tell me I am negative so I can go to the gym and find some more modeling work," I tell him as his eyes glance down and then back up again with an extremely serious look. He takes a deep breath.

"Kyle, I don't have good news. There is no easy way to say this. Your tests came back positive for HIV. I'm so sorry. The Eliza test, which is the standard antibody test, came back positive. When that comes back positive, we run another test for confirmation called a Western blot. Four out of the nine bands on that test were reactive, which confirms that your results are positive. I'm sorry."

I keep hearing his words replay in my head. *I'm sorry. I'm sorry.* I . . . can't . . . breathe. My heart pounds with repetitive hard thuds as if it were about to pop out of my chest. I'm not surprised if the doctor heard my heartbeats from his seat. My throat tightens. I heard what he said but the words didn't seem to ring true. They can't ring true. Me and HIV?

I gain a second of clarity.

"Did you say I'm HIV positive? Are you sure those are my results? This can't be. I don't understand. I was tested a year ago and I was fine. I play a lot but I'm careful. I grew up in the 1980s. I know what you can do and can't do with a guy."

At this point, Dr. Goldstein puts his hand on my hand and begins to explain the results, how they work, how lab technicians check and recheck all the results, the accuracies and inaccuracies of the test.

"We are going to do another test, to test your viral load, that's the number of copies the virus has made of itself in your system. We are also going to check your CD4 count, which is the number of immune T-cells you have, a prime target of the AIDS virus. We are also going to check for hepatitis, gonorrhea, and syphilis, to rule everything out," the doc tells me, sitting much closer now. He's only a few inches from my face and looking deep into my eyes, like that would make a difference right now.

"Kyle, I know this is hard to accept right now but let's wait until we get the results from the follow-up tests. I don't want to give you false hope, but sometimes people come back with a false positive and that could very well be the case here. It's very rare but let's hope for the best."

I hear his words again and they don't register. HIV positive. CD4 count. Viral load. How can this be? Is this a dream? Can I wake up? No. I can't be HIV positive. I won't accept this.

"Dr. Goldstein. There must be a mistake. Let's do the follow-up tests to confirm that you're wrong. This is not my destiny," I tell him as I stare out the window in the examination room. I see the cars zip by on Storrow Drive. There's a whole world out there for me to see and embrace. There's so much more I want to do in life.

"Kyle, the first tests are conclusive. The Western blot is done only if the first test comes back positive for the antibody. In the meantime, if you need to, I can set you up with an HIV counselor to talk to, in case you need to have someone to talk to. I'm here for you. Here's my pager number in case you want to talk and have more questions later on. I know this is horrible news, but if you were to have HIV, this is the time to have it. There are twenty-five medications to work with and people are living longer lives. It's not the death sentence that it once was ten years ago. There are patients here who have had it for fifteen years and then some," Dr. Goldstein tells me, almost sounding like one of those actors in an ABC after-school special.

As he talks, a friendly Haitian nurse comes in and withdraws several vials of blood. Another poke in the arm, just like in Provincetown. Her warmth calms me down momentarily but I can't hold back the tears.

I see the red individually fill the vials. I watch and think how this thing may be inside me, growing, photocopying itself, invading my system, decaying it from the inside out, having a party inside my beautiful body. No, it's not inside me. It's a mistake. It has to be a mistake.

"Kyle, do you have any family here to talk to? Or a close friend? You're going to need support. If not, the counselor can put you in touch with other people who are living with HIV who can help support you emotionally. You don't have to be alone at a time like this."

I think about his question and I'm surprised by my own answer.

"Dr. Goldstein, I don't have any real close friends here. I tend to travel a lot for work and modeling jobs. I can't tell my family. They've had a hard enough time dealing with me being gay and on *The Real Life*. But my best friend's mom back in Oklahoma, Bella Sols, is a radio psychologist, with her own call-in show. She was the first person I came out to and she's always been like my second mom. I think I'll give her a call because I don't understand any of this. This can't be."

Tears gush down my face. I am trying so hard to maintain my composure. Dr. Goldstein seems almost robotic in his responses, like a scientist. It fucking figures.

Half an hour has gone by and it seems like time has stood still. I keep hearing him talk about how the virus works, replicates itself, and how the tests were done. It's all scientific lingo. Being a gay man, I know enough of the basics, about how the virus works, but nothing about CD4 counts and viral loads and medications. None of it is sinking in because I refuse to believe I became one of them, an HIV gay guy, another statistic, another walking dead guy.

"These results should be in by Friday. I'll put a rush on it. Again, Kyle, I am so sorry. I'm here if you need me in the meantime." He shakes my hand and gently puts his arm around my back as I open the door that leads into the gloomy hallway of this gloomy ward on this gloomy day. I will never be the same Kyle Andrews after today, July 19. It's the beginning of my own personal 911 except the terrorists may be the three-lettered bug HIV.

Before I leave, drying my eyes and my cheeks with a tissue paper from the examining room, I look down so no one can see my tearstained face. I step into one of the unisex bathrooms. I stare at my blue eyes and imagine this thing inside me. And I cry my heart out. My mouth is open and the tears come down like a miniwaterfall. But my tears are silent, just like this killer inside me.

Chapter 22

TOMMY

"I like this condo but it's too small and pricey for what it is," I tell my realtor, Kathy Wright, who looks like a spitting image of actress Laura Linney, elegant yet attractive.

"It's a two-bedroom with 490 square feet for $220,000. I love the neighborhood here in Cambridge but I just can't do it," I tell Kathy as we climb the six steps back up to the ground floor. Did I mention this was a basement-level condo, where you see feet dart back and forth from the living room windows or close-ups of Goodyear tires from the cars parked outside?

Kathy gives me that polite but frustrated look of hers that screams, "I'm doing the best I can but there's not much here in your price range." She's been giving me that look through this whole month of July since I really began condo hunting. She's been such a good sport. I can be anal about these things beyond my regular OCD.

As we surface back up on the street level, outside the three-story brick building near the Massachusetts Institute of Technology, she says, "Tommy, you may want to try and look in Boston, specifically in Dorchester. You may find a condo there, maybe even a two-bedroom, in the low $200,000 range. I have nothing more to show you here in Cambridge that is bigger or cheaper than this. Here's the name of my Boston counterpart who covers Dorchester. His name is Bill Cook. He'll take care of you. If I come across anything else here in Cambridge that fits your bill, I will call you. But it won't hurt to see what is in Dorchester for comparison."

And with that, I hop back into the Jeep and head back to work at the *Daily*. I've exhausted most of my lunch breaks scouring for condos. I'm getting discouraged. I can afford a studio or a one-bedroom in Cambridge as a renter but not as a buyer. I guess this is what you call being priced out of the market. When I pull up to the *Daily*'s elevated parking lot, I dial Bill Cook's number. He was already expecting my call. That Kathy is quick.

"Mr. Tommy Perez. Good to hear from you. Kathy has been telling me about your search and what you are looking for. I have some possibilities if you'd like to meet up tomorrow, Thursday. I have a feeling we are going to find you a place on this side of the river and perhaps close to the *Daily*."

He sounds so pleasant and sexy. I can tell he's from the South with his slight syrupy twang. We agree to meet at noon the next day so he can show me two possibilities.

After seeing twelve places in Cambridge, it will be refreshing to look at a different neighborhood and type of building. All I've seen are old triple-deckers near Harvard and MIT. No cookie-cutter new developments here like in Miami.

The next day, I meet Bill at the rendezvous point we agreed on: a three-story brick row house in the Ashmont neighborhood in Dorchester. This is near the last stop of the subway's red line. It's not the best neighborhood—home to most of the summer wave of shootings—but it has potential. As I pull up to the row house, I notice no one is bicycling, or running or walking their dogs. Hmmm. It's like a Victorian ghost town. This is not a good sign. Where are the humans? I see one, a handsome face in a black Jeep Cherokee, sitting in the driver's seat. That must be Bill or someone about to mug me, because he spots me and emerges from his SUV.

"Tommy Perez, so nice to meet you. I'm Bill. Great to match a name with a face," he says with a powerful handshake. Bill has straight surfer-blond hair combed to the side like a page from a book. He has dark blue eyes like the water off Cape Cod and a pointy nose that works well with his face. He's tall, about six-feet-one, and semimuscular. Actually, he looks doughy but who cares. I am here to buy a condo, not Bill.

We shake hands and he points to the brick brownstone.

"This is it. Let's go inside," he says as I follow up to the third-floor unit. It's spacious and grand, with exposed brick walls, shining hardwood floors, and two small bedrooms. Asking price: $230,000. I'm intrigued by the unit because the owner apparently had renovated it to sell. It's in move-in condition and it also has a balcony in the back that overlooks Dorchester. You can see the *Daily's* bright-white neon highway sign from here.

I really like this place but the price is too high, I explain to Bill. I can see why the owner is asking her price. She has spent quite a bit of money giving this condo an extreme makeover. Too bad she can't give the neighborhood the same makeover as well. While this building is beautiful, the neighborhood is suspect. It's a *Law and Order* episode waiting to happen.

"She may budge a little on the price but she really wants the $230,000 so you may have some haggling problems there," Bill says, holding his organizer tightly against his chest and looking down at me with a grin. "The owner is a businesswoman who bought this as an investment five years ago when the market was soft. Now it's booming and she wants to cash out."

He said there was another unit nearby in a neighborhood called Lower Mills here in Dorchester. That unit was on the lower end of my price range and was also a two-bedroom.

"Where is Lower Thrills, ah, I mean, Lower Mills," I ask Bill, who is laughing at my apparent Freudian slip.

"Just follow me," he says.

So I follow him there, my Jeep trailing the Jeep. A few minutes later, we both pull up to the condo in a four-story red-brick building. It sits at the end of a quiet residential street of Victorian and ranch-style homes. What a beautiful little neighborhood, almost a hamlet. Bill explains to me how a former chocolate factory, the first in the country, is around the corner, now serving as loft condos that overlook the Neponset River, the unsung hero of the rivers here. It's where the first trading was done among the early explorers. A block away from the condo is the town of Milton, which marks the beginning of the South Shore, and it, too, feels like colonial America with its spacious lots of homes perched on small hilly roads.

Lower Mills, which got its name from all the old mills here along the river, feels more like a small suburban oasis in an urban setting. I had no idea this was here. *Que lindo.* As I get out of my car, I see people walking their dogs, people running, mothers with baby strollers. On the way, I saw a group of children following their teacher on the sidewalk. This neighborhood brims with life. I have a good feeling about it.

Bill and I walk up the five steps to the condo's front door and he smiles and says, "Tommy, this isn't the most beautiful building. In fact, it's the eyesore of the neighborhood. It's a plain-Jane brick building but you can probably get the seller to come down. She bought a house in Brockton with her husband so she needs to sell this ASAP. She hasn't had any offers yet. It's been on the market for two weeks. You'll see why when we go inside."

Five steps inside the unit, and I can see what Bill was talking about.

Walls are painted an almond hue and they are dirty with
handprints and smudges from God knows what. The carpeting
is off-white, worn, torn, and ragged. The living room seems dim
and cramped with the two brown sofas at each end. The two
bedrooms, one for the couple and the other for their five-year-
old daughter, share the same fossil carpeting. The bathroom
needs some TLC with its two-toned blue motif. It looks like
light blue was fighting with dark blue and both colors are at a
draw.

"Yes, the colors are competing against one another here,"
Bill says, almost reading my mind. As we walk back to the front
of the unit and into the kitchen, I stand around and feel im-
pressed with the space of the whole condo. The kitchen is
pretty grand, with its white-tiled linoleum floor (it's got to go)
and wooden cabinets (those are workable). The place needs a
little help, that's all. I don't see it as it is but what it could be.
I'm the Envisionator.

"The one good thing about this listing, Tommy, is the
space. It's 850 square feet. All it needs is *Queer Eye for the Gay
Guy* and you can fix this place up, and flip it. It may be a good
way to break into the market. The owner is asking $202,000
but I'm sure you can get her down, especially if she learns
you're a reporter at the *Daily* and that you are single. You're
single, correct?" Bill tells me with a quizzical squint from his
blue eyes, which easily match the tone of one of the two blues
in the bathroom. Can you tell I'm a sucker for blue eyes?

"Yes, I'm single as a dollar bill but worth much more," I say
with a giggle.

"I just broke up with my ex-boyfriend," I add, reminding
myself how much I hate that hyphenated last word.

"I kind of sensed that you were gay. Don't worry. You're
with family here. There are lots of gay men who live near my

home in Ashmont Hill and Melville Park, two other micro-neighborhoods in Dorchester. Will you be our new neighbor?" he asks with a smirk and a wink.

You know, Bill is really handsome and I have caught myself checking him out during today's condo search but my focus is my condo, not Bill.

I take another stroll around the condo, envision the second bedroom as my little writing cove, an office for my freelance work and for reading as well as a guest bedroom for when my sister Mary visits or for Brian if I ever get him to come up here. Coming from a studio that is 420 square feet, this condo is a palace. It's huge! It can be a work in progress. Besides, I only have my big blue sofa, a queen-sized bed, and my computer desk to move. Not much at all. This could be my first new home.

The condo is also only five miles from the *Daily* and near Boston Market, a prerequisite for anywhere I live or work. As I stand there and do a 180-degree turn in the kitchen, I stop and tell Bill, "I want to make an offer. I feel good about this place."

He pulls out his organizer and walks me out the door. "I'll get the paperwork going. This might be premature now but welcome to the neighborhood, Tommy," he says with another wink.

Chapter 23

KYLE

Those "KNOWING IS POWERFUL" HIV ads are pissing me off. Knowing is not powerful. It's a bitch. It's terrible. And all these ads are everywhere, screaming from bus benches, whispering from billboards, shouting from posters as if they are rubbing the news in my face. Knowing is shitty. That should be the ad.

Dr. Goldstein calls me today and tells me that my viral load is below 50, meaning it's undetectable, and that my CD4 count is 582, which is good and uncommon for someone with HIV.

"You are very healthy," he tells me over the phone. "You are the ideal where most HIV positive patients want to be. It's not common for patients to have such good results. Usually, a person who is infected with HIV has a viral load of 10,000, even 20,000 copies. You are below 50 and that is extraordinary. I have consulted with other doctors here in Infectious Diseases Ward and they suggested I refer you to a new study that looks at recently infected patients. If you qualify, meaning you were infected less than six months ago, they will draw blood from you every two weeks and monitor your immune system. Basically, it's knowledge for knowledge and free of charge, if you're interested. Because of your numbers, we won't need to put you on medication so at least that's good news. You are in the best scenario for someone who is positive."

I thank the doctor for the information. The news is bittersweet. I am healthy and I am not healthy.

"I'm still wrestling with this. I'm doing the best I can. My best friend's mother, who is a psychologist, happens to be in town for a medical conference and I told her that I needed to speak to her urgently. I could barely keep it together on the phone without falling apart and crying. So I will have someone to talk to," I tell Dr. Goldstein as I lie on my bed, staring at the millions of dots in my ceiling and trying to make sense of all this.

So I am healthy for now but how long will that last? There's this thing inside me and my body seems to be handling it well, per se. I guess I should be thankful. I just need to see Bella tonight. She has this inner light about her, something soothing that makes everything seem okay when it's not. She's good at what she does, taking calls on the radio from people with all sorts of problems. I need her to help me deal with this. I can't tell my parents, who have had issues with me being gay for years. I have no close friends here in Boston. Just lots of ex-lovers, fans, and former tricks. They don't matter much in a time of crisis.

I write down the name of the nurse who is handling the study and call her. I make an appointment for next Thursday for a consultation. I try to stay focused on a routine. Work out at the gym. Call my agent about more upcoming jobs. Maybe I should find a real full-time job, one with health benefits. I'm not going to stay healthy forever and those AIDS drugs, from what I have read, are pretty costly.

How did I get myself into this situation? This can't be happening. God, wake me up! I am Kyle Andrews, role model, reality TV star, a famous member of the gay community. Everyone wants to look like me in my ads. If word got out, that would be the end of my career and my sex life. Who gave this to me? I've only been with a dozen guys since last year and I remember being safe with them all. Something doesn't add up here. Something is wrong but the tests say I am positive and this is Massachusetts Regional Hospital, the best of the best in medical care in New England. If I am going to be sick, Boston is the city to be sick in.

Denial is the biggest obstacle. I feel fine. I look fine. I am fine. No trace of the disease externally but that's just the thing. You never know who has this bug. It doesn't discriminate. Fuck! The tears pour out again so much so that I taste the salt from them on my lips. *Breathe.* Take deep breaths. Relax, Kyle. I'm going to the gym and work off some of this tension. I can't be alone with my thoughts. It's too much now.

At 7:30 P.M., I start heading over to the Boston Back Bay Hotel to meet Bella. The hotel overlooks the Boston Common, the oldest public state park in the country. It's not that far from me here in the South End and it's a fifteen-minute walk from the gym/Club Café. I enter the majestic building with its spiraling bushes at the entrance, head up to her room on the fifth floor, and knock. All this emotion bubbles up inside me and I do my best to keep it at bay. I try to keep it together, to stay strong in front of someone I have admired for ten years and who is known as the "Angel of the Airwaves" back home. She's a Dr. Laura, but with heart and grace.

She opens the door and I see her smiling with green eyes that seem to twinkle like two gems. Bella has always reminded me of Julie Andrews, Ms. Mary Poppins. She has this grace, this elegance about her that draws people to her upon first glance. You just want her to hold you when you see her.

"Kyle, so good to see you. I'm so glad you're here in Boston. I was going to call you before you called me," she says, squeezing me into a big hug and giving me a sweet kiss on my neck. "This must be a sign that I was meant to be here and you needed to speak with me today."

I crack a smile, "Oh, Bella. It's so good to see you." She puts her arm around my back and rubs the lower part of it as if making invisible circles. She walks me to the table near the windows that overlook the lush beautiful green park below.

"I'm falling apart here. I can't handle this. I don't know what to do," I break down, burying my face into my hands.

She sits me down, leans in close to me, and cups my hands in her hands. "What's wrong, Kyle? I sense a hidden pain inside you. It's okay. Take a deep breath. You're in good company. I'm here for you. I'm here to help you, sweetie," she says in her caring tone.

"I thought I was doing a good community service so I got tested for HIV in Provincetown on the Fourth of July." I surrender to the tears pooling in my eyes. "And my results came back this week . . . I'm . . . positive! My doctor told me I'm very healthy. My viral load is undetectable and my immune cells are preserved. I don't understand, Bella. Why me? How could I get this? I'm safe."

She looks at me with those big soulful eyes of hers, squeezes my hand, and places her other hand on top of my hand.

"Kyle. I'm so sorry, honey. If the doctor said you're positive and the tests are conclusive, then you have to start taking care of yourself. This is not the end of your life. This is not a death sentence," she says, caressing and patting the tops of my hands. Her good energy reaches deep inside me. She has such a powerful presence.

"Kyle, I am going to connect you with hope. You are not alone in this. There is someone you know, someone you've known since high school, who is HIV positive, too, and has learned to handle this well."

I am so confused as she tells me this in her calm optimistic voice with calming eyes.

"Wait, are you telling me you're HIV positive, Bella!" I ask her.

She starts to chuckle.

"Ah, no, Kyle. Not me. I haven't had sex in years. I don't have time with my work schedule on the radio and my private patients . . . But Eric is HIV, your old friend, my boy. He's been living with it since he was a freshman in college. He caught it from his ex-boyfriend, the one who cheated on him, remember? That Scott."

How could I have not seen this? Eric is so full of life. He bought another condo in San Francisco and his computer ER business is doing well. He looked great in Ptown a few weeks ago.

As relieved as I am that someone I know has it and is doing so well, I am also extremely saddened.

"Eric has it? But he never told me. He looks so healthy. In fact, he's superbuilt. I would have never known, Bella," I tell her, wiping the tears coming down my face.

"Yes, he lives life to the fullest in San Francisco and he works out a lot to stay strong. If he feels strong on the outside, he'll feel good on the inside. He didn't want you to know because he didn't want your pity or for you to look at him differently. He likes the fact you look up to him. But I know my son, and I know he wouldn't want you to go through this alone. Call Eric tonight and tell him what you told me. He'll help you. He'll walk you through this," Bella says, rubbing the side of my cheek with her wrinkled hands.

"I've connected you with hope and that's all you will need right now. Knowing that Eric is okay, you will be okay," she says. "You need to imagine that you are surrounded by a healing, white light. It envelopes you and protects you from all negativity. That is your guiding light, your hope. Eric will be there for you and so will I. Remember, you're not alone, Kyle. You never have to be because you have us and we love you."

We spend a good hour talking about how I could have caught the virus, from whom, and how I should just focus right now with being comfortable with being HIV positive. She tells me how angry she was at Eric's ex-boyfriend for exposing him to the disease, for basically murdering a part of him. She talks about how he became terribly ill a few years ago and had to be hospitalized and go back on medication to stabilize his viral load. Now she says he takes an immune-boosting vitamin and drinks a lot of green tea, which is also good for the immune system. She suggests that I don't tell my family back in Oklahoma until I'm completely comfortable with the news myself, whenever that day will be.

"I want you to think hard about what you did sexually since your last HIV test, which was a year ago, no? The answers will come to you in time. And as you get more information about exposure and who gave it to you, you will have to call the person you suspect. He may not know he is positive and may be infecting guys, just like you. And that's not right. You are going to feel angry once this settles in and that's perfectly natural."

Before I leave Bella's hotel room an hour later, I thank her for her support. I feel so much better. If Eric has had this for years and he's okay, I should be okay, too. She asks me to call her in a few days but insists that I call Eric tonight when I get home. Bella leaves Boston tomorrow morning and she's on her way to speak at a psychologists' conference tonight.

"I know you're feeling better now because you know, deep down inside, you will be okay. Just like Eric," she tells me as she walks me to the door. I think she can read minds, too.

"Bella, thank you so much. You've always been like another

mother to me," I tell her, smelling the traces of her Estee Lauder's Pleasures perfume.

"And you, like another son," she says. "Stay strong. I believe in you. You will be okay, Kyle. You will. I promise."

I walk out of the hotel and cut through the Boston Common, strolling along the paved paths that crisscross throughout this mini–Central Park. I sit on a bench along the pond, watching the ducks bob in the water. The sky is dimming but there's still enough light outside to cast tree shadows against the pavement and grass. I sit here and think about Bella and Eric and all the guys I've been with in the last year or so. The hunky guy at the gym. My Puerto Rican ex. The Mexican guy in Miami that penetrated me but I remember him using a condom. I analyze what I had done sexually and I keep coming back to the same conclusion: I've been safe. Growing up in the 1980s, you're groomed from the early days of middle school about the dangers of unsafe sex. No sex without a condom and I had done that. Simple as that. I should be okay.

But then my mind begins toying with me. Did I slip up one night after I had too many drinks at Club Café? Possible. Did I taste some cum when I had a sore in my mouth after blowing some guy? Possible. Did a condom have a hole in it one time? Maybe. Anyone who gets caught up in the heat of the moment of hot sex, especially with a serious boyfriend, can let their guard down at times. Human nature. It happens but you never think something like this can happen to you.

I always believed HIV happened to those guys flying high on crystal meth and cocaine with their all night shag-a-thons with multiple partners. I don't know anyone like that and I don't belong to that scene although I've seen them at the White Fiesta and in Ptown.

As I sit here, I think about those HIV drug magazines featuring smiling healthy sculpted men running and hiking. The ads don't get around the fact that these men have to pop drug cocktails every day. It's just another way to mask the reality. I don't want to be one of those ads. I want to be the way I was, pre-HIV.

I pull out my cell and call Eric.

"Hey, Kyle, what's up?" he says from San Francisco.

"Eric . . ." My voice cracks. "Your mom told me. I need your help. I'm HIV, too."

I explain to him the results of the test, my talk with his mother. He's in shock.

"Kyle, listen, guy. You're gonna be okay. I will walk you through this. Trust me on this, okay? I will hold your hand throughout this whole thing," he says on the other end. "But you've always been safe. I know you know better than most guys. Have you tried getting another test?" he says.

"Well, the tests came back pretty conclusive and I volunteered for a study. I'm gonna find out if I'm eligible. Eric, why didn't you tell me you were HIV positive after all these years? I would have helped you with it," I ask him, throwing some peanuts from my man-purse, or my murse, to the ducks in the pond.

"Because I didn't want you to see me differently. Sometimes, people see the disease and not the person and I didn't want you, of all people, seeing HIV and not Eric, your old friend. Once you say it, you can't take it back. When I see you, I forget that I have HIV. It's just us, like when we were teens."

"Oh Eric. I love you so much. I wish I could have been there for you all those years ago. I would have held your hand and gone with you to the doctors."

"Thanks, Kyle. I know you would have but I didn't want you to have to go through this with me. The important thing is, I'm here for you now," he says.

For the first time since I talked with Dr. Goldstein, I really feel like I am going to be okay.

I keep talking to Eric about how his medications work and when to tell someone you're positive. The whole time, I walk along Arlington Street, passing all the churches and residential buildings on my way back to the South End under tonight's darkening sky.

"Kyle, the key is mind over matter and having faith. You have to believe you're gonna be okay and you will," he says.

I believe him.

Chapter 24

RICO

I'm on my way back to David's *Goliath* after work tonight. This is my second time coming over. First time was last week, after we met at Club Café. We went to his place, which is his boat, and we made waves. Shit, all night, too. I even slept over at the dude's house, I mean boat. It's wickedly weird to imagine living on a boat but I can see why David does it. The dude's got great views of downtown Boston. He doesn't pay rent. Heck, maybe I should buy a boat and move out of Savin Hill and my hole-in-da-wall room.

David lives in what he calls a floating neighborhood at the Boston Harbor Marina in East Boston. For all the drawbacks that he has there, he also has as many pros for aquatic living. He's got to shower in the marina office but he can park on the pier. No residential permits here, Mayor Menino! I wonder how David gets pizza delivered.

When I came over the first time, we were hungry but David couldn't turn the microwave on and have his lights on at the same time. It blows out the fuse. So he lit some candles and heated up some macaroni, my favorite. It was kinda sweet.

He's got to do laundry at the marina office. He gets his mail there. And he stores his clothes in small plastic containers he hides under his bed in the bunk of the boat. Talk about tight quarters. I practically slept on top of him, which wasn't so bad. Slurp!

His whole living space on the boat is like a small efficiency. While the boat is 28.7 feet long, and no more than 11½ feet wide, he lives okay here. Party of uno!

And all he pays is a $500 seasonal fee plus $37 per foot of the boat. So a 29-foot boat here would cost about $1,573 from May to September overall. So much cheaper than buying a place. With Boston's burning real estate market, you have to be a gazillionaire to afford David's downtown aquatic views on land. I know I can't afford to buy anything now but I'm penny-pinching as much as I can. Just last week, I rented seven units in the Back Bay and South End. Cha-ching!

"This is like great therapy," David tells me just after I hop aboard the boat on this Wednesday evening. "The way the waves lap against the boat, it's like you're in your own crib."

David likes to talk about his boat, a lot. *Goliath* is his baby. I've noticed he talks in aquatic metaphors. What's up with that? Is he Popeye the sailor or Aqua Man from the Justice League or worse, Captain Morgan?

He looks hotter than the first time I saw him. He's in a tight black tank top and baggy blue jeans that barely hang on to his hips. Again, the veins in his arm bulge. So sexy. So right. So yum. I want some.

He greets me with a hug and I bear-hug him back.

"Good to see you, Rico," he tells me as he climbs up a small ladder to the boat's small deck. "Come up here. You gotta check out this sunset. Just like in Key West."

I head back up and see a magenta sky, the sun dropping back into the west behind the skyscrapers of downtown, not far from where I used to work as an accounting clerk. I only hear the seagulls now and the water gentling nudging against the boat. Wow, this is cool.

"I had a great time Thursday," David says as we sit on the edge of the boat, our legs dangling over the water. I see swans bobbing on the surface. Ahh, this is great.

He leans in and puts his arm around my shoulder. I'm not into the whole touchy-feely thing but this feels nice. It feels right. I'm just going with the flow like the currents here in the Boston Harbor.

"Rico, what do you want to do in life?" he asks me, his leg gently bumping into mine. I need my sunglasses. The sunset's so bright.

"What do you mean?" I ask him back, my leg now nudging his leg back. They look like pendulums swinging over the boat.

"You know, what is your ultimate goal? What do you want to be? Where do you want life to steer you or where do you want to drop anchor?" he asks, now leaning his back against the boat, lying down and staring up at the dimming sky.

"Um, to make money. I want to pay off my debt and buy a house somewhere. Be great to have a dog," I tell him, looking back at that fuzzy-shaved head of his.

"That's it? You don't want a mate in life? You don't want to have kids? I've noticed all you do is talk about money. Money, money, money! There's more to life than dollar bills," he tells me, taking a sip from his wine cooler.

"Well, money does make the world go around. I want to be financially secure. I'm financially insecure right now but I'm working on that as we speak," I say, holding up my business card. "It'd be nice to have a boyfriend but I'm just not there yet. Maybe one day. For now, it's all about Rico. I gotta live life for me. Look at my friend Tommy. He falls in love with a guy and the dude's a big alcoholic and says he doesn't love him anymore. And my last boyfriend cheated on me like there was no tomorrow," I explain to him, now sitting beside him again and staring at the sky, too.

"I gotta put me first. Boyfriends come and go, Captain David!" I finish.

He smiles back at me, his toothy grin unleashed, and he starts rubbing the back of my neck, a minimassage. Aww, that feels so good. If I was a cat, I'd be purring. Meow. Wait, did I just call myself a pussy?

"Sounds like you're not ready to commit again. Sounds like you've been burned, like you've hit some rough weather in the sea of love. I'm ready for love. Been married to the sea for too long. But I won't force it. The universe will send me the right mate when the time's right. When the right wave comes along, I'll catch it and not let go," he says, offering me a sip of his wine cooler. I take some and just lie back with him. I am comforted by David's warmth and sincerity and his realness. This guy is so sexy.

We start kissing, softly, then strongly. He gets up, grabs my hand, and leads me back downstairs to the bunk. I follow, stripping off my shoes, shorts, and shirt along the way until I'm naked. David does the same thing, too.

Once in the bunk, we circle each other like two sharks on the hunt. We attack one another with boundless sexual energy. The boat sways back and forth. The water rocks against the sides. This is hot. For the next few hours, I thrust myself inside David, feeling the warmth of his body and his heart. I wouldn't want to be anywhere else tonight.

Chapter 25

TOMMY

It's early September and there's a slight nip in the air. It's breezy yet warm outside. I hear the trees that line my street swaying and the leaves on the ground swirling into microtwisters. *Adios*, summer! *Bienvenido*, fall. The sun is beginning to set at 7:30 P.M. instead of 8 P.M. And in a month, my new neighborhood will be marked by jack-o'-lanterns on every porch. I can't wait to carve one and put it out on my windowsill. I will call him Pepe the pumpkin.

I am thinking this as I gaze out the bedroom window of my new condo in Dorchester. I'm a DOT guy, as locals would say. I closed on the condo last week and spent all last weekend moving. Rico's bulging biceps and his truck were a great help. There's just so much you can stuff in a cranky Jeep Wrangler named QBAN. We did the move in three trips from Cambridge to Lower Mills. I didn't have a lot of stuff, just my big blue sofa, my Sears queen-sized bed, a small desk, and lots of Old Navy and Gap clothes. I'm glad I had Rico to help me out. Back in Miami, Papi would have called the Perez cavalry, all my male cousins who are mostly mechanics. It would have been a family affair followed by a good Cuban lunch. Boston's not like that, at least not for me.

So this is my second weekend in my condo on Adams Street, and it's been swell so far. I'm the only Hispanic on my condo board and, apparently, the only gay guy, too. So I'm a double minority but I've educated some of my neighbors about the wonders of Miami, how the Cuban coffee down there is called Cuban crack and the kinds of articles I write weekly for the *Daily*. Apparently, everyone here knew who I was before I moved in. So on moving day, one by one, my neighbors dropped by and introduced themselves to the new kid on their block.

"You must be Tommy, in Unit A-1. So glad to meet you. We've heard a lot of good things about you. We need good professional decent people like you," greeted Cecilia McGillicuddy, the vice president of our condo board. She looks a lot like Ethel, the bubbly neighbor on the 1950s show *I Love Lucy*. Cecilia said all this as I was lugging two really heavy boxes of books. I didn't want to be rude so I stood there, listening patiently, and accepted her welcome before my arms abandoned me.

As soon as I dropped off those boxes, Darren, the condo prez, stopped me outside my door and welcomed me to Lower Mills as well. He looked a lot like Captain Kirk from *Star Trek* when the show became a movie franchise.

"So you're a writer with the *Daily*? I've seen your byline. Good stuff. Maybe you can write about our neighborhood and make it look good," he said as I stepped out of my doorway. "The only news about Dorchester in the *Daily* or even the *Chronicle* is about the latest shooting or homicide. They forget that Lower Mills is a safe and nice part of DOT."

I told Darren, "I'll try. Thanks for the idea but I can't guarantee anything."

Similar encounters repeated at least six more times that day. Rico just nodded to everyone and kept hustling. He wanted to be done with this move as well. Apparently, the Italian Stallion had another hot date with the Skipper and his

Goliath in Eastie. I finally met the guy last week at Club Café, and Rico and the Skipper were all over each other like two dolphins splashing in the ocean.

I felt like a third lifejacket on their love boat. They only stayed around for an hour and then they set sail back to David's boat. I remember that night so well because I'm still feeling embarrassed over something I did. I think my mouth got me in trouble.

After Rico and Captain Morgan left, I stayed at the bar by myself and ordered my second Diet Coke with vodka. I was feeling pretty buzzed and I was there celebrating the closing on my condo set for the next day.

I saw the usual crowd of guys, the youngish late-teen set, the early twentysomethings in their AF uniforms, and the older guys wishing they were one of them all over again. Of course, Beyoncé was bouncing on the monitors, followed by Mariah Carey's megamix of her top number one songs from the nineties.

As I paid for my drink, I noticed Mikey with his new boyfriend in tow approaching the bar, coming my way.

Turns out Mikey and this guy, his name is Phil from what I hear, have been dating for a few weeks. I get reports from people who tell me where they've seen them, like I really wanted to know, but when you are part of such a small gay scene, everyone knows your business, whether you like it or not. And the pair is always here at Club Café, Thursdays and Saturdays. Tonight, an August Thursday, was no exception.

Mikey spots me, smiles, and nods his head to greet me.

"Tommy Boy, where have you been? How it's going?" he says before ordering a Corona at the bar. "Hey, this is my friend Phil," Mikey introduces us.

"Nice to meet you, Phil." I shake his hand. He's cute in a Jude Law kind of way but more rugged. He has wavy light brown hair with streaks of blond from the sun. and striking blue eyes. My hair has more volume than Phil's and I am leaner and I look younger. I guess Mikey likes lean guys. I'm not jealous. I repeat: I am not jealous. I swear. I am just cuter. That's all.

It's just awkward when someone you were in love with and so intimate with is now with someone else, doing the same exact thing and going to the same places he did with you a few months before. Phil is my blue-eyed substitute.

After the round of introductions, I tell Mikey that I just bought a condo in Lower Mills and that all is swell at the *Daily* and in life in general. He grabs his drink while his, ahem, *friend* waits for his from the ponytailed bartender.

"That's great to hear, cutie. I'm so happy for you," he says. "I figured you would have moved back to Miami eventually, since that's where you're from. But Boston seems to be work-ing for you," Mikey says before leaving. For a second, he seemed like the charming Mikey I met last winter.

Mikey turns around and I hear him tell Phil, "Cutie, I'm gonna go to the boys' room. Be back in a second." Mikey calls out. Ugh, he calls Phil cutie, too. How uncute of him. "Talk to you later, Tommy."

I hold up my drink. "See ya, Mikey," and I comb my right hand through the bush of curls at the back of my neck.

Mikey left Phil at the bar, right where I am. Can someone spell awkward with a capital A? The guy must know I'm his boyfriend's ex-boyfriend.

He turns to me and smiles, revealing his perfectly straight teeth. This guy can give Rico a run for his smile. When he smiles, small crow's feet form around his eyes.

"So, Tommy, how do you know Mikey? You guys seem to know each other pretty well, from what I can tell," he says, leaning in and looking straight at me. He doesn't seem aware of who I really am. Or could it be he's just a cool guy? I heard he's a real estate broker and used to be a teacher.

I think about how I am going to answer this. Who knows what Mikey has told this guy. But I am going to be honest. I've got a great buzz going and alcohol acts like a brutally honest truth serum for me. I want to sound sincere, not bitter, jealous, bitchy, or anything.

I take a deep breath, focus, and spill my Diet-Coke-and-Vodka-soaked guts.

"Mikey and I dated. We broke up a few months ago. He's a cool guy," I tell Phil, who looks surprised by my disclosure. As he takes in the news, Kelly Clarkson's song "Break Away" appears on the video monitor above us as if she's giving me a hint. But I can't break away. I just stand still in a moment like this, of unknown territory.

"You guys were boyfriends?" Phil asks, all surprised. "I had no idea. He said you guys used to hang out. Why did you guys break up?" Phil continues with his inquisition, taking huge gulps of a beer. He sizes me up, getting an eyeful of me and realizes that I am the guy Mikey most recently dated.

I slurp up half my Diet Coke with vodka, wondering how to answer this diplomatically. Obviously, Mikey didn't tell this guy the whole story. I'm going to be honest, even though Mikey hasn't. I can't speak for Mikey. I am going to tell this guy what I wished someone had told me last winter. Here I go.

"Phil, you seem like a really nice guy. I'm telling you this now because I wish someone had done the same for me. Perhaps I could have avoided a disaster of a relationship," I tell him. Phil is eating up every word I am saying.

"Mikey is a great guy with a good heart but he has some issues. My issue with him was the drinking. He wanted to spend every weekend here and get drunk. It wasn't cool and I got tired of it. I just want you to know what you are getting yourself into. Just be careful," I tell him. "Sometimes I couldn't tell who he was after two or three drinks. He became two different people.

Just keep your guard up and keep him away from the liquor. I wouldn't want you to go through what I went through. It wasn't pretty."

Phil seems stunned by the words, looking at me as if someone has just told him his car was stolen or that his house was on fire. He doesn't seem to know how to take what I have just thrown at him.

"Thanks, Tommy. I appreciate your candor. I'll remember what you said," he says, before pulling out his hand to shake mine. "Nice meeting you. I'm gonna go find Mikey. He's already had three drinks tonight."

I smile and finish the last of my own drink.

"Nice to meet you, too, Phil. Take care," as he walks away into the crowd of guys. I order another drink to deal with the damaging seed I just planted in their relationship. Why did I do that again? Oh yeah, because I wish someone had done the same for me and given me a preview of what was to come.

That was last week, and ever since then, Mikey hasn't acknowledged me in public. Phil must have told him what I said and they probably argued about it.

I don't blame Mikey for ignoring me. It wasn't my place to say anything, and if I hadn't been riding my alcohol buzz, I probably would have kept my big Cubano mouth shut. I know better for next time.

But I can't do anything about that now. Today is a new fall day and I am living in a new neighborhood and embarking on a new chapter in my life. It's a perfect sunny Saturday. I grab my CD player with my Gloria Estefan's *Greatest Hits* disc so I can hit the running trail that hugs the trolley line that connects commuters to the red line at the Ashmont stop.

Gloria starts to sing "Turn the Beat Around" and I start to run around.

"Turn the beat around . . ." she sings.

Chapter 26

KYLE

So since Bella, Eric, and the doc suggest I try and focus on my work and everyday routine, I'm heading to Club Café to cavort and let off some steam. Nothing like making love to a tall cool glass of Apple Martini. Since I'm healthy and alcohol is one of the few things I enjoy, I'm gonna drink up whatever life has to offer.

I walk in on a September Thursday night. Love the breeze coming from outside. I'm wearing a sleeveless red shirt, revealing my tanned arms and my baggy blue Diesel jeans. My hair is all spiked up. I managed to straighten out my soft curls. I look fierce. No one would ever know I had this three-lettered bug inside me. As long as I practice safe sex, what I have is no one else's business, thankyouverymuch. It's been a few weeks since I found out the news and since I met with the nurse for the newly infected HIV study. She's supposed to get back to me this week with the results. Because HIV research tends to get little funding and is often the first to get axed during state budget cuts, she said it may take a few weeks for the results. Maybe tomorrow. I'm sure I won't learn anything new other than what I already know. I'm another queen with HIV.

I make a beeline to the bar. The bartender pours me a

glowing green Apple Martini. I slurp up some of the tart drink. So delish. It's just past 11 P.M. and the boys are trickling in. There's Tommy coming in with his red hoodie. We actually match tonight. He sees me, waves, and walks toward me.

"Tommy Boy, how have you been, Mr. Cuban Clark Kent," I tell him, giving him two air kisses while containing my martini from any spillage. If I had to, I could probably balance my glass on his brown curly hair. The boy needs to trim that bush down a bit.

"Hey, Kyle. Good to see you. How's the modeling going?" he greets me, craning his neck to look up to me as he talks. I am so much taller than him.

"Things are going great. I've been taking some time off just to gather myself. Between all the hosting parties and college lectures, I needed some downtime."

I walk with him to the front bar, where he orders his usual.

"Diet Coke and Vodka," the bartender says and Tommy nods and smiles.

"I love how we don't have words, Tommy," the bartender flirts back with him. "I know what you want just by looking at ya."

Tommy tells me about his most recent story, about the lack of radio programs for Hispanics in Boston and why the city can't support its own full-time Spanish language radio station.

"*Por que?*" I ask Tommy in my bits of broken *español*.

"Because the advertising market hasn't recognized Boston, even though it's 16 percent Latino, as a viable Hispanic market. It will get there, like Miami and Chicago, but Boston is just not there yet, Kyle," he tells me in between sips of his DCV. "There is enough of a population here for a full-time Spanish radio station. But in the meantime, Boston Hispanics are being tuned out, if you know what I mean."

I look at Tommy, at those big brown eyes of his, and say "Hmmm. Bery interesante, señor."

We chat for a little bit and I'm feeling the first martini swimming through my body. I'm feeling good. So I order another Apple Martini, or Mansana Martini, as the Hispanics would say.

As I stand here and chat, I think of how healthy he is. Tommy can have any guy he wants. He's negative. He has his whole life ahead of him and he wasted a few months of it with that drunk Mikey. Who knows if they had safe sex? Who knows how many of these young guys are positive and aren't saying a word about it, like I am. Who knows how many don't know what their status is? I'm a living example of that. I really thought I was negative.

I must be thinking too much to myself because I suddenly hear Tommy calling my name repeatedly.

"Kyle . . . Kyle . . . oye! Are you with me?" he says. "Are you okay? You looked really angry for a second there," he tells me, putting his hand on my shoulder.

"Yeah, I'm fine, better than fine. I can't complain, Tommy. I'm healthy as I can be." I look down at my drink and then scan the bar for any cute boys.

They all look so happy, laughing among one another and drinking and grooving to Carrie Underwood's country dance mix, followed by Daddy Yankee's reggaeton mix. That's the first time I hear the veejay playing him here.

These club guys don't have a care in the world. They are probably all negative just like Tommy and they don't even realize how lucky they are. I wish I could turn back time and transform my positive status into a negative. What would I say if I took one of these guys back to my place to mess around with and he asked me if I was HIV positive? I never even thought about that. I've been so caught up in the science of the disease, the viral load, and the CD4 counts, that I haven't really dealt with the emotional part, the possible rejection. I can't afford for word to get out that Kyle Andrews, *Real Life* celeb, is sick. Word would spread faster than an instant message in a male-for-male chat room. My modeling career and speaking engagements would dry up faster than this martini.

"Well, Kyle, you seem a little bit down. If you need to talk, give me a call," he says with a warm smile. I'm so touched by his kindness. We've never really had heavy talks, just superficial ones, but the last person I would want to share the personal details of my life with is a reporter. This is a story I can't afford to have published in the *Daily*. No offense, Tommy Boy.

"I know we're not that close but I know what it's like to be a newcomer to this city. Besides, I'm a good listener," Tommy continues. "That's why God gave me big ears, to listen to others," he says, laughing at his own joke. He always does that.

He shakes my hand and I give him a hug-hug and kiss-kiss on the cheek.

"Tommy, that's so sweet of you, but I'm fine. Go find your wingman Rico. I'm sure he's waiting for you somewhere," and so he goes, disappearing into the crowd of guys.

Seeing all these cute twinks living it up without a worry in the world only inflames my anger. Why me? God, what did I do to become positive? Who gave this to me? I order another martini to numb the pain and this warped reality I've become a resident of. Am I now the star of *The Real Life: HIV*?

I don't care if I get drunk, anything that will prevent me from harping on HIV. I go to sleep and it's there. I wake up and it's there. No matter what I do during the day, working out or talking to my agent, it never goes away. You can't outrun yourself.

I finish up my third drink and leave the bar. I don't want to take the chance of slipping up to someone that I have this thing. I venture back out onto the brick-paved Columbus Avenue and walk alone up and down the South End streets, crying my heart out. The fall breeze comforts me, tickling my face. I walk up Columbus, then down Berkeley, then up Boylston Street until I tire myself out like a flickering candle.

God, damn you! I pass out in my bed, trying to forget.

The next day, my drunken stupor is awakened by my ring tone, "My Humps," by the Black Eyed Peas, thumping on my cell.

"What you gon' do with all that junk," the phone sings.

Yes, that's my ring tone because, well, I love my humps. I don't recognize the 617 number. I pick it up.

It's Nicole, the nurse from the hospital conducting the HIV study.

"Kyle, good morning. I hope I didn't wake you up," she says in her pleasant voice.

"Ah, nah. I'm up. So how am I doing? Can I be in the study?" I talk to her with my eyes closed to shut out the prism of light pouring in from the bay windows in my bedroom.

"Kyle, I have some good news. We can't use you for the test," she says before I interrupt her.

"Well, that's not good news because that would mean I was infected more than six months ago," I fire back. She jumps back into the dialogue before I can pop another word in.

"No, you don't understand, Kyle. Let me finish. We can't use you for the HIV study because your antibody test came back negative. This is very good news, but we need to run another test to break the tie we have with your positive result from Provincetown and this negative result in Boston."

I prop right up in my bed. This must be a dream.

"Wait. I'm negative. I don't understand. How could I go from positive to negative?" I ask her, climbing out of my bed and staring at myself in the mirror with a confused expression on my face.

"Kyle, I don't want to give you false hope but it seems that one of the tests is a mistake, most likely the first one. I hand-delivered your vials to the lab from the test we took a few weeks ago and you were the only one tested that day so the chances are slimmer that there was a mistake," she explains, a mix of enthusiasm and concern in her voice. "I have alerted Dr. Goldstein about the results and he wants you to come in later today or Monday for a retest. I am hoping the best for you, Kyle. This is very rare."

I pace back and forth on my hardwood floors, elated yet concerned, euphoric yet confused about the news she just woke me up with. I'm now drunk with happiness even as I feel a bit hung over from last night.

"Because of your viral load and CD4 counts from the fol-low-up test a few weeks ago, which show you to be un-detectable, there is good reason to believe you are probably negative," she says.

I'm in shock, and yet I'm not sure what to believe. This was a mistake the whole time? Oh, lucky heavens!

"Nicole, thank you so much. You just made my day, my week, my life. I'm calling Dr. Goldstein to come in today for another antibody test."

I hang up and jump up and down in my bedroom like a cheerleader. I call Bella and then I call Eric and share the good news.

"Kyle, that means you *are* negative. They screwed up your tests, boy!" Eric tells me on the phone from his loft in San Francisco. I woke him up. I forgot about the three-hour time difference.

"I'm so happy for you. I knew something was off when you told me your viral load and CD4 counts. Your numbers are too good for someone with HIV."

I am still jumping up and down from joy as I talk to Eric, which makes my hardwood floors creak.

"As happy as I am to learn I may be negative, I wish you were negative, too, Eric," I tell him.

"Yeah, me, too, Kyle. I never thought I would get this either," he says in a sullen tone. "But you have to make the best of your situation and I am not going to let this beat me down. Now, Kyle, get off your ass, go get retested, and then celebrate. I am happy for you, dude!"

Chapter 27

RICO

"Hi, Powerpuff girl! It's me. Buzz me in." I'm talking to Tommy on my cell outside his building, which looks like a four-story former brick schoolhouse. I've been buzzing his condo but he hasn't answered. He's probably listening to La Gloria Estefan on his new stereo or something. "I'm buzzing you in right now. Come in," he shouts from the intercom as Conga jams in the background. I knew it! He's in Gloria mode right now. A few seconds later, after walking down five steps from the building's front door, I'm at Tommy's wooden door, A-1, just like the steak sauce.

It's a cooler September afternoon than the others, which hints that our warm days are pretty much fading. Winter's not too far away. Shit. Gotta pull out my snow boots in a few weeks.

I was in the neighborhood trying to rent out an apartment for a guy in Pope's Hill and I thought I'd say hi to Tommy Boy. I haven't seen his place since I helped him move in at the end of August because I've been hanging out a lot with David. Thinking of him makes me smile. I kinda like the guy.

"Dude, you've done a lot in the past two weeks. Shit, do you want to fix up my bedroom in Savin Hill?" I tell him as I check out the Pergo wood-laminate floors he installed in his hallways and living room to replace that icky white carpet that was here. He painted the walls a soft light yellow, a big improvement from its former cum color.

"Are you sure the guys from *Queer Eye for the Straight Guy* didn't stop by and give your place an ambush extreme makeover?" I check out the colorful poster prints of Cuba, Miami, and Fort Lauderdale in Tommy's living room. It's obvious how much he loves South Florida and his background. He's also proud of his place, too. He worked hard for it and it's paying off. As much as I'd like to have my own place one day, I can't help feeling very happy for *mio amico*.

"I've been working around the clock on the weekends. This condo is like me. The more I work on it, the more I work on myself," Tommy says, standing in his bedroom now, which he painted a seafoam green. He then shows me the second bedroom, now a small office with a Pier I Import denim love seat.

"So what's been going on, Rico," he says as he fixes me a glass of lime Gatorade. We're now sitting in his kitchen on a small breakfast table that is shaped like a Milano cookie, long and oval. "How is Popeye?" he says, giggling to himself. Tommy really is Velveeta personified with his cheezy jokes but what can you do. He's my friend. I accept him for all his flaws, no matter how corny they are.

"David and his *Goliath* are cool. We've been hanging out on his boat watching the sunset, going out to dinner and having fucking great sex. He's such a cool guy. No hang-ups or emotional baggage. Just a free spirit. Takes my breath away, Tommy. Really."

Tommy takes a big sip from his Diet Coke can. I noticed in his refrigerator that he has two shelves stocked with Diet Coke and another one just for bottles of the green Gatorade. Talk about OCD. If you were to cut a vein on his arm, Diet Coke would probably pour out. He probably pisses pure Gatorade.

"So, Rico, why not date the guy? You obviously like him. You keep sleeping over on his boat and you guys go out to eat and drink. What's the big deal? Date the guy before he gives up on you the way you give up on all these other guys you take home," Tommy says before letting out a big burp.

I can top his burp. *Burrrp!* Take that.

"Whoa. That was foul, Rico. You're the burpinator," he says.

"I don't know, Tommy. I like him. I really do. I haven't felt like this in a long time. Yeah, we have fun in and out of his sack. I just don't want to commit, that's all. They're too many fish in the sea. Oh shit, that sounds like something David would say." I take more gulps of the Gatorade.

Here comes Tommy now, giving me the whole why-I-should-date speech.

"See, that's what I don't understand about you. You're a great guy, hot, smart, and a little cheap but that's another story, and here you have a guy who seems to really care about you. Sometimes, you have to take a chance when it comes to dating. Who knows what you're passing up with this guy. Eventually, he's gonna want a commitment if you keep up seeing him as much as you do. I know I would. You can't always put up this don't-fuck-with-me invisible force field. Every once in a while, you've got to let someone into your heart, Rico. Date the dude, Rico!"

"Don't Rico-me, Tommy Boy." I've heard this speech, or was that a queer cheer, from Tommy before but it's hard for me to articulate my reluctance to date. It's not that I don't want to date one day. I . . . just . . . can't . . . date anyone right now. I just want to fuck and play. I don't want to get to know someone only to have them betray my trust. I can't let my guard down. No fucking way.

"There's nothing wrong with being single and content and having fun. One day I'll settle down with someone. I just don't want to get hurt and deal with all the emotional fallout afterward. It's taking me so long to get back on my feet," I tell Tommy.

"This past year has been about me. I don't want to get too close to anyone right now. I'm not like you, Tommy. You love being in a relationship, like the one with Mikey, at least when he was sober. I like being alone. I'm a lone wolf." I start howling like a wolf.

Tommy finishes up his drink, rolling his eyes.

"But sometimes, even lone wolves are never alone for that long," he says with his boyish grin. "Well, one day, I hope you find that right guy even though I think he's on a boat called *Goliath* in East Boston and his name is David, not that I'm trying to say anything. I just want you to be happy and Captain Morgan seems to make you happy, that's all." He now lets out another burp.

"What are you doing this Saturday?" Tommy asks.

"David's gonna take me sailing while it's still somewhat warm outside. I can't wait. Never been sailing. It'll be just us and the ocean."

"That's so romantical, Rico. See, you guys are a couple without even having the label. Reel the guy in. He's a keeper. That's so sweet that he's gonna take you out on the boat. He probably doesn't do that for just anyone," Tommy says, twirling one of his curls.

"Yeah, it'll be fun to get away from the city for a bit. I want to see him work the boat. Weather should be good Saturday," I say, topping his previous burp.

"Take that, Tommy Boy!" and he fires back with another Diet Coke burp.

A few more times and we sound like a symphony of burps. We break out laughing on this funny-looking Milano cookie–shaped table and I high-five Tommy when he manages to belt a really loud burp.

"Welcome to my home," Tommy says, opening his arms out in a welcoming gesture. "*Mi casa es tu casa.* Drop by whenever you want."

I wink back, "Thanks, Tommy Boy. *Burrrrp!*"

"Ugh, Rico, that one smelled. Gross!"

Twenty minutes and twenty burps later, I say goodbye to Tommy (I won the burping contest, by the way) and I hop back into my truck. As I drive on the winding Adams Street in Dorchester through Lower Mills and Cedar Grove past the cemetery and the giant nursery, Tommy's words resonate in my head. "Every once in a while, you've got to let someone into your heart, Rico. Date the dude!"

Why am I so fucked up? I have this great guy who adores me and I'm resisting him, keeping him at bay like an unwanted barge. Why can't I just give him an express pass to my heart? He's sort of in there and I'm not interested in being with anyone else right now. The thought of him being with someone else actually grosses me out, makes me want to barf. I'm just gonna take it day by day. Maybe I'll get bored and find some other guy to fuck around with. But the idea of David taking me sailing, something I've never done before, warms my Italian heart. When I see him, I just melt inside because he radiates this kindness I rarely see in guys lately. I can't wait to see him and go out on the water with him. A few minutes later, I pull up into Savin Hill and into the driveway of the house and I think of how long it's been since someone did something nice like that for me. It feels good and I'm kinda getting used to the feeling.

Chapter 28

KYLE

Thank fucking God! I got the results this afternoon from my follow-up blood test with Dr. Goldstein at Mass Regional Hospital. He called me to tell me the news at 11 A.M. today, Thursday.

"Kyle, it looks like the results are what we hoped for. You're negative. This test is consistent with your test from the study. Congratulations," he said, in that scientific, robotic tone of his.

"Thank you so much. This never felt right to me," I told him. "So if I got the false positive, that means someone has a false negative?" I told him in a serious concerned tone. "Look, I know people make mistakes but this is a huge one, mister! Someone out there thinks he's negative when he's really positive. You need to get to the bottom of this. The potential catastrophic consequences are too great."

Dr. Goldstein sounded nervous when I said that. He began stuttering.

"Ahh . . . I . . . I know. I've never dealt with something like this before. Neither have our fellow doctors. We suspect your first blood sample was contaminated with someone else's blood. We are conducting an internal investigation about this and we've contacted the blood bank," he explained. "Kyle, I am

so sorry. Here you are, doing a good deed to inspire other people to get tested and this mistake has turned your life upside
down. On behalf of the hospital, I apologize profusely. This
shouldn't have happened to you. I promise you, we will figure
this out."

As relieved as I am about the results, I shudder to think
what would have happened if I hadn't volunteered for the
study. My instinctual reaction was to send my hand through
the phone and choke the doctor for taking away my peace of
mind for the past few weeks. For making me think I was
gonna die sooner than I had expected, for making me question
my own reality, my own sanity.

It could have been worse. I could have *been* positive. This is
a blessing in disguise. Absolutely. I will never take things for
granted anymore. *Carpe diem*, as the teen Ethan Hawke shouted
in the movie *Dead Poets Society*. Live for now! And that's what
I am gonna do. This is the new Kyle, the 2.0 model, the one
that feels right and who will not get worked up over silly little
things.

I feel like I have been given another chance. And so with
that, I've decided to put my fame to good use. Since I know
what it was like to be positive, even for a little while, I have this
unique perspective. I know what I'd want someone to say if
they were in my shoes. This scare was my epiphany, my reality
check. No more bar drama or drunken nights with Apple
Martinis or Cosmos. No more whining about life and not getting my fair share or the better end of the stick.

Today, I called the organization that handles the "KNOW-
ING IS POWERFUL" ads and offered to volunteer. Turns out
the coordinator, Rene Sanchez, is a friend of Randy's, from the
Gay and Lesbian Community Center here in Boston. Rene
was enthusiastic about my interest in volunteering with the
condom distributions at Club Café and about lending my good
name and fame to the cause.

"You could make a big impact and be an inspiration to all these younger gay guys. They don't have a lot of openly gay men their age to look up to," Rene said over the phone earlier today. "We are about to embark on a new "KNOWING IS POWERFUL" campaign. I think it would be great if we could photograph you for one of the ads, Mr. Andrews." he said.

"Call me Kyle. Mr. Andrews makes me sound like a teacher or something. Not!" I told him.

I call Eric and Bella again and leave voice-mail messages already confirming what I had believed before. I'm negative. I'm alive and I'm on top of the world again. I'm gonna go celebrate in my own Kyle way.

Half an hour later, after changing into my blue jeans and red sweatshirt, I head toward the Prudential Center in Back Bay, a few blocks from me. I coast up the escalators to the second level and stroll inside the brightly lighted mall, which cuts through the heart of Back Bay and the South End. Passing the kiosks that sell candles and Russian dolls, I see the sign, the one with the little cow on the front, and it leads me to my destination.

"Can I help you?" the teenager in the green apron asks me from behind the cool counter.

"Yes, I would like to have a giant cup of milk chocolate ice cream with a thick peanut butter swirl, extra nuts, and whipped cream," I say, tapping at the glass. I love Ben and Jerry's Ice Cream and I couldn't think of a better way to celebrate being un-HIV.

"Coming right up," the boy in green says.

Two minutes later, he hands me the heavy frozen cup and a pink spoon. I give him a $5 bill from my jean pocket and leave him $2 in his tip box. I'm feeling that good. I never want to take anything for granted again.

I sit in the mall's food court at a corner table that overlooks Boylston Street and all the shoppers and workers scurrying like metropolitan work ants in a midday rush hour.

I smile to myself and dig into my ice cream like it was the first one I've ever had, enjoying the explosion of peanut butter, chocolate, and nuts in my mouth. So yummy that it tickles my tongue. This celebration is a party of one. Thank you, God!

Chapter 29

RICO

"All aboard!" David shouts my way as soon as he spots me walking on the dock toward the *Goliath*. I leap onto the boat and he gives me a hug once I land.

"Good to see you, man," he says.

"Same here, captain!"

"You're gonna be my first mate on our cruise today," he says, rubbing his hands into my hair. My body tingles whenever he touches me.

I brought a picnic basket with a P and J sandwich, a turkey sandwich, and a veggie sub. I wasn't sure what he likes. I also brought some beers and Sprites.

David looks yummier today than on other days. The fall sun highlights the soft light brown hairs on his forearms and on his shaved head. He's wearing a loose white T-shirt and baggy jean shorts that fall over his bare hips.

"Are you ready to hit the Atlantic?" he says, standing over me, his frame eclipsing the sun behind him as I put the basket down near the wheel.

"Anytime you are, skipper. I'll do whatever you say, Captain Nemo!" I say, wondering where to park my Italian ass on this narrow sailboat.

"Go ahead and take a seat wherever you want and we'll be on our way," he says. He starts to untie the two lines that moor the sailboat, which bobs gently in the calm harbor waters. The veins on his arms tighten from the action and I'm all turned on already. The other boats are bobbing in the water, too, like trinkets on a charm bracelet.

"Put on the lifejacket there by the steps of the cabin door-way," he says. He then does a last-minute general check of the boat.

I find a seat in a corner, with a perfect view of David's ass and his lean, GI Joe body.

"Sit back, relax, and enjoy the ride, Rico." He returns back to the wheel. I watch David do his thing. Shit, he's hot and he's doing this just for me, taking the boat out. I really appreciate it. I'm all about adventure, but yet, I've never been on a friggin' boat.

I grab a lifejacket and tie it tightly around me. I forgot to mention to him that I can't swim. Never needed to in the Berkshires and I just never got around to it. I only hit the beach to get some sun and check out the guys, not the water. So I would be lying if I didn't say that I'm a little nervous and hopefully I'm not showing it or anything. But I can't help but feel safe in David's hands. If anything happens, David will be my lifejacket. I'm wearing a sleeveless shirt to get some sun on my arms cuz I won't be able to dress like this in a few weeks.

The boat slowly drifts away from the dock and David turns the key to start the small engine. It comes to life with a low mechanical hum. Slowly, David begins to back out of his slip, which is flanked by other liveaboards and boat lovers. Within a few minutes, David clears his slip and *Goliath* gently churns the tranquil marina waters as he navigates it out of the murky green channel.

We pass other boaters on our way out of East Boston, then Dorchester Bay with the sun-filled sky filling out the rest of the scene. Fellow boaters wave to us when they see us, and David returns their aquatic greeting as if they're old friends. We pass by the necklace of small Harbor Islands such as Thompson, Spectacle, and Lovells islands as we slowly cruise out of Boston Harbor and into the Atlantic. Terns fly above us and the other boaters like voyeurs watching on any given reality show. The wind begins to pick up steam out there on the lip of the coast. I totally dig this. I can see why David just likes being on the boat. No worries. Just you and the sea.

As Boston grows tiny in the distance, we're out to sea but not too far that we can't see the picturesque Colonial and Victorian houses of Squantum in Quincy. In the distance, I see the old weather observatory at the top of the Blue Hills. I went up there once hiking and you can see the entire city, the Atlantic, and the South Shore from all sides. They're called the Blue Hills because the early explorers said the hills gave off a blue sheen from the coast, just like I'm seeing now.

At this point, David cuts the engine and we just cruise slowly. All I hear are the waves lapping against the boat.

"Rico, I'm gonna go and raise the sails. You ready?" he says from the wheel. "We're gonna catch us some wind."

"You're gonna break wind, what?" I'm not sure about what he just said because his back was turned. I'm just sitting here riding shotgun.

"No, we're gonna catch the wind, silly. Be careful with that beautiful face of yours. I'm gonna swing the boom your way. Duck or you'll end up taking a swim overboard," he says. Suddenly I feel like Sarah Jessica Parker's character in the movie *Failure to Launch*, when Matthew McConaughey takes her sailing.

I duck to be on the safe side even before he does anything. As soon as I do, David moves this large pole carrying the sail, I suppose, above me to catch Mother Nature's breath. David adjusts the position and he uses the lines to secure it just right.

The sails go up. They fill up with air, billowing like sheets flowing in a backyard. He tightens the lines and the boat hits fifth gear or something because we pick up lots of sudden speed. Back at the wheel, he shifts his weight on his sculpted calves and keeps his arms on the wheel. Every now and then, he turns around and glances back, making sure I'm still on board and alive. I'm turned on. The quick manuever got me even harder. I like a guy in control of things. This is all so new to me. I'm excited.

David keeps the boat on course as it glides along the coast-line, with a small whitish wake in the front. I'm enjoying this aquatic joyride. The wind brushes up against my face and the sun keeps me warm. When we hit a big dip in the waves, I feel the soft spray of the ocean misting my face and arms. We sail for a bit along the coast for about half an hour or so when he slows down the boat. We drift slowly toward Plymouth Harbor, where he then drops the anchor in an inlet here. He comes over to my seat and kisses me.

What is it about this guy that gets under my skin? Maybe it's the way he takes control of his life the same way he controls this boat. He seems to live life on his own terms, his own way. No direct boss. If he doesn't like where he is, he literally picks up and goes somewhere else. But there's more to him. He is kind, sexy, and just, real. I've never met someone so levelheaded and easygoing. He doesn't seem to care if others like him or what they think of him. He projects a "whatever" attitude about things in general, and at the same time, he has this zest for life and doing things his way. He's only been completely good to me ever since we met and we've gone out on a few dates. And the sex? Like two brushfires coming together in a forest and burning hot. I'm sitting here on the boat with a giant boner that's about to break out of my black athletic shorts.

I just feel comfortable with this dude. I'm drawn to him. I haven't felt like this in so long.

"Are you hungry? I brought some sandwiches," I tell him after we kiss a bit. I taste the salt above his lips from his sweat.

"Great. I can eat anything," he says, going through the basket of sandwiches. He grabs a Sprite and the turkey sandwich. I grab the P and J and a beer.

"This tastes great, Rico. You make a killer turkey sandwich," he says in between bites. I used low-fat mayo, fresh turkey, tomatoes, and lettuce on wheat bread.

"You taste great," I tell him and he laughs under his breath with his mouth full of food.

"You're too much, man. You crack me up." I bite into my sandwich and all I really want to do is bite into David. He starts explaining to me the ins and outs of sailing, why he keeps the engine handy, and how sailing saves on gas. As he talks, I notice a line of airplanes heading north, on their way to Logan. The sunlight bounces off each of their bellies, which makes me squint as cumulus clouds drift across the sky. I guess we're sort of under a landing path. The planes come in over the ocean as they descend over Boston.

"On a day like this, we could sail down the coast to Ptown and the Vineyard in no time. But this spot is quiet off Plymouth and it's nice to watch the kites float about the park right over there. See?" He gestures over starboard, and in the distance, I see some red and blue kites dancing in the air. I guess the day's perfect for that, too. I can stay here all day with this guy. I feel like I learn so much by being around him. He calms me.

"I've been wanting to ask you something," David says, wearing this beautiful tender expression. I lick the peanut butter off my fingers and listen.

"Go ahead. I'm all yours," I tell him.

"Well, we've been hanging out quite a bit and I've been growing pretty fond of you," he says, the boat rocking like one of those mechanical cribs parents buy these days for their newborns. David leans closer and my stomach tightens. This guy just turns me on like no one else has.

"I know you said you're not looking for a boyfriend and you just want to have fun and play and I totally respect that but I prefer to be one-on-one with a guy. I'm getting to that point with you that I rather it just be us. I like to be monogamous and you're the only guy I've been with and want to be with for now," he says. He lifts his hand and rubs the back of my neck. I'm getting goose bumps.

"That's sweet of you, dude. Really. But I don't want a boyfriend," I deadpan. I don't even know why I'm saying this anymore. I'm pushing him away. I don't want to trust and then be betrayed. I don't want to let someone into my heart, only to reject it by going off with another guy. I see all these couples who cheat on each other and that seems to be the norm in gay relationships. I haven't been able to make them work. So what's the point? I'd rather push someone away before they get too close to me. I'd rather do the pushing than have them shove my heart off a cliff. They can't hurt me if I hurt them first.

"Rico, I know you're scared. I can sense it. You're a tough dude and a strong guy, but with the matters of the heart, you've been hurt pretty bad. I just want you to give me a chance. That's all. I'm not saying for us to get married or anything but I just want to know that you'll at least try and be monogamous with me. Give me a chance, you Italian stud," he says with a warm smile, which melts my heart although I don't show it.

"You don't understand, David, how hard it is for me to trust someone again. I feel the same way you do. I like you a lot and you're opening up my heart. It's just . . . hard, you know," I tell him, looking out at the water and the small white-tipped waves. The wind makes David's white T-shirt ripple, and it's rubbing up against his small hardened nipples. I love those small nipples, yum. I wouldn't want anyone else to have access to them except me.

"Just think about it, Rico. That's all I'm saying. Just think about giving not just me a chance, but us a chance. Who knows where this can go? All I know is that I like you and want to be with you even more," he says. This guy says all the right things. Where did he come from again? Next thing I know, the words come out of my mouth, as if by reflex.

"Okay," I say. "I'll think about it." He breaks out into a wide grin and he grabs my hand and kisses it. I close my eyes and feel the warmth of his hands and his lips.

"Thank you, Rico, for giving us a chance," he says, snuggling himself in between my legs as I caress him in my arms, feeling the fuzziness of his shaved head on my chin.

"You won't regret it," he says. "You'll see. I spoil guys I like."

"Oh yeah, David? I think I can get used to that, and afternoons like this. Thanks again for this great afternoon. It's one of the sweetest things anyone has ever done for me."

"Well, it's not over. I want to jump into the water with you for a bit and go swimming. I want to see your sea legs in action," he says, all excited.

I take three gulps of my bottled water and imagine myself drowning and flailing my arms in the water, the headline in tomorrow's *Daily*: RICO COULDN'T SWIM! HE TOLD NO ONE.

"Well . . . about that. There's something I need to tell you first, David."

Chapter 30

TOMMY

Damn, it's chilly tonight! A premature cold front has interrupted whatever was left of the cool and warm weather we were having in Btown. *"Coño!"* as Mami would say.

It's Thursday night, and as usual, I'm back at the CC. So much has happened this past year. I fell in love, fell out of love, bought my condo, and wrote some great stories for the *Daily*. My next story will be on . . . well, I'll get to that in just a second.

I feel at peace with myself and it's not bad being single. Rico's rubbing off on me. Playing is fun. No commitments and you can walk away anytime. But I'd rather have a boyfriend to come home to, someone to share my thoughts with at night, someone to be with in that special way. But the single life ain't bad either. I feel like the gay version of Carrie Bradshaw on HBO's *Sex in the City* but I'm less puny and I prefer my Old Navy threads to her Prada and Jimmy Choo labels.

So that's why I'm here, looking for the newest members of this Boston boys club, who are somewhere around here cruising the bar and listening to Britney, Beyoncé, and Missy Elliott. The veejay really needs to get some new music. I am having flashbacks to last year's hits. The songs are getting so old that they are beginning to sound retro. The veejay needs to spice things up a bit. I am going to suggest to him that he play some Gloria Estefan, since she's coming up here in concert this November as part of her last road tour. I have an interview already set up with her. Whoo-hoo! Funny how I used to live a few miles from her in Miami Beach and it's in the land of Paul Revere and baked bean cuisine that I get to meet the Queen of Conga.

"C'mon, shake your body baby, do the conga!" I would hear her blasting in 1985 from the small kitchen radio back at Papi and Mami's house. Whenever that song came on, Mami would grab me, no matter what I was doing, and start twirling me around the kitchen, where we would dance, dance, and dance. But that's a whole other story, perhaps a submission for the *Chicken Soup for the Latino Soul* book.

After taking a lap around the club, I stop at the front bar and wait for Rico. He's running late again. He'll probably show up with David. No matter what Rico says, I know he likes David deep down inside and he doesn't want to let this fish get away. He's precious cargo, one of those rare finds in the gay world that you just want to hold on to. One day, I'll find my mate, too. For now, though, it's work, the condo, and playing (plowing) the field, in a nice way. *Ahhh*, life is good.

So as I wait at the bar, I scan the guys browsing at the hard bodies on display in the nooks of the bar. Even though it's chilly outside, about 45 degrees, the guys inside are still sporting their summer wear—sleeveless shirts or tank tops with jeans and flip-flops.

Across the bar, I see Mikey with Phil, who looks completely annoyed, or just constipated. I can't tell the difference between the two facial expressions. I know exactly what's going on through his mind. Mikey looks tipsy as usual and this will probably be another night of taking care of Johnnie

Walker. He just doesn't get it. I still wish he would get it and get some help. His Corona bottle is almost empty. So nothing changes and everything is the same over there.

In the dining area, I see judge Jack McGlame with his partner Dermot, eating some shrimp and salad as they both sip bottled water. He sees me from across the room and waves. I boomerang the wave and mouth "Hola!" and nod up with my almost-empty drink and a smile.

By the coat check, I see Josh, that new Channel 7 weatherman. I remember Rico telling me how he hooked him up with an apartment in Back Bay—and with his dick. The weathergirl is checking in his blazer from tonight's 10 P.M. newscast. Over by the bathroom door, I see that young guy Rico also hooked up with last winter, the Josh Harnett lookalike, Topher. Maybe it's a good thing that Rico is running late with David because all his old tricks are in the CC house tonight. It could make for an interesting night. Drama, no one does it better than Rico.

A crew of lesbians sits in the front lounge, laughing out loud and sharing drinks and stories about their week. Turns out one couple recently got married here in the Bay State, which is more of a Gay State thanks to the legalization of gay marriage. They are toasting their glasses of champagne with much revelry. They remind me of the circle of lady friends on Showtime's lesbo series *The L Word*. The cool thing about that show is that the "L" word can mean love, lust, liberty, lesbian, life, or lactating. It's fun watching these women just let loose, feeling so comfortable with each other and being them gayselves.

As I ready to order another drink from the bartender, he has beat me to it. He's already sliding me a nice cool tall glass of Diet Coke and Vodka. The Coke still fizzes.

"There you go, Tommy," says Rudy, the ponytailed bartender who splits his time between Club Café and The

A-House in Provincetown. "I can read minds, you know," he says, lifting up his left eyebrow.

"Yeah, yeah, yeah. That's what you always say," I answer back, placing a crisp $5 bill on the slick wooden counter. "Good thing I'm so predictable, right?" And we share a laugh.

I turn around and I see Kyle waltz into the club, walking like the diva he has always been, but he seems to walk with more purpose lately. People are coming up to him and saying hi and asking for his autograph.

Ever since he's become a spokesman for those "KNOW-ING IS POWERFUL" ads, Kyle's career has found its second wind. He travels the city to talk about HIV prevention and he is expected to speak before Congress about all these funding cuts to state HIV clinics and programs. His face graces those ads on buses, subways, and billboards and not just in Boston but around the country. One of those posters is in the bathroom here at the club, by the towelette dispenser.

The ad says, "KNOWING IS POWERFUL. GET TESTED TODAY!" with him looking seriously intense while holding another cute guy's hand.

I have to admit, Kyle has really become a quasi–gay man's hero. For all his antics on *The Real Life*, he seems to have grown up and found a new calling.

I call him over from the bar. He spots me and walks over to me with his mouth wide open from shock. I guess he notices my new look.

"Tommy Perez . . . oh . . . my . . . gosh! Your hair! It's gone! You shaved it off. You look like Demi Moore in *G.I. Jane*!" he declares as if making some important discovery. "How have you been? I heard you bought a condo! Congratulations!" He greets me with one of his hug-hugs and air-kisses. But this time, he rubs the top of my shaved head as if he were trying to make a wish from a genie's bottle. Kyle is wearing khaki pants and a light blue T-shirt that reflects the blue in his eyes. A button on his shirt repeats the HIV ad's slogan.

"Kyle, good to see you, too," I tell him after we hug. "Yeah, I finally mowed down my hedge of curls. It was getting out of hand. It was growing out of control. It was like a Chia Pet. The more it got wet, the more it grew. I had to tame it. So you like?" I tell him as we both sit down on two bar stools at the corner of the bar.

"Yes, I like very much. You look more distinguished. I see some Cuban gray hairs popping up in there," he says. "It looks very George Clooney when he was on *ER*."

That's a nice compliment. George Clooney is hot. Maybe he'll be in *Ocean's 13*. But I need to get back on track here.

"So I want to talk to you about something and it's not my hair or lack of it. I've been seeing your ads and I've been hearing about all the work you have been doing on behalf of AIDS awareness and how you've been really working hard to reach out to young people. You've been doing a lot of good work," I say as Kyle starts blushing, his dark brown eyelashes flapping like Minnie Mouse's in one of those vintage black-and-white Disney cartoons.

"Oh why, thank you, Tommy. I appreciate that," he says with a grin as he continues to play with my fuzzy brown hair. "I just want to make a difference, you know. I feel so blessed, Tommy. It's been such a life-changing year."

Kyle seems so centered, a paragon of inner peace. I wonder what changed in him. Maybe he'll tell me after I make my pitch.

"So, I want to write a profile on you for our Features section in *The Boston Daily*. I think you would make a great story, Kyle."

Kyle's face lights up, becoming ever so animated. He's such a character.

"Why G.I. Jane, what a *great* idea!" he says. "I see the headline for the story: THE REAL KYLE!"

We burst out laughing in our corner of the bar and he gives me his new business card so I can call him up and set up an interview for next week.

"I'm gonna go walk around and say hi to the masses, Tommy," Kyle says as he rises from the bar stool. "I'll catch you in a few. Thank you again for offering to write a story about me. I think a lot of people might learn something from what I have to say."

We toast our glasses.

"I agree. I'll call you next week. Have fun," I tell him as he smiles and walks away into the throng of men in the main bar.

As Kyle leaves, Rico finally arrives with David. They spot me from the entryway, where a video monitor blasts the new Mariah Carey song, which has been playing over and over all summer.

Rico nods up and walks in with David in tow. I've never seen them hold hands together. They look like . . . *a couple?*

"Tommy, what's going on?" Rico greets me with his usual bear-hug.

"Same 'ole, same 'ole. Just here with my drink scoping out the place," I tell him without trying to sound cynical. "Maybe I'll find another story for the *Daily* here or something else. You never know."

David is more reserved and shakes my hand. He is more of the quiet type but Rico says he's pretty loud in bed. They make waves on that boat pretty often.

"Hi, Tommy," David says, standing thisclose to Rico.

Rico begins to tell me how they had a great dinner down the street at another nameless South End restaurant known only for its address, kind of like in New York. They wanted to stop in here for a drink before heading back to David's boat for some late-night lovin'.

I can't help taking advantage of the opportunity right in front of me. "*Well*, you guys look like a couple," I tell Rico and David, who is smiling as if I just voiced what he's been thinking—and hoping—all along. They really did look like a couple and would be if Rico would just take a chance and let his heart lead him instead of his cock.

Rico smirks my way and says, "Yeah, something like that." I smile back at Rico, wink, and whisper in his ear, "Well, that's a start. You go, boy!"

After two drinks, the Captain and Rico decide to leave and have their own private party aboard the *Goliath*. I wish them well. I am really happy for Rico. He is on his way to coupledom.

I still wish I were on the same path. Now it's just me here at the bar with the bartender, and I don't mind at all although it would be nice to date again. Who am I kidding, I love having a boyfriend, a companion, but I won't settle for less.

Watching the parade of men go by makes me realize there are so many men out there to date and perhaps, one day, I will fall in love again. But for now, I'm sitting back, enjoying my Vodka with Diet Coke and just feeling *good, hella* good, as Gwen Stefani would say. Suddenly, a voice interrupts my train of thought.

"Excuse me, do you have a light?" says the Voice, which reminds me suddenly of Miami.

I turn around on my bar stool, and to my surprise, I see this handsome man, European looking, with wisps of black short curly hair, thin black eyebrows, and light brown eyes the color of caramel. He looks like he's in his mid-to-late twenties and very Orlando Bloom-ish.

"Ah, no. I don't smoke," I respond, gazing into those piercing eyes of his. I look at his shirt and again I am surprised. The shirt reads CUBA, and it features two small baseball bats underneath it. I just had to ask. Inquiring Cuban minds wanna know.

"Are you Cuban?" I inquire with such a big smile that I could have swallowed my entire glass whole.

"Yeah, I just moved here this summer. I valeted my raft outside," he says with a wink, looking at me like I would understand his inside joke. People think most Cubans came to the United States on a raft or inflatable tires from the mid-1990s Cuban raft crisis so I get the joke. People are surprised when I tell them my parents and my aunts and uncles came here on a plane in the 1960s.

"My name is Carlos but my family calls me Carlito in Miami. What's your name? Do you speak Spanish?" he asks as I stare at his long sexy black lashes that seem like they could reach out and touch my face. I'm so tickled to learn that he is (a) Cuban and (b) from Miami. What a coincidence! This is too good to be true. A cute *cubano* in Boston, from MIA.

"I'm Tommy, short for Tomas. My family calls me Tomasito," I tell him, and we seem to delight in the similarity in our family nicknames. "I moved here from Miami Beach and *soy un cubanito*, too. So now there are two gay Cubans in Boston. We just doubled the Cuban Census count here."

We both start laughing and share in the magic of the moment. I guess he forgot about his nicotine dance because he then ends up hopping up on the bar stool next to me and he orders a drink, a Cuba Libre. What isn't Cuban about this dude? He seems so proud of his Hispanic heritage, something refreshing to see in this sometimes icy-attitudinal town.

We plunge into a heavy conversation, about our families, what made us flee to this winter tundra; how Gloria Estefan needs to find some new music; whatever happened to Jon Secada. Carlos has a slight Miami accent as he talks, which immediately transports me back to Miami's bright colorful streets, its electric vibe, the tropical vapor, home. He tells me he moved to Boston to work as a freshman English teacher and he wanted to get away from his family for a bit to find his independent self. He lives in Somerville right on the Cambridge border. He tells me that his older sister Cristina and his parents drove up in their Chevy minivan and helped him furnish his one-bedroom apartment with Pier I furniture. Carlos has a tabby cat named Havana. How funny. I'm sure if he had a pitbull, his name would be Fidel.

"You know, you can leave Miami but it doesn't leave you," he says, sipping his drink and then twirling the little red straw in the glass to fully mix the elixir. His eyes are locked on mine like he has me in his sights. "But you can always go back. This was my first summer here in Boston and I just started teaching at a high school in Dorchester. I really don't know many people here."

This guy is so handsome, the kind of handsome that is unassuming. Everyone would think he's hot but he doesn't carry himself like he would believe it himself. As he talks and twirls his straw, I suddenly imagine us lying in my bed shirtless in our boxer shorts. He is grading his students' papers and I am reading *Entertainment Weekly* or revising one of my stories. I see us turning out the lights, whispering to one another in Spanglish, and spooning, my face buried in the back of his neck. He smells like a mix of Calvin Klein Escape and baby powder. His body is tight and lean with a little bit of dark brown chest hair that thinly funnels down to below his navel. Ahhh. *Que rico!* That's so typical of the guys back home in the 305.

"Well, you do now. You have a fellow *cubanito* here to hang out with," I offer, and I start telling him how I survive from turning into a Cuban popsicle in the winters. Basically, you layer yourself like a ball of yarn and stay indoors. I rattle off the places to find the best Cuban *arroz con pollo* and *bistec.*

There's something about Carlos. I feel so at home talking to this guy. I'm not one to date Cubans. I usually like my guys as white as Dandy bread but Carlito may be an exception. We seem like we have so much in common and he's such a cutie. I can't break away from his stares. I can see myself introducing him to Papi and Mami and eating flan in our kitchen.

"This is great, Tomasito. I thought I'd never find another Cuban here in the city, especially one as cute as you," he flirts back. When he laughs, his head leans back and his curls become ruffled from his happy energy. "I'm surprised we don't know each other from Miami. It's not that big of a town."

I agree. I don't remember him at all from Miami either but that's not a problem. He's a fresh, okay, hot face from a city that is now home. And his home was my home.

As he drinks his Cuba Libre and I finish up my Vodka with Diet Coke, I can't help but feel a great cosmic connection with Carlos. *Amigo* or future boyfriend, I feel like he is going to be some great Cuban comfort in Boston. We lean in pretty close as we talk at the bar. I have a funny feeling in my stomach, one that I haven't felt since last winter, when I met What's-his-face, Mr. Corona-beers. This is a good feeling. I'm glad it's back.

"To Miami!" he toasts my glass. I return the toast. "And to Boston, to new beginnings, and to new friends."

Chapter 31

MIKEY

What am I doing heah? I'm sitting in the corner of this basement level room inside the Cathedral of the Holy Cross in the South End. There are twenty people heah, mostly men, sitting in a circle around a large table. The room is well lit. You can heah the cars outside zipping by above us and the footsteps from people walking on the old wooden stairs outside. How did I get heah?

"I'm Robert and I'm an alcoholic. I haven't had a drink in four months," says the older guy across from me.

"HI, ROBERT!" the room welcomes him.

This is my first AA meeting and I almost didn't make it. My counselor gave me this address to attend weekly meetings to talk about my drinking. But when I got here, I ended up in the wrong support group. The men and women kept talking about their sexual cravings and compulsions when I walked in, and then I realized I was in the sex addictions group and not AA. That one was next door in the basement. I thought I was going crazy or something. Well, I finally got up and found the right room and here I am surrounded by other alcoholics.

"My name is Tim and I've been sober for six months," another dude introduces himself.

"HI, TIM!" the group cheers.

Last week, after leaving Club Café all plastered, I hopped into my Toyota Matrix and hightailed it back to Duxbury. I got into a fight with Phil and I ditched him at the bahr. The last thing I remember was getting off Exit 11 to Duxbury. Next thing I remember, a state troopah was banging on my window. I had slammed into a pine tree off Birch Road, not fahr from my house. I totaled the cahr and I bumped my head against the steering wheel. My airbag deployed and probably saved my life. The rest is a blur. The troopah gave me a breathalizer test. I failed. I was taken to jail for DUI. Ma and Pa picked me up from the police station to take me home. I'll never forget the look of disappointment on their faces. It's forever etched in my mind, along with the talk we had once I sobered up the following afternoon.

"Mikey, you are better than this," Ma told me.

"We're gonna get you some help. We're here to help you, too. We love you," Pa told me.

I appeared in court the next day, charged with DUI. Since it was my first offense and since the judge knew I was a guidance counselor at an elementary school and that my parents were educators, he ordered me to do 100 hours of community service and attend mandatory weekly AA meetings. I have to meet with a counselor once a week as well in downtown Boston. I was able to get a hardship license to drive to work and to my meetings so I'm still able to drive. I replaced the Matrix, a total loss, with a Subaru Forrester that Ma and Pa helped me buy, as long as I promised to do as the judge said and seek counseling. I agreed. I came to this AA meeting in the city because I had a meeting with a counselor in downtown Boston so this was on my way home tonight.

"Hi, my name is Jack and I haven't had a drink in twenty-eight years. Geez, I could have had a son by now," an older man in his early sixties introduces himself. Everyone seems to know him and laughs at his last remark. He looks familiar.

"HI, JACK!" the group welcomes him.

I loved drinking. It took away all my pain, loosened me up, made everything feel right. I felt alive, so free. But it was taking over my life, at least on the weekends. I looked forward to drinking at Club Café and I couldn't stop after one. I had to have one more, and another. No matter how many times I woke up with a wicked headache the following day, I forgot about it once I felt back to normal. I feel horrible for everything I've said to people while wasted, especially Tommy Perez. I really did love him and I probably still do, but I wasn't ready to deal with his finger-pointing about my drinking. I've learned in counseling that denial is the worst part about this disease. It tells you that you're okay when you're not. I had to lose my car, and potentially my life, to realize I had a problem. Oh, it's my turn to introduce myself. Heah I go. I'm so nervous.

"Hi . . . um . . . I'm Mikey and this is my first time heah. I've been sober for a week. I'm an alcoholic."

"HI, MIKEY, AND WELCOME TO OUR GROUP!" the group welcomes me with an applause. It feels good, like I'm doing the right thing.

After the round of introductions, people start sharing their stories and we read from one of the passages in the twelve-step program booklet. I don't feel alone in this at all. So many of these guys have had similar experiences to me, blacking out, driving drunk, being cruel to the people we love. It's like hearing my own experiences through someone else.

An hour later, the meeting wraps up and everyone starts talking outside. On my way out, the older dude named Jack stops me and introduces himself.

"My name is Jack McGlame and I just wanted to welcome you personally. I know it's hard being here but it'll get better. I was where you are twenty-eight years ago. Just remember you're not alone here. We're here to help each other," he says, patting my back.

"Thanks, Jack. I'm Mikey. I appreciate your kind words. By the way, you look very familiar. Were you ever in the *Daily*?" I ask as we stand outside the steps of the church on this chilly fall night.

"Why, yes. There was a story about me in the *City* section about the short stories I write about the people who appear before me in court. I'm a Boston circuit court judge."

"Yeah, I remembah that story. It talked about your struggles with drinking, too. I knew the writer," I say, feeling sad about the way I treated Tommy all those months ago.

"You know Tommy Perez? He's such a good fellow. He's a breath of fresh air for the city. We could always use more good sweet Latinos here."

"Yeah, he's a good guy," I say. Jack gives me his numbah in case I need someone to talk to with me being new at all this. The more support, the bettah.

"See you next week," he says. "You're gonna be okay. Just believe in yourself. Have faith, Mikey."

A few minutes later, I'm on 93 South heading back to the South Shore. I pull over at the Barnes and Noble in Braintree to find some books about drinking and coping. I wouldn't mind getting a mocha latte while I'm there. After pulling into the parking lot, I walk inside and stand in line to order. The guy in front of me looks familiar, sort of. I only see the back of his short hair.

"Hi, Tommy, the usual, right? The brownie?" the salesgirl tells him.

"Yeah, you know me. I gotta have my daily ultimate chocolate chip brownie," he tells her.

When he pays for his order and grabs his dessert, he turns around. I recognize those Disney-deer-brown eyes immediately. It's Tommy. His hair is so short but he's still a cutie, just more handsome. He looks surprised when he sees me.

"Um, hi, Mikey," he says.

"Hi, Tommy. So good to see you. What are you doin' around heah?"

"Well, I now live on the Boston-Milton border and I'm only seven minutes from here so I come here every night for my brownie run," he says with a smile. "What about you? You're a ways from Duxbury."

"Do you have a second? I just wanted to talk to you a bit, if you could give me a few minutes?" I ask him.

"Um, okay," he says.

I grab my mocha latte and we sit in the corner of the café area, where we can have some privacy. I tell him about the drinking, the DUI, the accident, my AA meeting tonight, everything.

"I just wanted to apologize for being such a jerk to you all those times. You didn't deserve that. All you were doing was trying to help me," I tell him. He seems surprised, stunned by the revelation. He sits and listens to everything I have to say, like he used to.

"Mikey, thank God you weren't seriously hurt. You could have been killed. I'm just glad that you are getting help and that you have all this support. That is truly great. I'm so proud of you," he says, putting his hand over my hand.

"In order for me to help you last summer, I had to walk away from you. You had to figure this out on your own," he says. "I wasn't helping you by enabling you."

"Yeah, I know, Tommy. You tried so hard and I couldn't see it. I appreciate everything you tried to do for me. You're a special guy, you know that? Listen, it would be great if we could have lunch sometime, maybe as friends? I know this great place that makes great turkey carver sandwiches. Maybe you've heard of it. I think it's called Boston Market," I say with a grin.

He laughs and looks downward. Then those beautiful expressive brown eyes meet mine again.

"Yeah, that sounds nice. If you need a friend, I'll be there," he says. "As long as you're getting help, I'll try and be your friend. I've always wanted you to be healthy, Mikey."

We catch up on our lives for the next half hour at Barnes and Noble as if we picked up where we left off so many months ago. It's the first day of a new friendship.